CU

Letting his MDR from its holster high on h: expensive, and the ammo wasn t cneap, either, but Flint enjoyed the finer things, and he didn't want to go through this mission without having had a chance to kill someone with his new toy.

The nearest security guard was flat on the ground, trying to get a call through on his phone. Flint's first shot went through the tire and punched into the man's collarbone. The phone clattered to the asphalt as the man screamed. Flint's double-tap silenced him as he hooked around the hood of the vehicle and scanned for the next target.

He *liked* the FK BRNO. It felt like shooting a .40, but was packing as much muzzle energy as a .44 Magnum. The workings were smooth and tight. He blasted the next guard, a blond kid in a cheap black suit, in the face. The kid jerked as the bullet punched through his brain, and his head bounced off the pavement as he dropped.

BRANNIGAN'S BLACKHEARTS

ENEMY UNIDENTIFIED

PETER NEALEN

Printed in the United States of America
http://americanpraetorians.com

Also By Peter Nealen

The Maelstrom Rising Series
Escalation
Holding Action
Crimson Star

The Brannigan's Blackhearts Universe
Kill Yuan
The Colonel Has A Plan (Online Short)
Fury in the Gulf
Burmese Crossfire
Enemy Unidentified
Frozen Conflict
High Desert Vengeance
Doctors of Death
Kill or Capture

The American Praetorians Series
Drawing the Line: An American Praetorians Story (Novella)
Task Force Desperate
Hunting in the Shadows
Alone and Unafraid
The Devil You Don't Know
Lex Talionis

The Jed Horn Supernatural Thriller Series
Nightmares
A Silver Cross and a Winchester
The Walker on the Hills
The Canyon of the Lost (Novelette)
Older and Fouler Things

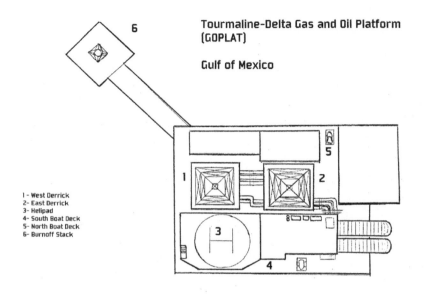

Tourmaline-Delta Gas and Oil Platform (GOPLAT)

Gulf of Mexico

1 - West Derrick
2- East Derrick
3- Helipad
4- South Boat Deck
5- North Boat Deck
6- Burnoff Stack

CHAPTER 1

Officer Lou Hall had been on the San Diego PD for about a year. He'd just gotten off night shift, and frankly wasn't sure whether the tradeoff had been worth it. Sure, he got to see the sun a lot more, and with the sun, in San Diego in the summertime—the winter tended to be pretty gray and damp—usually came the California girls, dressed in as little clothing as they could get away with.

But his partner, Fred Dobbs, was a surly, balding cynic, he wasn't getting paid *that* much more, and most of those same attractive California girls turned up their noses as soon as they saw his badge. He'd even gotten berated by one for, "just wanting to shoot minorities." He was half Mexican, himself, so he didn't know where the hell that had come from.

Then he looked on social media, and didn't have any more questions.

Dobbs was grumbling, as usual, and Hall had tuned him out after about the first five minutes, as usual. It was always the same thing. Dobbs was in the process of a nasty divorce, and couldn't talk about anything besides what a bitch his soon-to-be ex-wife was. So, Hall was scanning the sidewalks and trying not to think too hard about how much he hated his life, and really should have applied to El Cajon, or somewhere that actually paid their cops well.

Something caught his attention, and Dobbs' incessant bitching faded even farther into the background noise. At first he wasn't sure why he was looking at the parked taxi so intently, then he saw that it was unoccupied.

Taxis parked in Horton Plaza were nothing new. There was always far more traffic than there was available parking, and most people didn't try to drive to Horton Plaza. But an unattended cab?

Maybe the driver just went to take a piss. Yeah, that was probably it. He knew full well what a full day sitting in a car was like.

He didn't notice the second cab parked just around the corner; there was no reason to. It wasn't out of place. But the man sitting behind the wheel certainly noticed the San Diego PD car cruising past the abandoned taxi. He toyed with waiting, but there was a crowd coming out of the Lyceum Theater at the same time. *Perfect.*

The man ducked down below the dash and touched a remote. The unoccupied taxi exploded, the detonation shattering every window within sight, including the windshield of his own cab. He was showered with fragments of safety glass, as the vehicle rocked on its shocks. He'd parked a little too close; the concussion hammered him into the floor of the cab, and he blacked out for a moment.

When he came to, he had to kick the door open. The Plaza was a nightmare hellscape. Where the taxi had been parked, only a crater filled with twisted, fiercely burning wreckage remained. The cop car was burning, the windows shattered and the side panel crushed in and peppered with shrapnel, both men inside obviously dead. The sidewalk was littered with bodies and parts of bodies. People were screaming, the noise only then managing to register to his deadened hearing. His ears were ringing from the explosion. A young woman staggered away from the crater, bleeding, half of her face flayed away by the blast.

The man staggered out of the cab and joined the mass of screaming, panicking humanity fleeing the blast zone. Wounded people were being trampled. The panicked mob was going to seriously impede the first responders; it was just too cramped in downtown San Diego.

The man felt no particular satisfaction in what he'd done. He'd been well paid for it. It had been a job, nothing more. He blended into the crowd and disappeared.

***

Ann Sumner was bored. And hot. Directing traffic at Phoenix Airport hadn't been what she'd been expecting when she'd pinned on a badge. Sure, she was there to "protect against terrorism," but what she mainly ended up doing was either breaking up traffic jams outside the terminal or escorting overly excited passengers away from the desk agents they were berating.

And that was when she wasn't just standing there somewhere in the terminal, her hands crossed in front of her duty belt, watching people and counting down the seconds until her shift was over. Which was what she was doing right at that moment.

She glanced over as an airport shuttle pulled up to the glass doors. She couldn't see the hotel logo, but it looked just like any other van full of airline passengers disgorging its human cargo so that they could go stand in line and get treated like cattle.

This assignment is making me way *too cynical.* She almost had to laugh at the thought; what cop *wasn't* cynical about people, at least after the first year or so?

She had dismissed the van as just another part of the scenery even before the side door slid back and the two M240Gs were swung up and opened fire.

The muzzle flashes would have been almost invisible in the Arizona sun, had they not been shielded by the darkness of the inside of the shuttle. The roar of gunfire, the shattering glass, and the screams of people either hit or suddenly panicking as they

3

realized they were unarmed, defenseless, and under machinegun fire, however, was unmissable.

Sumner was mowed down in the first couple of seconds, though not because she'd been targeted. There had been too much glare for the gunners to see who was on the other side of the glass clearly enough to pick out any one figure for their attention. She'd just been near the left-hand limit as the gunner swept his muzzle across the terminal.

Both guns kept up the fire, pouring bullets into the "Arrivals" doors until their belts ran out. Then they hauled the doors shut and yelled at the driver, who floored the pedal and pulled away from the curb.

The shuttle was heavy and sluggish, and took some time to accelerate. A pair of police vehicles were already closing in, lights flashing and sirens wailing, and one of the men, still wearing his balaclava, hastily reloaded, turned his smoking M240 toward the rear, and settled in behind it as the other one kicked the back door open.

The door swung wide, hitting the end of its hinge and then smacking against another car. It came most of the way closed again before the gunner could open fire, and he swore as his buddy kicked at the door again. This time it stayed mostly open, and he opened up on the two police vehicles.

A line of bullets stitched across the hood and the lower corner of the windshield of the lead car, and the cop suddenly swerved to try to avoid the fire. In so doing, he swung out in front of the second car, and they piled up against the concrete barrier on the side of the road.

Then the shuttle was racing away, the rear door still flapping. The men inside weren't too worried about it. They'd ditch the van down by the Salt River in a few minutes and be gone.

With what they'd been paid for this one, they could live be living the high life a long, long way away from Phoenix for months.

4

"What the hell is that?"

Border Patrol Agent Jorge Tarrasco looked up, squinting into the West Texas sun. He couldn't immediately see what the new guy, Ottoman, was looking at.

"What the hell is what?" It was hot, he was getting close to the end of his shift, and he was ready to go home. It was never pleasant, there on the border, with Cuidad Juarez within spitting distance. The violence over there had been overtaken by other cities in Mexico, but that wasn't saying much, since Mexico had topped even the Syrian Civil War for body count lately. And being Border Patrol, right there in El Paso, meant hours upon hours of just waiting for all hell to break loose. There was enough traffic through the border crossing that *somebody* was bound to be trying to get across illegally, and quite possibly have enough firepower to object rather...strenuously to being denied.

Ottoman pointed. Tarrasco squinted behind his sunglasses. *So help me, if the new guy's going on about some desert bird or something...*

That wasn't a bird. He wished he had binos, or an RCO optic on his patrol rifle, but he could only shade his eyes and squint. The sun was definitely glinting off of some kind of aircraft. It looked about the size of a small private job, but it was getting way too close to the border crossing, and it was flying low.

He realized that it was even smaller than a crop duster about the time the twin rockets roared off the rails under the wings, arrowing toward the border checkpoint.

There wasn't time to yell, to duck, or to do anything but stare. The drone had been far closer than Tarrasco had realized, and it took less than a second for the two rockets to hit.

They weren't Hellfires, not quite. But they were still packing a fifteen-pound warhead apiece, and it was enough. The first rocket hit a truck that was just pulling across the line, coming out from under the overhang that sheltered the Customs and Border

Patrol officers from the sun. The truck exploded, fire, smoke and shrapnel rocking the vehicles to either side. The CBP officer who had just waved the truck through was knocked senseless, possibly dead.

The second rocket hit within a yard of Tarrasco himself, punching through the overhang above before detonating, sending fragmentation sleeting through metal and flesh alike. Tarrasco was hammered on his face on the pavement, bleeding profusely from several shrapnel wounds.

The rockets were only the precursors, though. With the muted buzz of its propeller, the drone plunged into the middle of the border crossing before anyone could even react to the rocket impacts.

Loaded with one hundred pounds of high explosives, the drone detonated as soon as it hit the ground. The border crossing, and most of the people within a dozen meters, disappeared in a flash and a billowing cloud of dust and smoke, as the resounding *boom* rolled off the Franklin Mountains and the Sierra de Juarez.

***

"Time now," Flint said, checking his watch. "Hit it."

Beside him, the man known to Flint and the rest of the team only as "Scrap" touched the dial key on his phone. It was a crude, ad hoc way of triggering an IED, but it worked, it wouldn't point to anyone in particular, and there was exactly zero chance that anyone had phone jammers working in Matamoros, of all places.

Matamoros seemed like a weird place to have a meeting like this, but if Flint had given it thought, he would have figured that the nearness to some of the newly constructed oil platforms off Point Isabel might have something to do with it. He knew that the targets were discussing new exploration and security concerns with the increasing violence in and around Mexico. Beyond that, he really didn't care. He had his mission, and that was that.

The bomb had been carefully placed well ahead of time. The meeting was going down on the El Saucito Golf Course, just

6

south of Matamoros, and Flint and his team had posed as contract workers to get the charges planted the previous week. It always helped having good intel, and employers who weren't shy about sharing it. So, there had been nearly twenty pounds of PETN stuffed in a planter just inside the elevators leading into the conference room long before the various VIPs had showed up.

The big glass windows facing the golf course blew out with a shower of shattered glass and ugly black smoke. Fire alarms started going off, and faint screams could be heard from inside.

The security personnel were on point; Flint had to give them that. A dozen vehicles in the parking lot fired up at once, and men started piling out of their cars and running inside, trying to get their charges out. Most of them, thanks to Mexico's strict gun laws and regulations regarding foreign contractors, were unarmed; their entire job was simply to grab their principal and run away.

Wrong day for that. With Scrap and Gibbet beside him, Flint pulled the van's door open and piled out, making sure his balaclava was up before the door was all the way open. He brought his MDR to his shoulder and double-tapped the man closest to the resort doors on the run.

The .300 Blackout rounds weren't suppressed or subsonic. They took the man in the armpit as he reached for the doors, and he dropped like a stone, his heart and lungs destroyed. Flint was already tracking in on the next, even as Scrap dropped the guy right behind the first one, and then Gibbet just started dumping rounds into the security men as fast as he could pull the trigger.

A ripping burst of machinegun fire roared from behind them, as Lunatic and Funnyman opened fire on the vehicles themselves with a pair of MAG 58s. The Belgian machineguns were still some of the best in the world, and Flint had insisted on getting at least a couple of them. His employers hadn't been happy with the expense, but they'd come through. Hundreds of 7.62 rounds tore through the thin-skinned vehicles, puncturing tires and shattering glass, and Flint shook his head. They hadn't even bothered with up-armors.

The last of the unarmed and helpless security men had figured out that they were under fire and dove for cover. Unfortunately for them, the only cover in the parking lot was more thin-skinned vehicles, and they didn't have any way of laying down their own covering fire.

Flint pointed Scrap and Gibbet toward the doors. Their "guests" would be coming out shortly. Villain and Chopper followed, while Psycho and Reaper ran for the far side to make sure none of their targets squirted out through the golf course. They had another team on the far side, just in case, but Flint wanted to have everything tied up in a nice little package, right there in the building.

Letting his MDR hang, he drew his FK BRNO Field Pistol from its holster high on his thigh. The 7.5mm pistol was hideously expensive, and the ammo wasn't cheap, either, but Flint enjoyed the finer things, and he didn't want to go through this mission without having had a chance to kill someone with his new toy.

The nearest security guard was flat on the ground, trying to get a call through on his phone. Flint's first shot went through the tire and punched into the man's collarbone. The phone clattered to the asphalt as the man screamed. Flint's double-tap silenced him as he hooked around the hood of the vehicle and scanned for the next target.

He *liked* the FK BRNO. It felt like shooting a .40, but was packing as much muzzle energy as a .44 Magnum. The workings were smooth and tight. He blasted the next guard, a blond kid in a cheap black suit, in the face. The kid jerked as the bullet punched through his brain, and his head bounced off the pavement as he dropped.

There were only four left, and they were scrambling for the trees, trying to stay low and move from vehicle to vehicle. Flint grinned tightly behind his balaclava, lifted his pistol, and shot each one as they showed themselves. The first one went sprawling, keening in pain, while the second one vaulted his body and dashed for a limousine that had already been thoroughly ventilated by either Lunatic or Funnyman. The hood was full of holes and smoking. The fleeing security guard was smashed off his feet by another burst of 7.62.

The last two did not show themselves again, though the bursts of machinegun fire continued for several seconds. Flint reloaded and holstered his FK pistol with a grunt of dissatisfaction. He'd wanted to account for all of them himself, and either Funnyman, Lunatic, or both had robbed him of his score.

Oh well. He turned back toward the doors.

They burst open in almost the same instant, a knot of suited security men leading a clump of obvious VIPs out of the building. The security men stopped dead at the sight of the bodies and the smoking vehicles, but they were too late.

Scrap, Gibbet, Villain, and Chopper opened fire before any of them could react. Hidden from the door, they caught the security guards by surprise, and in moments, the leading elements were dead. The screaming had started anew, and the VIPs were trying desperately to shove their way back inside, against the press of people trying to get out, away from the blast site.

Flint and his team were right on top of them, however, and the security personnel were starting to understand just how badly outmatched they were. Flint cranked three 7.5mm rounds into the ceiling as he advanced on the milling crowd in the lobby.

"Listen up!" he yelled. "You've got two choices. You shut up, do what you're told, and come with us, or we just go ahead and skullfuck all of you, right here, right now. It's really no nevermind to me, either way. But it's up to you. Come along with us, or die right here." He leveled his Field Pistol at the nearest woman's head. She shrank away from the muzzle, huddling on the floor. Flint smirked, even though his face was covered, and she couldn't see the expression.

Nobody tried to play hero, nobody offered any resistance. He found he was slightly disappointed. Oh, well, maybe the Mexican authorities would come out to play. He recognized at least one Pemex board member, a high-ranking Mexican Policia Federal officer, and what had to be several staffers from the *Congreso de la Uniòn.*

Inmate came in the doors from the van. "Birds are inbound," he reported. "Five mikes."

"Good to go," Flint replied. "Everybody on your feet!" he yelled. "Get moving out onto the green! Let's go! Nice and orderly! I'd hate to have to just shoot all of you and leave. Actually, you know what? That might be fun. So, go ahead, take your pick!"

Once again, nobody decided to test him. Of course, the smoking vehicles and bullet-shredded bodies out in the parking lot were a good incentive to play along. The team herded the crowd out onto the golf course, pushing and prodding with rifle muzzles where needed, or even just where a stumble or half-panicked flinch was going to be amusing.

Flint didn't bat an eye as Scrap shoved a woman in a too-tight skirt and three-inch heels. She fell against the man in front of her, who didn't dare try to help her, and stumbled onto the ground. Even with his balaclava in place, Flint could see Scrap's leer. "Come on, senorita," he said. "No time for that now. You can lie down for me later." He reached down and grabbed her cruelly by the upper arm, wrenching her to her feet. He shoved her, and she stumbled again. "Let's go."

The helos were already getting closer. They weren't overtly military; that would have been a bad idea. They were brightly-painted blue-and-green Eurocopter EC225s. They weren't armed, either; they wouldn't have raised any red flags on takeoff, in fact not until they'd suddenly diverted from their respective flight plans when Inmate had called them in.

The three transport helos came in close together, their rotors beating at the humid air and whipping the smoke from the bomb and the damaged vehicles into fantastical whorls, landing where there were clear and reasonably level spots on the golf course. Flint and his boys had already surveyed the landing zones previously, during the initial recon and prep for this hit.

No sooner had the first helo touched down, flattening the nearby vegetation with its rotor wash, than Flint was splitting the hostages and his team of shooters into three groups, pointing Villain with one group and Psycho with another toward the helos off to either side. He let Scrap herd the remaining hostages toward the center bird, following and turning back to check for incoming security forces.

He wasn't expecting much. Matamoros had been relatively quiet for the last few months—though with places like Acapulco and Cabo San Lucas becoming war zones, it was clear that there was no place in Mexico that could be counted as *safe*—so most of the *Federales* were probably otherwise occupied, even the ones on the take to the cartels. And they were far enough out from the city itself that it would take any response force a few minutes to get there.

Scrap and Gibbet were shoving and kicking the hostages onto the bird. They weren't getting any resistance, but it paid to let the cargo know who was in charge. Flint glanced over at the other two helos, got thumbs-up from both Villain and Psycho, and climbed up the ramp himself. "Let's go!" he yelled forward, though the pilot couldn't possibly hear him over the scream of the EC225's engines. Reaper was up front, though, and leaned into the cockpit to pass the word. A moment later, the helo was rocking into the sky and turning east, toward the coast.

***

Flint was one of the first to step off the ramp onto the helideck of the Tourmaline-Delta platform. The two skeletal derricks of Rigs One and Two rose into the brilliant blue sky over the Gulf of Mexico, but Flint didn't spare them a glance.

"Get the hostages below!" he bellowed to Dingo, who had come jogging up from the ladder with several more of the group. "Then get the defenses ready! I think that we're going to have company soon!"

"We are!" Dingo yelled back, his voice straining to be heard over the roar of the helicopters. "There are four helos about thirty minutes behind you! Looks like Mi-17s!"

Flint nodded. Mexican Marines. Had to be. Well, he was about to show them that these weren't cartel bully-boys they were going up against. He slung his MDR across his back and started for the edge of the helideck, facing back toward land. There were several munitions cases set along the side, and he hastily cracked one open.

The lean tube of a Mistral Surface to Air Missile launcher was nestled inside, and Flint drew it out and prepped it. Behind him, the hostages were being hastily—and none-too-gently— chivvied down the stairs into the depths of the oil platform. The helos were already pulling away; their task was done, and they'd be carefully sanitized once they got to their final destinations. There wouldn't be any loose ends for this job.

As the third helicopter growled away into the distance, Flint sat on the side of the helideck, his boots dangling above the forest of girders leading down to the blue waters of the Gulf, scanning the sky for the telltale specks of the incoming Mexican helicopters. Dingo came and joined him, pulling another Mistral out of another case.

"We've had a snag," Dingo said.

"I don't want to hear about 'snags,'" Flint warned him.

"Not our fault," Dingo replied. "The sub's not here yet."

"Any word as to why not?" Flint asked. He was still watching the horizon. Their way out being delayed was bad

12

enough news, but it would be worse if they didn't deal with these Marines first.

"Nothing," Dingo answered. "But then, everybody was supposed to be comm-silent once this show kicked off, anyway."

Flint spat over the edge of the helideck. "Well, I guess we're going to have to go to Plan B, then," he said. "Another few hours shouldn't be too bad. If we can hurt this assault force bad enough, they should leave us alone for a while, until we can get off." He grinned behind his balaclava. "Besides, with a few of the split-tails in that bunch, some of us could even have some fun before we run out of time."

"Is that really a good idea?" Dingo asked.

Flint glanced at him. He hadn't picked Dingo, and knew next to nothing about him. But that wasn't the sort of question he expected from the wolves and meat-eaters that he went looking for. His bunch were *warriors*, in his mind, the kind who could take what they wanted from those who were too weak and pathetic to stop them. "Right" and "wrong" were concepts for weak people.

"Don't worry," he said, even as he caught a faint glint of sunlight on metal in the distance and hefted the Mistral. "Everything'll be fine."

***

The group of four Mi-17 Hips accounted for almost a sixth of the Mexican Navy's full inventory, and almost all that were available on the east coast. It was quite a response, given the amount of violence wracking the country, and in fact, the attack at the golf course had been relatively small compared to some of the massacres being perpetrated by various narco armies in other parts of Mexico. But there had been enough connected people among the hostages that *something* had to be done, and so the Marines had been mobilized as quickly as possible.

They were bearing down on the Tourmaline-Delta platform, flying fast and low. The pilots were skilled, and the Marines in the backs of the helicopters were all veterans, having

13

been blooded in the non-stop narco war. The Mexican Marines were still considered one of the last remaining untouchables, the last incorruptible paladins in the forces fighting the narcos. Which meant they got called on to kill a lot of narcos.

And the combat-hardened men in the backs of the helicopters, their P90s between their knees, weren't always terribly concerned about what it took to accomplish that mission. "Collateral damage" wasn't high up on their list of priorities.

The Mexican Narco War had gone far past that point, a long time before.

Even so, they were used to pretty much uncontested command of the skies. The *Càrtel Jalisco Nuevo Generaciòn* had managed to shoot down an Army helicopter back in 2015, but for the most part, the Naval helicopters had been untouched. So, when missile warnings started to go off in the cockpits and the pilots started evasive maneuvers, nobody aboard was ready for it.

Flint, Dingo, and the others, scattered along the western side of the platform and all armed with Mistrals, had waited long enough that the Russian-built helicopters didn't have a prayer. It took the shoulder-fired SAMs barely a few seconds to streak over the water to their targets, homing in on the blazing heat of the helicopters' engines.

The lead helo took a direct hit and exploded. Debris spun away from the black-and-orange fireball in the sky, and rained down into the Gulf. The second managed to avoid a direct hit, but the missile detonated barely three feet from its engine housing, and it was soon in a flat spin toward the water, trailing thick, ugly, black smoke.

The third helicopter banked hard to get away from its missile, and flew right into the second one that had been aimed at it. There was a brief puff of the exploding missile, and the helicopter rolled over and plunged into the ocean.

The fourth had managed to avoid being hit, and was diving and banking at the same time, but couldn't avoid the section of

14

destroyed rotor blade that fell into its own rotor hub. The hub exploded in a shower of grease, smoke, and flying parts, and the helicopter crashed.

Only a few moments after the first missile had been fired, all that was left of the Mexican Marine task force was a bit of blackened debris floating on an oil slick on the surface of the Gulf of Mexico.

***

Contralmirante Diego Huerta stared at the radio. It had been jammed with little more than screaming and desperate calls for help for about thirty seconds, and then had gone dead.

The radar operator looked up at the *Contralmirante*. "We have lost all their transponders, Señor," he reported.

Huerta clenched his fists. He was a beefy man, of middling height and going bald. He'd actually done some time as a Naval Infantry skullcracker in his youth; that was how long this war had been going on. He might have risen as fast and as far as he had thanks to family connections, but he was still a Naval Infantryman at heart regardless.

And those were his men who had gone down on those four helos. He had no doubt that that was what had happened. He didn't know who these *pinche cabrònes* were, but they were well-prepared; far better-prepared than the narcos usually were. And it was adding up with everything else he'd seen of this incident so far to make him very, very nervous. These *maricònes* were far more dangerous than he was used to. And given some of the monsters his Naval Infantry had faced, that was saying something.

Huerta slowly straightened. An officer must be dignified. He couldn't swear like an enlisted man, or rage at the loss of his men. He had to maintain his decorum.

And he had to consider the consequences of his actions, from a political point of view as well as a tactical and strategic one. And the political consequences were embodied in the form of the young woman standing in the command post, dressed in a white pantsuit.

Olivia Salinas had shown up amazingly quickly after the incident; she said she was a Special Liaison from the office of *El Presidente*, and she had the credentials to prove it. And her presence therefore carried the full weight of that office, looking over his shoulder.

He turned to her. "Señora," he said calmly, "I know that our government will not appreciate this suggestion, but I have to make it. My Naval Infantry are spread thin, dealing with the narcos. I just lost two platoons in a few seconds. I don't have the resources to replace them easily. We need to ask the gringos for help."

"Absolutely out of the question, *Contralmirante*," Salinas replied coldly. Her hair was pulled back severely, and her sharp cheekbones jutted below calculating black eyes. "The Mexican people need no help from the *Norteamericanos*."

Which was obviously crap, and both of them knew it. Huerta could deal with narcos; he had been for some time. But whatever had just happened was something bigger than a narco turf battle. And his available assets had just been cut down to almost nothing.

Still, relations between Mexico City and Washington were strained, to say the least. He knew there were still a few American SOF units in Mexico, but they were strictly there in a training capacity for the Mexican armed forces.

"This is a hostage situation," he pointed out reasonably. "Time is of the essence. The American Delta Force or SEALs can be here to assist more quickly than I can put together another strike force."

Salinas glared daggers at him. "Was I unclear, *Contralmirante*?" she asked. "The answer is no. This is a Mexican problem, and will be solved by Mexican forces." She turned away

16

from him, looking out to sea, toward the distant oil platform and the wreckage floating above the bodies.

Helplessly, Huerta glanced in the same direction, then turned away. He had work to do.

***

It was late when Huerta finally left the command post. He was trudging through the dark toward the trailer that had been set up as his personal quarters when his cell phone rang abruptly.

He pulled it out and frowned. He didn't recognize the number, but given his position, that wasn't unknown. He answered it. "*Hola*?"

"Hello, Admiral," a strange voice said in English. "I think we need to talk."

"Who is this?" Huerta demanded. "How did you get this number?"

"My name is Van Zandt," the other man replied, "and I have my ways. Now, time is pressing. You have a bad situation on your hands, and I think I might have a solution…"

CHAPTER 2

"No," John Brannigan said. "Not only no, but *hell* no."

"John," Hector Chavez started to remonstrate with him, "we're not talking about some half-assed Pemex contract, here."

The two men were facing each other across a table in the Rocking K, the best—and essentially only—diner in tiny Junction City. It wasn't the sort of place most people would immediately think of when it came to planning covert operations, but it was the closest meeting place to Brannigan's mountain hideaway, and so Chavez had pegged it as their contact spot, more often than not.

John Brannigan was a towering, six-foot-four former Marine Colonel, his hair gone shaggy and gray on his head and his face. He shaved his cheeks and his chin, but his handlebar mustache was bushier than ever. He might have had a few more crow's feet around his gray eyes, especially after his recent turn to mercenary commander. Activities like a hair-raising mission on the island of Khadarkh in the Persian Gulf, followed by a jump into northern Burma to take down a North Korean liaison operation in the Golden Triangle, were not calculated to keep a man young.

Brannigan was dressed in his usual flannel shirt and jeans, his "going to town" clothes. Chavez had dressed down since his first visit; he was wearing a leather jacket and jeans. The third man at the table, however, stood out a bit more.

Mark Van Zandt, his hair still cut in a close military regulation cut, clean shaven and straight-backed, was dressed in his usual khakis and a polo shirt, and leaning back in his chair, wisely keeping out of the conversation.

Van Zandt had been one of Brannigan's last commanding officers. He'd also been the one to bear the news that Brannigan would be forced to retire from the Marine Corps. There was little love lost between the two of them, even though they had entered each other's orbits once again when Van Zandt had been looking for a deniable team to send in on the Burma operation.

"You want me to take my boys into *Mexico*," Brannigan said, leaning back in his chair and folding his brawny arms across his chest. "Mexico *defines* 'non-permissive environment.' Gringos are not welcome, particularly gringo contractors. I've done my homework, Hector. If you think there's a snowball's chance in hell that I'm going to go into that killing field unarmed, relying on Mexicans of dubious loyalty for protection, you've got another think coming."

"This isn't that kind of contract, John," Van Zandt snorted. "Which should be abundantly obvious, since we're coming to you. The guys who blew up Khadarkh and jumped into northern Burma aren't exactly the go-to for a petroleum security operation, now are they?" Acid sarcasm dripped from his voice. Brannigan turned his glare on the retired general.

"Not the point," Brannigan retorted. "We get spotted down there, there's gonna be hell to pay."

"Which is different from your last two jobs how?" Van Zandt pointed out. "Come on, John, now you're just being difficult."

"Why us?" Brannigan asked, after taking a deep breath. He *really* didn't want to go into Mexico. He knew too much about the horror-show that was the Mexican narco-war. Khadarkh had been a simple in-and-out, on a tiny island, no less. Burma had been different, but for all the atrocities happening in Burma—some of which his crew of mercenaries, the self-styled "Brannigan's Blackhearts," had witnessed first-hand—Mexico was an entirely different scale. It had beaten out the *Syrian Civil War* for body count.

"The same reason I came to you for the Burma job," Van Zandt said coolly. "You're deniable. Which, I might add, is a *huge* selling point for *Contralmirante* Huerta right now, as well."

"Who's Huerta?" Brannigan asked.

"He's the commander of the Mexican Marines who tried to retake the oil platform where our mysterious terrorists took their hostages," Chavez said. "He lost most of a company in a few minutes, has been getting stonewalled by Mexico City, and wants payback."

"So he'll cover for us?"

"He's assured me that he will," Van Zandt said. "He's under strict orders that no US military forces, including DEVGRU or Delta—who are about the only ones who could handle this otherwise; we don't exactly have a MEU in the vicinity—are to be called upon. The platform is technically in Mexican waters, and therefore it is a Mexican affair. They don't want help. Well, the PRI doesn't want help. Huerta does."

"And if he sells us down the river as soon as the job's done?" Brannigan asked quietly.

Van Zandt shook his head. "It's a possibility, but I've talked to the man. I think he's on the level. *And* I made it clear that if anything goes wrong that he might have prevented, recordings of all our conversations would somehow reach the President."

Brannigan nodded. "I expect that's a pretty good deterrent, all things considered."

"It should be," Chavez said. "The PRI's so damned corrupt, they might not even bother to put him on trial. At least not before they've disappeared his entire family."

Brannigan looked down at the table, frowning. It was true enough that he'd already started feeling the itch for another mission, another fight. And his Blackhearts were the kind of mercenaries who went into impossible situations and managed to kill their way out. They'd done it twice already, and Van Zandt wouldn't even have considered them for the job if it had been anything else.

But he couldn't shake the bad feeling that Mexico gave him. He'd been there, many years before, before the narco wars really kicked off and the corpses started piling up. He'd liked the country then. But he'd watched as the violence, corruption, and increasingly brutal and sadistic killing had spread even to the tourist safe havens of the country. Going into Mexico struck him as the equivalent to marching into a Hieronymus Bosch painting.

"With the level of sophistication and preparation the opposition has shown," Van Zandt said quietly, "I don't think it's an exaggeration to say that you could well be those people's only hope of getting out alive. Especially with the Mexicans refusing official help."

Brannigan blew out a sigh. "What do we know about the opposition?" he asked. The decision was made. He'd go. He knew his men would go, too, at least the original team.

Damn, I still haven't recruited a new medic. He'd avoided it after Doc Villareal had gone down in Burma. Losing Doc already hurt bad enough, in addition to the guilt he felt for having taken the man back into combat, which had been his own personal hell ever since Zarghun.

"Next to nothing," Van Zandt replied. "In the first half hour or so, several of the attacks were claimed, piecemeal, by various jihadist splinter groups, but we're pretty sure now that none of them were in on it. It was too coordinated, and none of them had the foresight to wait until the dust settled and claim responsibility for the whole shooting match. Whoever's behind it still hasn't uttered a word.

"The guys you're after are the only lead we've got, and they left no witnesses at the golf course," he continued. "Their faces were covered, and they wore gloves, so we don't even know

22

what color they are. They are packing some serious hardware, though; bullpup rifles and SAMs at the least."

"Insert?" Brannigan asked. He was already going over the logistics of the mission in his head. It was his great skill and something of his curse; as soon as he knew he was doing something, he started planning it.

"Don't know yet," Van Zandt replied. "Air appears to be out of the question; the Mexicans lost four Hips trying to take the platform back. A surface approach at night *might* be possible, but if they've got night vision and thermals—and I suspect that they do—then that could be suicide, as well. We'll have to figure that out. Preferably without bringing the Navy into it." He grimaced.

"The good news," Hector Chavez put in, "is that Matamoros and the platform are both close enough to the border that you shouldn't have to stage inside Mexico itself. You should be able to stay in Texas until it's time to go."

"Small favors, I suppose," Brannigan said absently. His mind was working a mile a minute. Then his eyes sharpened, focusing in on Van Zandt. "Unless you've got any more intel for me, I need to get moving. If you're right, time is pressing."

"Unfortunately," Van Zandt said, "that's it. That's part of the problem."

"Fine," Brannigan said, standing up. "I'll let you know if we find any intel on the platform."

***

"Why did I let you talk me into this?" Joe Flanagan asked.

Flanagan was what some might call "ruggedly handsome." His hair and thick beard were so black as to look almost blue in certain light, his eyes were a light blue in a tanned face starting to show a few lines, and his broad shoulders and narrow waist were in keeping with his previous occupation as a Recon Marine. They were also in keeping with his current occupation as a mercenary, but that wasn't something most people knew about.

The short, muscular man next to him grinned, pearlescent white teeth showing starkly in an ebony face. "You finally saw sense and agreed that Uncle Kevin has your best interests in mind, Joey boy," Kevin Curtis said. "It's been how long since you've been out to meet girls?"

"Don't call me 'Joey,' Kev," Flanagan growled, as Curtis pulled the door open. The shorter man just grinned wider. Curtis was built like a tank; he was a bodybuilder when he wasn't being a gambler or a mercenary. He even had sponsorships, something that Flanagan had expressed surprise about, given that he was a midget.

That exchange of insults had been epic.

The lights of the bar gleamed off Curtis' shaven head as he waved Flanagan past him. Flanagan, for his part, stood in the doorway a second, his eyes narrowed.

"You're blocking the fatal funnel, Joe," Curtis remonstrated. "It's not having the dramatic effect that you probably hope it is. The girls will not be impressed."

"So help me, Kev, if I agreed to this crap just to try to amuse the fat, dumpy friend…" Flanagan muttered as he stepped inside.

"Would *I*, who have been trying to get you a date for, well, forever, do that to you?" Curtis asked as he stepped inside and let the door close behind them.

"In a heartbeat," Flanagan said flatly.

The bar actually didn't look like Curtis' usual speed. When he could be said to have a home at all, it was in Las Vegas, where he made most of his money when he wasn't in exotic places, packing a machinegun. His usual bars were Vegas chic, with lots of neon and the kind of sleek décor that Flanagan generally found sterile.

But this place was different. The bar was wood, with wooden-and-brass stools along it and a brass foot rail. The lights were all soft and yellowish, instead of garish, multicolored neon. It actually looked classy.

"You wound me, Joe," Curtis said, looking around. He nudged Flanagan with an elbow. "Come on. The girls are already here."

He led the way toward the far end of the bar, where two young women were sipping their drinks. Flanagan's eyebrow went up.

One was quite obviously Curtis' type; she was a little bit shorter, with a curvaceous figure that her dress showed off to great effect. Her hair *might* have actually been blond, but there was enough dark in it that it was impossible to be sure. Curtis went straight to her, slipped a thick arm around her waist, and said something into her ear as she giggled and kissed him on the cheek.

The other woman was definitely *not* the "fat, dumpy friend." She sized Flanagan up over the lip of her glass, a glint of approval and amusement in her dark eyes. She was slender and willowy, wearing a dark-blue dress that hung just below her knees, with thick, wavy black hair that fell past her shoulders and framed a flawless, heart-shaped face. She was stunning.

Flanagan realized he was staring at her like an idiot, glanced at Curtis, who was watching him with a huge, shit-eating grin on his face, swallowed, and stepped closer. "Hi," he managed.

"Hi," she replied with a smile. "You must be Joe." She held out her hand, and he shook it, suddenly struck by how warm it was.

Get ahold of yourself, idiot. He was suddenly acutely aware of how long it had been since he and Mary had broken up.

"That would be me," he answered, having to raise his voice to be heard over the noise of the bar's clientele. "I'm afraid that Kevin wasn't particularly forthcoming about you, though."

"I'm Rachel," she said, smiling even wider. "It's nice to meet you, Joe. What are you having?"

Over the next thirty minutes, Flanagan found himself entranced. Rachel was smart, warm, and had a way of drawing him out of his shell that he'd never encountered before. He caught Kevin and the blond girl giving them sly glances from time to time. He realized he'd been set up. But by then, he really didn't care.

Then his phone rang. And so did Curtis', at almost the same moment.

Frowning, he pulled it out. He recognized the chime. It could only mean one thing. "Sorry, Rachel, I've got to check this."

"Sure, honey," she said, taking another sip of her beer. He felt himself get warm around the collar. She noticed, too, and smiled.

He looked down at the phone. It was a message from Brannigan.

Got a job. Get to Corpus Christi ASAP. Time Sensitive.

"Damn it," Flanagan muttered. The one time he really, really didn't want to get interrupted...

Curtis, as usual, was a bit louder and a bit more emotional. "Son of a bitch! Not now!" He looked like he was about ready to throw the phone. "No. No, we're not going on this one! We can sit one out..."

Flanagan was already shoving his phone back in his pocket. "I'm really, really sorry, Rachel," he said, trying to make himself heard over Curtis' rantings. "But this is important. We've got to go."

She smiled sadly, and then, to his surprise, leaned forward, kissed him lightly on the lips, and pulled his phone out of his pocket. She held it up. "You're going to need to unlock this so that I can put my number in," she said.

He blinked in surprise, then smiled, took the phone from her, and unlocked it as she'd asked. She took it back, put her information in his contacts, and handed it back to him. "Call me when you get back," she said. "I'm looking forward to finishing our conversation."

"So am I," Flanagan said sincerely. Then he was hauling Curtis toward the door. The shorter man was still railing about how unfair it was.

"I've been setting this up for weeks!" he exclaimed. "Dammit, dammit, dammit!"

"We can't let the rest of the boys go without us, and you damned well know it," Flanagan said, as he dragged Curtis through the door. "I'll drive; you check if flights are going to be quicker than driving."

***

Sam Childress was moving up in the world. He wasn't living in his aunt's trailer anymore. He had his own apartment now. And he was paid up for most of the year.

It was an unfamiliar feeling. He hadn't been this flush for cash in a long time. Certainly not since he'd gotten out of the Marine Corps. But all the same, he was suddenly restless.

The Burma job had meant that he hadn't needed to go back to the temp agency and beg Julie Keating for work. He'd found that he really didn't have anything he *needed* to do. He was flush enough that he could be his own man for once. And he didn't know what to do with himself.

So, he found himself working out, watching a lot of TV, and searching for the end of the Internet. It was starting to drive him nuts. There really wasn't that much on TV, and the less said about some of the stuff he found on the Internet, the better.

At least he had plenty of time to work out. He was getting stockier and more muscular than he thought he ever had been in his life. He still looked a little gawky; that was just a fact of his facial features and his beak of a nose.

His eyes were glazing over as the fiftieth commercial for something he'd never use and didn't care about came on, when a heavy knock pounded at his door.

He shot off the sofa and moved quickly to the door. He wasn't expecting anyone, but right at that moment, any diversion from his boredom was welcome.

He pulled the door open. Somehow, he was not surprised to see Carlo Santelli standing there.

Santelli had been his Battalion Sergeant Major when he had still been on Active Duty. The short, balding fireplug of a man had had occasion to bawl Childress out with his thick Boston accent quite a few times, and even sign off on his Non-Judicial Punishment that had busted him down a rank. Twice.

But those times were past. Now both men were civilians. They were also both mercenaries working for the one commander both of them would follow into anything: John Brannigan.

"I'm not broke this time, Sergeant Major," Childress said quickly, remembering the grief that Santelli had given him for spending all the money from the Khadarkh job before they'd gone into Burma.

"Great, Sam, I'm proud of ya," Santelli said brusquely. "Not why I'm here. Got a situation, and I need another set of hands. Grab ya crap and let's go."

Childress had long ago stopped hesitating when Carlo Santelli told him to do something. The fact that, unless they were on a job, Santelli had no more rank than he did didn't ever quite register to him until later, or until Santelli reminded him of it. But there was no reminder coming this time; the stout Italian had a thunderous frown on his pugnacious face, and was hardly looking at Childress.

Childress grabbed his jacket, checked that he had his key—that was a mistake he'd made far too many times after he'd first moved into the apartment—and then stepped out into the hallway with Santelli.

"What's up?" he asked, managing to just barely check himself before he added, "Sergeant Major." For a man who was slightly notorious for having little to no filter on his mouth,

Childress was always strictly respectful when he talked to Santelli or Brannigan.

"We've got some of the boys who are feeling their oats and getting a bit too loud, if you take my meaning," Santelli said as he led the way down the hallway, about as fast as his short legs could take him. Childress had to stretch his own stride to keep up.

He didn't ask any more questions. The hallway of his apartment building wasn't the time or place, anyway.

Santelli led the way downstairs and out onto the street. His car was clearly a rental; the plates were from Arizona, and living in Boston, Childress didn't know if Santelli even owned a car, much less a mid-size SUV like the blue Pathfinder sitting on the curb. Santelli swung into the driver's seat, while Childress folded himself into the passenger's seat.

"The new guys?" he asked, as Santelli pulled away from the curb.

"Mostly," Santelli answered. "I got a call from Bianco; seems that a few of them decided to have a get-together."

"Where?" Childress asked, hanging on for dear life. He hadn't known that Santelli drove like a maniac.

"Just up the road," was the reply. "Seems that Jenkins is based around here, too."

They got to their destination in short order. The "Shirts and Skins" Sports Bar was set just off the highway, and the parking lot wasn't yet packed at that time of the early evening. Santelli pulled the SUV into a parking space and threw his door open.

"Did you come all the way out here just for this, Serg...Carlo?" Childress asked, as he hurried toward the door in Santelli's wake.

"Nah, I was already out here," Santelli replied. He slowed just enough to give Childress a look. "Are you kidding? How fast do you think airline flights move?"

"Never mind, dumb question," Childress muttered.

Santelli pushed through the doors, into the slightly darkened interior of the sports bar. Flickering light from at least a dozen TVs filled the room. The bar was a square island in the center, surrounded by small, round tables with cheap, black-upholstered chairs.

The Blackhearts group was easy to pick out. They were, by and large, more fit than anyone else in the room, and at that moment, also considerably louder.

Aziz, Jenkins, and Wade were arguing over a war story, specifically who had been where at what time. Childress immediately identified the place as the village in northern Burma where Doc Villareal had been killed, and they had gone into a system of tunnels after the North Korean advisors to the Kokang Communists/drug runners. It sounded like they were avoiding actually getting specific about the place, but this was bad enough.

Santelli stalked toward the table, murder in his eyes. Jenkins looked up as he and Childress approached. The former SEAL looked a little glazed; he'd clearly had a few already.

"Hey, Childress, check it out!" he said, pulling his sleeve back. He'd gotten a new tattoo, still under a wrap of clear cellophane. It was a black heart, with a fighting knife through it and crossed rifles behind it. "We've got a logo, dude!"

Santelli was suddenly, despite his height, looming over Jenkins. "And what the *fuck* made you think that that was a good idea?" he hissed. "Hey, why don't we do merchandising, maybe get a movie deal? That sound good, too? Then we can have all sorts of government agencies looking at what we've been doing lately! Sounds fucking great!" He looked around the inside of the bar. "You been having fun, regaling complete strangers in public with stories that can't possibly have *any* repercussions for any of us?"

"We haven't said anything specific, Carlo," Wade said quietly. The former Ranger NCO was a big man, clean-shaven and brown haired, with pale blue eyes and an intensity that was coming

30

out in the form of a growing anger at being dressed down this way. "We're not stupid."

"Coulda fooled me," Santelli snarled. "Talkin' about this shit in public." He jerked a thumb at the door. "Let's go. Colonel's got a job for us, and time's wasting." He glared at Jenkins and Aziz. Bianco had been sitting toward the back, his arms folded across his beefy torso, saying nothing. He didn't look like he'd gotten the Blackhearts tattoo. Aziz, somewhat to Santelli's surprise, also had cellophane showing beneath the cuff of his sleeve. Aziz had been a soldier and a professor, and hated both alternately. He tended to act like he was above the other Blackhearts, just because, and getting a tattoo like that didn't seem in character for him.

Childress glanced at Bianco. The big man's face was blank, and he pointedly wasn't looking at Aziz, who was glaring daggers at him. Childress thought he understood. Bianco had protested, and Aziz, being Aziz, had done it just to put the "newbie" in his place.

Hell of a stupid reason to get inked. But it wasn't his hide, so Childress just shrugged.

With Santelli glowering at them, and the other patrons watching the group curiously, the Blackhearts paid their checks and headed for the parking lot.

***

Alex Tanaka would have had to admit that he'd been a little surprised to get the text from Brannigan. He shouldn't have been; he'd acquitted himself well in Burma, and Brannigan, Hancock, and Santelli had all said as much. But he couldn't shake the feeling that, as a former basic leg infantryman, he didn't belong among these former Special Operators.

He was currently trundling down the dirt road that had led to his first introduction to "Brannigan's Blackhearts." He'd been driving past Don Hart's farm on the way to the airport to fly to

Corpus Christi, and figured he'd swing by and see if the other man wanted to ride in with him.

He pulled into the driveway leading up to the white-painted farmhouse. Hart's truck was still sitting by the barn, so it looked like he hadn't missed him. He brought the car to a halt and honked.

There was no reply, no movement. He frowned, shut the engine off, and got out.

He thought he heard some sounds from inside, but they were faint. Still frowning, he stepped up onto the porch and knocked.

Was that a mumbled cry? Was Don hurt? The former Marine was an amputee; maybe something had happened. Sure, he'd jumped into Burma with no problems, but you never knew. He knocked again, harder.

"Don?" he called. "It's Alex! You okay?"

Before he could tell if he'd heard a response or not, the sound of gravel crunching under vehicle tires came from behind him. He turned to see a silver sedan pulling up next to his car, and then Roger Hancock got out.

Roger Hancock had been Hart's platoon sergeant in the Marine Corps; Tanaka knew that much. He also knew that he was Brannigan's right hand man, even more so than Santelli. Lean, sharp-featured, and with his head shaved bald, Hancock seemed to see everything, and Tanaka had to admit to himself that he found him a little more intimidating than even Brannigan himself.

"What are you doing here, Alex?" Hancock asked as he mounted the steps onto the porch.

"I was driving by and thought that I'd see if Don wanted to share a ride," Tanaka explained. "But he's not answering the door."

"He's not answering his phone, either," Hancock said. He reached past Tanaka and opened the door. It had been unlocked, but Tanaka noticed that Hancock had a key in his other hand.

Hancock pushed inside, and Tanaka realized he may as well follow. He felt a little nervous, just walking into Don's house without being invited; he knew that most of the Blackhearts probably wouldn't react well to such an intrusion, and he expected that most of them were well-armed.

He knew he sure was.

But they weren't greeted by a shotgun blast. As his eyes adjusted to the darkness of the entryway, taking in the open living room leading into the dining room, he heard Hancock say, "Oh, for fuck's sake, Don."

Tanaka stepped around where Hancock was standing, his hands on his hips, and saw what had him so pissed off.

Hart was lying on the floor, mumbling, a mostly-empty bottle of Wild Turkey in his hand. There were similar bottles all over the room, most of them empty. Tanaka could smell the booze and acrid sweat from ten feet away.

"Come on," Hancock snapped. "Help me get him up."

Tanaka circled around Hart, who yelled something unintelligible and took a swing at him as he tried to take the bottle away. He dodged the punch easily, but looked up at Hancock. "Should we even take him?" he asked.

"Sounds like we're going to need all hands on deck," Hancock replied, as he fended off Hart's flailing and got a hand under his arm. He lifted the burly, bearded drunk easily; Hancock was a strong dude. Given that Tanaka had heard that he did all sorts of extreme sports stuff on his off-time, that probably shouldn't have been surprising. "And if anybody's earned a chance to straighten himself out, I think it's Don. Come on. We'll put him in my car; it's a rental, so if he pukes the only one who's going to have to worry about it's gonna be the poor bastard getting it ready for the next renter."

CHAPTER 3

"Colonel Brannigan, I presume?" *Contralmirante* Huerta stood up and extended his hand. The Mexican officer was in mufti, a dark suit and shiny blue shirt.

Brannigan shook the proffered hand. He towered over the Mexican admiral, who was showing a bit of gray in his slickly-parted hair and mustache, though not nearly as much as Brannigan was.

Brannigan had dressed up a little for the meeting; he was wearing khakis and a sport coat, in contrast to his usual "retired" outdoor wear. He was still wearing boots, though, and the sport coat hid the Wilson Combat 1911 on his hip. Even with Van Zandt and Gomez in the room, he didn't trust this Mexican officer very far. He knew too much about how much the bad guys had infiltrated the instruments of the Mexican government.

Van Zandt was in a suit, and was standing back to one side, watching the two men meet. Gomez had posted himself up at the door, watching everything impassively with his hard, black eyes.

Gomez had become a Blackheart in the plus-up that Hancock and Santelli had conducted prior to the Burma job. Nobody knew much about him. He didn't talk much. In fact, getting more than a handful of words out of him on any particular subject was often an exercise in frustration, if not outright futility. He was lean and hard, with short black hair that was almost as dark as Flanagan's, and features that made him look like a younger

35

version of Geronimo. If he was an Apache, he never said as much, even when asked, but he sure looked the part.

He'd just shown up in Corpus Christi, unannounced, and had been waiting at the meetup when Brannigan had gotten there. True to form, he hadn't said much, but had simply taken up a position as Brannigan's bodyguard. Brannigan had just made out the outline of a pistol butt under his shirt when he'd moved just right at one point.

"I'm kind of surprised to see you up here," Brannigan said to Huerta, "this far from your command at a time like this." They were meeting in a suite in the Radisson Hotel. Outside the window, the surf washed the North Beach of Corpus Christi, and clouds were gathering over the Gulf of Mexico.

"My command is doing very little at the moment," Huerta admitted. "And the farther away from my government's authorities I am for this conversation, the better. I could get in a great deal of trouble for even talking to you. I have been strictly instructed not to approach the *Norteamericanos* for anything pertaining to this situation."

The three men sat down at the table, while Gomez maintained his silent, watchful vigil. Fortunately, they were in Texas, so either Gomez or Brannigan carrying weapons wasn't likely to raise any eyebrows, even if they were seen.

Huerta was clearly uncomfortable. The room was cool; the air conditioning had been going full blast when they'd gotten there, so the heat and humidity outside should have been negligible, but the Mexican admiral was sweating.

"You don't seem too happy to be having this meeting at all," Brannigan observed, leaning his elbows on the tabletop.

Huerta looked him in the eye. "I am not," he admitted. "I am a *Contralmirante* of the Mexican Naval Infantry. Terrorists have taken hostages from Mexican soil, including several highly-placed industrialists and politicians, and are holding them aboard a Mexican-owned oil platform in Mexican waters. This is a Mexican affair, and I should be able to deal with it myself, with my forces. That I cannot is an embarrassment, and that I am here in the United States, begging a gringo mercenary for help, is a shame that I do not wish to ever feel again."

Brannigan supposed he ought to feel insulted, but couldn't bring himself to. He understood Huerta's sentiments; he'd probably feel the same in his shoes.

"Well, the plus side is," he pointed out easily, "if we're successful, no one should ever know that you had to stoop so low in order to resolve this situation."

Huerta's eyes narrowed a little as he observed the American mercenary commander. He hadn't expected that. Brannigan kept his face carefully neutral, suppressing the faint smirk that threatened to lift the corner of his mouth under his bushy mustache. He found he was getting more comfortable with the idea of being a mercenary, if a mercenary who operated under certain strict rules. And the presumed contempt of his newest client only amused him. After all, what did it say about a merc when he was approached to do a job that regular forces had tried and failed at?

Either that he's really good, or that he's just more expendable and crazy enough to willingly go into a situation that is likely to get him killed. Don't let it go to your head.

"What do you know about the opposition?" he asked.

Huerta shook his head. "Next to nothing." Which was disappointing, but not unexpected, given what Van Zandt had already told him. "They are well-armed and well-equipped. We have not been able to get an aircraft or a boat near the platform since the first failed assault, thirty-seven hours ago. There has been no communication; they have issued no demands. They have just set in and shot at anything and anyone that comes near."

"What about the rest of the attacks?" Brannigan asked. "Any leads there?"

But Huerta shook his head again. "Most of those on the Mexican side of the border were executed by cartel *sicarios*," he said. "Some are known to us. Some are apparently small-time, for-hire killers. Those are the ones we know about. A few, like those on your side of the border, we have no idea *who* conducted them. The attackers were gone before anyone could react."

Brannigan rubbed his chin between the chops of his mustache. "Still no credible claims of responsibility for any of it?"

Both Huerta and Van Zandt shook their heads. "Nothing," Van Zandt confirmed. "Which is damned peculiar. Al Qaeda claimed 9/11 quickly enough. A major, mass-casualty attack—or attacks—like this should have *somebody* saying *something*."

"Fine," Brannigan said. No point in belaboring what they didn't know. "Numbers? Equipment?"

"The security footage from the golf course suggests about ten or twelve," Huerta said. "They were wearing plate carriers and helmets, and carrying bullpup rifles and pistols, with at least two machineguns. There appear to be more on the platform, from what little information we were able to get from our helicopters before they were shot down. None of our few drones have been able to get close enough to get an accurate count since then, either."

Brannigan nodded. "We should probably expect at least twenty men, then, possibly as many as thirty," he said. "Figure ten or twelve for the hit, and another ten or so to secure the GOPLAT in preparation for their exfil." He looked down at the imagery that Van Zandt had brought, where it was spread on the table. There were photos and diagrams of the Tourmaline-Delta platform. It was big. "Hmm. Maybe as many as fifteen to take the platform," he mused. "Better to estimate high than to lowball it and find out that we're facing a bigger force than we thought."

He looked up at Huerta. "Which brings me to a rather delicate matter," he said. "Since this is not, and can't be, a US government operation…"

Huerta's lips thinned in distaste, but he simply asked, "How much?"

Brannigan named a figure. He saw Huerta's pupils dilate in shock. He just shrugged. "Military operations aren't cheap, you should know that, Admiral. And under the circumstances..."

He knew the odds were against Huerta having that kind of funding readily available. On the other hand, he knew something about a lot of the Mexican military leadership's financial habits. The Mexican Marines might have the reputation of being the Mexican military's "untouchables," but there were always exceptions to the rule.

"I do not have that kind of money," Huerta said flatly.

Brannigan glanced over at Van Zandt, who was impassive, but glaring disapproval at him. Van Zandt had assured him that the Blackhearts would get paid, but Brannigan was playing a different game, and he'd let Van Zandt in on it later. He was doing his former boss a favor. If this really was going to be deniable for whatever back-room agency Van Zandt worked for, US government funds—even black ones—had to be kept out of it.

After a long moment of silence, Huerta sighed. "But I might be able to obtain it," he said reluctantly. "My family's company is a long-established economic power in Mexico, and we have considerable resources available to us, including resources that might not be...reported to certain authorities."

That could mean that they had a hand in the drug business, and were keeping it on the down-low from the government for obvious reasons, or that they were simply cautious, and keeping some of their assets hidden from the well-known, rapacious corruption in Mexico City. After all, the PRI had created the network of corruption, bribery, and kickbacks that had *been* the governing apparatus of Mexico for over eighty years.

"What does your family's business do?" Brannigan asked blandly, even as the wheels started turning in his head more quickly.

"Quite a number of things," Huerta sighed, apparently seeing where Brannigan was going. "Yes, they can provide a certain level of discreet logistical support, including getting men and…items of equipment into otherwise inadmissible places."

"Good," Brannigan said, making a mental note to caution the boys to be *extra* paranoid. Not that his original team was necessarily going to need the reminder; they'd crossed paths with both an Arab organized crime syndicate and the Russian mob in Dubai during the insert into Khadarkh. "Don't worry about weapons or ammunition; I've got some of my people already looking into that." Santelli was scouring every gun store in Nueces County, looking for what they'd need. "Though we might need some…discreet transport." By which he meant smuggling. That Huerta didn't bat an eye when he said it only confirmed a few of his suspicions.

"Insert is going to be the hard part," he continued, turning his eye back to the imagery on the table. Neither of the other two men sitting there contradicted him. He looked Huerta in the eye. "Does your family company by chance have any sort of maritime 'discreet transport' available?"

But Huerta shook his head. "No," was all he said. "I am afraid not. I do not know how to accomplish it."

"Are civilian charter boats getting shot at, too?" Brannigan asked.

"Apparently so," Van Zandt said.

"And we have set in an exclusion zone around the platform, enforced by the ARM *Hermenegildo Galeana*," Huerta said. "We cannot allow any further civilian casualties through carelessness."

"Well, we'll have to figure that part out," Brannigan said. He was mentally gauging distances over the water, and didn't like what he saw.

Huerta had little more to offer in the way of information. Brannigan wasn't inclined to press him for equipment; they'd source as much of it themselves as possible, in large part because then he knew that they weren't going to get shoddy crap in the interests of making sure they disappeared after or during the mission. Huerta certainly *seemed* sincere, but Brannigan hadn't fallen off the turnip truck the day before. He knew something of the political pressures the man was under, and what it could lead men to do, especially once they'd already gone off the reservation in the first place.

And for a man like Huerta, hiring gringo mercenaries to do a job that his Mexican Marines had failed at would be going way, way off the reservation. Which meant he had to be carefully watched.

He wondered if there weren't Mexicans watching the hotel, since Huerta had gone in there in the first place. His absence from the trouble zone had to have been noticed.

Their meeting at an end, Huerta saw himself out, Gomez stepping aside to let him out the door, unblinking black eyes following the Mexican Admiral every step of the way. Brannigan saw Huerta look the dark man in the eye for a brief moment, then look away.

He had to hand it to Gomez; the man could be intimidating. And his silence only contributed to the air of menace he radiated.

"What do you think, Gomez?" he asked, after the door shut behind Huerta. He hadn't had much more success in engaging the quiet mercenary in conversation than most of the rest, but he'd give it a shot.

"Long swim," Gomez said, stepping to the table and looking down at the imagery. "Might be doable, but it'll take time, and we'll be tired by the time we get there."

Brannigan watched him keenly. "You a diver?" he asked.

Gomez peeled back his t-shirt sleeve to show the Recon Jack tattooed on the inside of his arm. Brannigan grinned tightly. He hadn't known that Gomez had been a Recondo, but immediately felt a renewed kinship with the taciturn man.

"Been a few years since I've been on a Draeger," Gomez admitted, "but it'll come back to me. Trouble is, I don't know that we can run dive school for Tanaka or Wade in a couple of days."

"We can't," Brannigan agreed. "And we may not even have a couple of days. This being a hostage situation, we could have hours, presuming we're not already too late. And on top of that, Santelli never made it to Combatant Diver, either."

"Scuba shouldn't be hard," Van Zandt pointed out. "Sure, there's the bubbles issue, but if you stay deep enough until you get to the platform, then any bubbles should be dispersed enough to avoid detection. Especially at night."

"Except that Gomez' point about fatigue is a valid one," Brannigan replied. "That platform's twenty miles from shore. That's a *long*-ass swim. We'd be lucky to make it in a night, especially if not everybody's used to finning, and I know *I'm* not used to finning anymore." He shook his head. "No, we need to get closer. Which means a boat, at the very least." He stood up. "Let's head back downstairs; see if the rest have any ideas."

***

They could already hear raised voices as they got closer to the suite that was serving as the Blackhearts' temporary meeting place. Brannigan was already pissed from the bits and pieces he'd heard clearly by the time he pushed the door open.

"We're not in the mil anymore!" Jenkins was protesting. "I don't have to put up with this shit!"

"Okay, you're not in the mil anymore," Santelli growled, his meaty fists on his hips. "That does *not* absolve you from getting stupid and talking out of fucking school!"

"Look, maybe the tats were a bad idea," Wade said. "But we weren't talking out of school. Sure, we were telling war stories, but it wasn't like we were openly talking about where we were at the time, or even when it happened."

"It's still bullshit," Jenkins exclaimed. "Who the hell are you to get in my ass, Santelli? You're not a Sergeant Major anymore."

"But he's my right hand, and I run this outfit," Brannigan snarled, looming behind Santelli. "You want to work? You want to get paid to be a shooter again? Then you do what Carlo Santelli tells you to where it pertains to the job and security about the job, and you keep your damned mouth shut, or one of us is going to shut it for you. Permanently. Get my drift, Jenkins?"

***

George Jenkins suddenly realized that he was getting none-to-friendly stares from most of the other Blackhearts in the room, most especially from the original Khadarkh crew.

His initial reaction was to get even more pissed. Who the hell did these guys think they were? He had been a *SEAL*. Sure, some of them had been Recon Marines, but they hadn't been in JSOC. The fact that he hadn't been either was something he didn't particularly think about much. Sure, he hadn't been up to DEVGRU selection. He'd had an off week. That was all. He was sure that he'd have made it if he'd gotten another chance.

But he'd still been a *SEAL*, and still had that Trident tattooed on his chest. The SEAL teams were the best and greatest warriors on the planet. Everyone knew it. So who did these *Marines* think they were, talking down to him?

But the somewhat more common-sense part of his mind was registering that some of those not-so-friendly looks weren't just pissed. And the implications of Brannigan's threat to shut his mouth "permanently" were starting to work their way through his mind.

"You wouldn't," he started to say, then faltered as Brannigan's eyes flashed dangerously.

"Wouldn't what, Jenkins?" Brannigan said softly. "We've already invaded two sovereign countries for pay. What do you think we wouldn't do to maintain our security, and make sure nobody knows about the Blackhearts who shouldn't?"

For a moment, Jenkins looked into the big Colonel's eyes, and suddenly felt his blood run cold. Brannigan wasn't impressed by his Trident, or his resume, and Jenkins suddenly got an idea of just how dangerous the big man really could be. He'd seen Brannigan in combat, of course, but he'd never imagined him to be anything but an officer, until now.

He swallowed, and at the same time, got even more pissed. He didn't like being afraid. He didn't like being forced to acknowledge that maybe, just maybe, he wasn't the best, most dangerous man in the room.

"Fine," he said, his voice coming out more high-pitched and hoarse than he'd intended. He cleared his throat. "Fine," he repeated. "I'll shut up. But this isn't over."

"Yes, it is," Wade suddenly growled. Jenkins looked over at the big Ranger's pale, pitiless eyes. "I'm with Brannigan on this," Wade continued. "Sure, I got carried away. I screwed up; we shouldn't have gotten the tats. But we're a team, and a team needs to be on the same page. We're not in high-school. We work for Colonel Brannigan, and he says Santelli's word goes. So it does. And if you turn on the team for the sake of your fucking ego, I'll cut your throat in a heartbeat."

Jenkins saw the truth of his words in Wade's eyes. The big man's stare always looked a little too intense, a little crazy. Jenkins suddenly knew that Wade would follow through on his threat without batting an eye.

Fighting back tears of rage and humiliation, he subsided. "Fine," was all he said. He turned away from the rest and headed for the back corner of the room.

As he did, he caught a glimpse of Aziz watching him. The message in the other man's eyes was just as clear.

Hey, it ain't me this time.

***

44

It took a few minutes for the tension from the confrontation to die down. Tanaka had been keeping as far back toward the wall as possible; the look on his face was that of a kid watching his parents fight. The original team had mostly been standing behind Santelli, and Bianco and Wade had been flanking Jenkins, only facing him instead of backing him up.

Hart had still been sleeping it off in the other room.

Hancock had gone to retrieve Hart, who was disheveled but somewhat more coherent. He was deeply, almost embarrassingly apologetic for being too drunk to make his own way to the meeting, and promised repeatedly that it wouldn't happen again. Santelli and Brannigan had simply stared at him and made it clear that it had better not.

Then they got down to the business of planning.

CHAPTER 4

The *Grupo Huerta* rep was a thin, weaselly-looking man, with a pencil mustache and long, wavy hair. He was wearing a light-gray suit, and lounging in the booth where Brannigan and Hancock had been instructed to meet him, looking at his phone.

He looked up as the two Blackhearts approached the booth. The small diner in Corpus Christi seemed like a strange place for a business meeting, but given the nature of the business they had with *Grupo Huerta*, the low-key surroundings were probably better than any corporate conference room.

The little man looked up at them, with the kind of languid insolence in his eyes that Brannigan had come to expect from gang-bangers, not corporate drones. Of course, he had to wonder just how much separation there really was, given *Grupo Huerta*'s "discreet" elements.

He slid into the booth across from the little man. "You must be Señor Cavaldes," he said.

Cavaldes might have nodded. It was more of a toss of his head, as if to say, *Whatever, gringo.*

"We have some business to discuss," Brannigan said. Hancock had grabbed a nearby metal-backed chair, flipped it around, and straddled it, folding his arms across the top of the back.

"I don't think so," Cavaldes replied. There was a notable, if faint, sneer in his voice, that almost extended to his expression.

Brannigan usually prided himself in controlling his emotions and his expression, but his eyes flashed at the little man's tone. Cavaldes noticed it, too. He didn't flinch; not quite. But he sobered a little.

"You're going to have to repeat that," he said, leaning partway across the table, his voice dropping to a threatening rumble. "Because if I came out here just for you to waste my time, I'm going to be a little...upset."

Cavaldes glanced over at Hancock, who was watching him with that hawkish, unblinking stare that Hancock got when he was watching a target, or a wayward subordinate who needed a severe thrashing. He blinked, and looked back at Brannigan, who was watching him with the same sort of intensity. The thin man licked his lips, apparently suddenly realizing that the gringos he was meeting with were every bit as dangerous as the *sicarios* running around his country.

"I'm here to tell you that the meeting is off," Cavaldes said, sounding a bit more subdued. "Only the fact that *Contralmirante* Huerta set it up kept me here. You should go home and forget all about this."

"In case you hadn't noticed, sport," Brannigan said, "*we* are home. You're on American soil." It was a minor point, but this guy was pissing him off, and he felt the need to correct him. "Why is *Grupo Huerta* reneging on the deal?"

"It is a security matter," Cavaldes answered. "The *Grupo* cannot risk doing business with you."

"Is that so?" Brannigan countered. "Given some of the under-the-table deals that the *Grupo Huerta* has been involved in, I find that rather hard to believe." He didn't exactly have a complete dossier on the company, but Van Zandt had managed to get him just enough background to know who he was dealing with. "You've made deals with cartel front companies, transnational criminal organizations operating under NGO status, and even countries that do not have your nation's best interests at heart. You've laundered drug money, looked the other way while your ships and aircraft have been used for gunrunning, and facilitated the siphoning of your country's natural resources to China." He watched Cavaldes' face go pale as his litany continued. He was hitting the mark, and had to wonder how much more was under the surface that he didn't know about.

"So don't try to tell me that you're suddenly worried about either dealing with dangerous people, or breaking the law, Señor Cavaldes," he continued. "Neither one has stopped you before."

Cavaldes' jaw worked for a moment, and then he suddenly tried to bolt. He didn't get far. A diner booth is not the best spot to try to make a quick getaway, and he got jammed between the seat and the table, just long enough for Hancock to get in his way, suddenly looming over him, that same piercing stare pinning him to the bench, a hand hovering in just the right spot to make it clear he had a pistol under his shirt.

"What's the deal, Cavaldes?" Brannigan asked. He hadn't moved, letting Hancock head off their suddenly reticent contact. "Did you get paid off? Or has one of the top people been threatened?"

"Maybe both?" Hancock suggested, keeping Cavaldes pinned with his basilisk stare.

As he watched Cavaldes, Brannigan couldn't help but feel an intense *déjà vu*. Their first contacts in Dubai, on the way into Khadarkh, had been the Suleiman Syndicate, a rare Arabic criminal organization, and they had turned on them. This wasn't as hairy; they hadn't been counting on Huerta for the weapons or ammo, but more for transport and other, more minor logistical items on a short timeline. But now that looked like it was out the window, and he couldn't help but wonder why. Corruption? Or something worse?

Cavaldes seemed to have realized that he'd misread the situation badly. He had quickly gone from casually contemptuous to near-panicked. "Look, I don't know why, man!" he protested. "I'm just the messenger!"

"You've got to know something," Brannigan said quietly, keeping his voice low and dangerous. "Maybe we should take you for a ride and wring you out a little."

Cavaldes was shaking his head. "They didn't tell me anything," he insisted. "I was supposed to meet with you, and then an hour ago I got a call that I had to tell you that the deal was off."

Hancock glanced at Brannigan, who was still watching Cavaldes with narrowed eyes. "An hour ago?" he asked.

Cavaldes nodded spasmodically. "Yeah, just about."

It didn't tell him much, but it told him that something had definitely changed. Maybe someone had gotten to the *Grupo Huerta* leadership? Or some new bit of information had surfaced? Maybe the attackers were connected, higher than Huerta had imagined.

That was a thought. Might it explain why Huerta's hands were apparently tied?

"Look man, I don't know what else to tell you," Cavaldes said, his eyes flicking back and forth between Hancock and Brannigan. "All I know is, the *Grupo* won't work with you. I can't change that."

Brannigan watched him for a long moment, then jerked his head toward the door. "Get out of here," he said curtly.

Hancock didn't say a word, but stepped away, granting Cavaldes an escape route. The skinny man took immediate advantage, scrambling out of the booth and moving quickly toward the door. He didn't run, not quite, but he made tracks.

Brannigan sat back in the booth and looked at Hancock. "What do you think, Roger?" he asked.

Hancock watched Cavaldes' retreat, a faint crease between his eyebrows as he thought. "Is that a 'what do you think we should do' question, or a 'why do you think they backed out' question?" he asked.

"Both," Brannigan answered.

Hancock sat down in the booth across from his boss, where Cavaldes had been sitting. "As for the second, I wonder if Huerta wasn't under surveillance by somebody connected with the opposition, whoever they are," he said. "It's the only way I can think that somebody might have gotten wind of our involvement in the first place. I know you don't entirely trust Van Zandt; neither do I. But the leak coming from him doesn't seem right."

Brannigan nodded. "I think you're right. Van Zandt has plenty of reasons not to like me; I've got even more reasons not to like him. But this doesn't smell right to be him. There's definitely *something* going on; this is way too big and too bloody to be a setup."

"So, the bad guys have bird-dogs out, keeping an eye on their opposition," Hancock concluded. "Which means that this is even bigger than we thought."

But Brannigan shook his head fractionally at that. "No, it was already plenty big. Nobody coordinates an attack on that scale without being in it for all the marbles. September 11th was big, and that was half the number of targets this was. It was relatively simple, too; capture four airplanes and kamikaze them into buildings. This was coordinated hits, across state and international lines. Somebody big's involved; somebody with a lot of resources."

"Which brings us back to the original question," Hancock said. "What do we do now?"

"What do you think?" Brannigan asked.

Hancock mused for a second. His glance suggested that he knew what Brannigan was getting at; the Colonel had made it clear before Burma that Hancock was his second-in-command, and needed to be on top of things in case Brannigan went down. Brannigan was pushing him to think and strategize.

"Chavez got us the initial contacts with the Suleiman Syndicate in Dubai," Hancock said after a moment. "I know, it didn't work out, but that was an on-the-ground decision by that Al

Fulani asshole. The point is, Chavez knows ways of making contact with the 'gray area' of commerce. I think we need to have him do some digging."

Brannigan nodded in satisfaction. Roger hadn't been ready when Brannigan had told him he was the go-to to take over the Blackhearts if and when the time came. He'd still been doing what he'd always done, pursuing adrenaline. Often at risk of life and limb.

Since that day, when Brannigan had watched his subordinate and old friend nearly wipe out on a racetrack, he'd noticed a change in the former NCO. Roger didn't take as many risks. He was always thinking, always observing, always pushing to assemble as much information about their situation that he could get. He'd taken Brannigan's words to heart, and it was a good thing to see.

"I agree," Brannigan said, sliding out of the booth, making sure his shirt was still covering the butt of his 1911. "Let's give Hector a call."

***

"I don't know how we're going to get all of this without attracting attention," Santelli worried, looking down at the loadout list that he and Brannigan had put together. "We're gonna be on a watch list by noon, if not wrapped up by the cops."

Tanaka laughed. Santelli looked up at him, frowning.

"You need to spend more time away from Taxachussets, Carlo," Tanaka said, still chuckling. Gomez was smiling, a strange expression on the taciturn man's otherwise immobile face. "This is *Texas*. We'll probably get a discount."

Gomez was driving the big cargo van, with Santelli in the right seat and Tanaka strapped into the single seat in the back. The sides of the van were windowless, making it unlikely that anyone was going to look into their cargo, even though, as Tanaka had pointed out, they were in Texas, and unlikely to be interfered with, or even draw a second glance.

"We're close enough to Mexico that *somebody*'s going to think we're gun-running," Santelli protested.

"Except that most of the gun stores around here won't even show their 4473s to the Feds without a warrant," Tanaka explained. "Most Texans take the Second Amendment *very* seriously. We'll spread things out, make sure we're not spending too much in one place, but we'll be long gone before anybody thinks to start looking into the purchases we're making. Don't worry about it."

Santelli looked out the window, a dubious expression on his face. He'd have to admit that he wasn't familiar with Texas' gun laws. For that matter, he'd spent most of his Marine Corps career either on Okinawa or in California, and the rest of his life in Boston. None of those places had the reverence for the Second Amendment or the gun culture of Texas.

"Why are we heading out of town?" he asked. They were nearing the outskirts of Corpus Christi, with no sign of stopping.

"Because if we're going to spread things around," Tanaka said seriously, "it's better to start with the small-town gun stores. Most of them have better selection, anyway."

An hour later, they pulled up next to "Ray's Guns and Ammo," a solid adobe structure with bars on the door and windows. The parking lot was pretty full for a Thursday afternoon, but neither Tanaka nor Gomez appeared at all surprised as Gomez parked the van and Tanaka pulled the side door open.

"Come on," Tanaka said. "Let's see what they've got."

Tanaka led the way inside. Santelli's eyes widened a bit as he entered the place.

Past the bars on the doors, "Ray's Guns and Ammo" was a clean, brightly-lit emporium, with racks along the walls positively packed with everything from expensive shotguns to the newest "black" rifles. Shelves on the floor were loaded with ammunition, slings, holsters, reloading supplies, targets...anything that a shooter might need.

Tanaka moved to the counter in front of the newer firearms. Santelli recognized a few of them; the AK and AR patterns were unmistakable. He saw a few SCARs, PTR-91s—not unlike the G3s that they had jumped into Burma with—and several newer designs that he wasn't familiar with. Most of them were illegal in his home state.

"Howdy, gentlemen," the young man behind the counter said as they approached. "Anything I can help you find today?"

"We're looking for some LWRC M6s," Tanaka said.

"All three of you?" the younger man asked, looking around at them.

Tanaka nodded. "We're putting together a carbine course," he explained. "Aiming for standardization among the instructors." If it wasn't true, it was at least believable, and the kid had no need to know the details.

"I think we've got a few in stock," the younger man said. "Let me check."

***

Half an hour later, they were loading the cases for three LWRC M6A2 rifles, three FN-45 pistols, along with two cases per man of both 5.56mm and .45 caliber ammunition into the back of the van. "That was easy," Santelli remarked.

"I told you," Tanaka said. "Texans aren't big on being busybodies when it comes to guns."

"I know people back home who would be horrified," Santelli said. "They'd immediately ask about criminals getting the guns so easily."

"We still had to fill out 4473s and do NICS checks," Tanaka pointed out, referring to the FBI's National Instant Criminal Background Checks System. It was part of the paperwork involved in legally obtaining a firearm in the United States. "If we'd been felons, it would have popped up and we'd have been denied. People who think that reasonable gun buying only enables criminals don't know what they're talking about. Besides, once again, this is Texas. You pull a gun to commit a crime in most places around here, and the locals will pull *their* guns and shoot you."

"If it's this easy, why did we go with the sixteen-inch barrels?" Santelli asked. "Why not get the tens, given where we're going?"

"Because Short Barreled Rifles are a whole different can of worms," Tanaka answered, as he climbed into the van. "We don't have an extra eight months to wait for the ATF to issue a tax stamp."

Santelli nodded thoughtfully. He realized that he'd never really had to do this kind of weapons procurement; Hancock had handled the deal with the Russian mobsters in Dubai, and Van Zandt had done all the logistics prior to the Burma job. If he was going to be Brannigan's right hand for this sort of thing, he needed to know more. He was glad he had Tanaka along.

Gomez climbed in behind the wheel, and looked over his shoulder at Tanaka, who was looking at the maps on his phone. "'The Minuteman' is next," Tanaka said, reading off the directions. "I've been there before. If you thought Ray's was good, wait until you see this place."

***

It was evening by the time the van pulled into the hotel parking lot. Curtis glanced out the window. "Looks like they're back," he reported.

Brannigan just nodded. He'd just gotten off the phone with Chavez. They had a contact. And he really wasn't sure what he thought about it. But the clock was ticking. And they didn't have much choice.

When the three men who'd gone on the procurement run came up to the suite, Santelli was shaking his head.

"I've been living in the wrong neighborhood," he marveled. "We'd never be able to get this stuff up north. Maybe I should move."

"Would Melissa be okay with that?" Bianco asked.

Santelli grimaced. "Probably not," he conceded. "She doesn't like the heat much."

Brannigan looked at his former Sergeant Major and old friend briefly. Santelli had been convinced that he and Melissa had been on the rocks before Khadarkh. Somehow, though, it seemed as if his discovery of new purpose after forming the Blackhearts with Brannigan had saved that relationship; the two of them seemed closer than ever lately, even with Santelli haring off to risk his neck on the regular. He hoped that it would last, for Carlo's sake.

"We've got the hardware?" he asked.

Santelli nodded. "An LWRC M6 rifle, with Aimpoint T2 sights, and FN-45 pistol for each man, eight rifle mags and four pistol mags, and about four hundred rounds rifle, one hundred rounds pistol each. We even got holsters and slings. No chest rigs yet."

Brannigan nodded. "Jenkins is on that. He's got a buddy in the business."

"What about the rest?" Santelli asked.

"*Grupo Huerta*'s a bust," Brannigan said, curtly explaining the result of his meeting with Cavaldes. "But we've got another contact, with a company called Ciela International. I'm leaving with Joe and Kevin here in the next few minutes."

CHAPTER 5

"This sucks," Curtis said, as the three of them stepped out into the parking lot. "Having to run around on business just as prime clubbing time comes around."

"It's Thursday," Flanagan pointed out.

"Haven't you ever heard of Thirsty Thursdays, Joe?" Curtis retorted. "And I'm not just talking about thirsty for booze, either, if you know what I mean. Cougars galore!"

"What about that fake blond?" Flanagan asked dryly, as if he already knew the answer.

But Curtis didn't rise to the bait. "Oh, I know what this is about," he said slyly. "Seriously, Colonel, I wish you hadn't called when you did. You wouldn't have believed it. Mopey Joe here was actually talking to a girl! A hot, hot, *hot* girl, too. *Way* out of his league."

Struck by a sudden suspicion, Flanagan turned a glare on his shorter companion. "Why do I suddenly suspect that the entire thing was a setup?" he growled. When Curtis put a hurt expression on his face, Flanagan's eyes narrowed further. "Let me guess; she was primed already. Was she an escort, Kevin?"

Curtis' hurt expression turned to indignation. "Don't you put that evil on me, Joseph!" he snapped. "That girl is a saint! You would not believe the lies Cindy and I had to tell her to get her to come out, about what a great, handsome, charming guy you are! You should feel grateful that she has such horrible taste that she

57

not only believed us, she even apparently *still* believed it even after she met your grim, suspicious ass."

Flanagan still eyed him suspiciously, but Curtis' indignation seemed genuine. They fell silent as Brannigan led the way to the car.

"Seriously," Curtis said after a moment, "you owe that girl an apology for even thinking that, Joe. As if I'd stoop that low. *I* don't even hire girls like that!"

"Sorry," Flanagan said, feeling somewhat ashamed. "She just seemed a little too good to be true."

"That's because you're an Eyeore," Curtis replied. "You need to have a little more faith in people. Including your friends."

Flanagan realized that he'd genuinely hurt his friend. But a moment later, the thought was erased as his eye settled on the face dimly visible on the other side of the auto glass, watching them from beneath one of the bright streetlights that illuminated the hotel parking lot.

He took two long steps to catch up with Brannigan. "We've got company," he said quietly.

Brannigan took a brief glance over at the car when Flanagan inclined his head toward it. "Maybe," he replied. "Or maybe they're just here to make a score, and are watching everybody coming out. We've still got places to be." He pulled the car door open and folded himself in behind the wheel. It was an awfully small car for such a big man to fit into.

Flanagan shrugged and ducked into the passenger seat, leaving Curtis to get into the back. No sooner had Curtis' door closed than Brannigan was putting the rental sedan in gear and backing out of the parking space.

They rolled down the slope and out of the parking lot. Flanagan was watching the rear view as best he could, though he had to crane his neck a little to see more than the side of the car. "They're following," he said.

"Just keep an eye on them," Brannigan replied, sounding unconcerned. "They might be surveillance, or they might just be going the same way. Both you boys strapped?"

"Yeah," Flanagan replied. His own STI Tactical was at the small of his back. Behind him, he could hear Curtis checking his M&P .45.

"Stay frosty," Brannigan said. "We'll see what develops."

Brannigan drove normally, but turned away from their planned route. The dark sedan behind them followed, but as the Colonel had said, that could just be a coincidence. The other car might just be heading in the same general direction. But Flanagan kept his eye on the other car in the rear-view mirror.

"Kevin, quit craning your neck to look out the back window," Brannigan said as he drove down the street. "If they're really following us, let's not give them any cues that they've tipped their hand."

Flanagan could hear the rustle as Curtis turned back forward. He could almost feel the smaller man's frustration. Curtis might often say that he was more of a lover than a fighter, but Flanagan knew better. His friend was a hell of a fighter, and while he could be as patient as he needed to be in the bush, he wasn't terribly subtle once the enemy was in front of him. He was at his best with a machinegun in his hands, after all.

Brannigan kept glancing in the rearview mirror as he drove. There was still a fair bit of traffic on the streets; it was getting dark, but it was still early in the evening. Flanagan found that he was having a harder time picking the target car out of the rest of the traffic as they wove between other cars and trucks on the road.

Brannigan turned left at the next major intersection, continuing to take them farther away from their destination. He was clearly taking the threat seriously.

"They're still with us," Flanagan confirmed, peering in the mirror.

They continued down the street, pausing at the next light. The car was still behind them.

Brannigan turned right. The sedan followed.

At the next light, Brannigan suddenly floored the accelerator as the light turned yellow. The other car abruptly accelerated to follow, running the red light to get through the intersection after them.

"Well, that tears it," Brannigan announced. "Three turns and a red light. You called it, Joe. They're definitely a tail." He turned his eyes back on the road. "I don't think that whoever got to *Grupo Huerta* is too happy that we're still around."

"What do you want to do about 'em?" Flanagan asked.

"I'm driving," Brannigan replied. "Find me a spot to go to ground. And get the rest of the team spun up. Might as well get those brand new LWRCs broken in."

***

For the next half hour, they traced a twisting and turning route through the major thoroughfares of Corpus Christi, Brannigan careful never to turn down a side street or possible dead end where they could be cornered. If their shadows were just surveilling them, they might be all right with only three pistols. But it did not pay to walk into an ambush, particularly not so lightly armed.

Curtis had leaned over the center console, looking over the imagery on Flanagan's phone, the two men's bickering over some girl forgotten in the face of the threat. That was why Brannigan had never been bothered by the continual back-and-forth between the two wildly different characters. When it needed to quiet, it did. They were pros, both of them, and he wouldn't want to go into a mission without either of them.

Once they had a destination picked out, Curtis had retreated to the back seat, where he'd called Hancock to report the situation and where they were headed. After that, it had simply been a matter of burning time.

Finally, Brannigan headed out of town, hitting Interstate 37 and heading northwest, toward the bridge that crossed the Nueces River and dumped out into San Patricio County. The sedan kept pace, and unless he was mistaken, looking in the rearview mirror, it had been joined by a pickup and an old, rattletrap Suburban that looked like it was half rust.

He sped up the freeway, the three vehicles maintaining pace and changing lanes as he did. None of them tried to pass the others, and the Suburban had to be straining to keep up, which further reinforced his suspicion that they were all part of the same crew.

Picked on the wrong guys, jackasses.

He took the ramp to cross over to the west, turning briefly onto US 77 before quickly exiting onto Highway 624 and heading west. The trio of vehicles kept pace, not far behind them.

At least nobody's started shooting yet. He honestly wasn't sure whether it was because the bad guys were waiting for a better spot to hit them, or if they were hoping that they'd go somewhere with less traffic, where violence might not be as out in the open, and therefore less likely to attract the attention of law enforcement.

He sped past the residential neighborhoods and small barbeque restaurants on the highway, only mashing the brake and turning off the highway once they were past the last houses and getting out into the fields. The sedan's wheels squealing on the asphalt, he floored it, mentally cursing the rental's anemic whine as it accelerated north toward the river, far too slowly.

There wasn't a lot of terrain that they could use; that part of Texas was pretty flat. There was, however, thick growth along either side of the road; mostly scrub trees and tangled underbrush. And that was what Brannigan was counting on, whispering a quick prayer that the rest of the team was in position.

To his right, Flanagan was half-turned in his seat, ready to throw himself out the door, his STI 2011 in his hand. Curtis was out of sight behind him, but doubtless in a similar posture, his

61

Smith & Wesson ready for action. The only one of the three without a gun in his hand was Brannigan.

The road dead-ended up ahead. Brannigan kept hurtling toward it as fast as he could reasonably get the little car going, until he could just see a tailgate around the corner ahead. That was the signal. He stomped on the brake as he passed the road on his right, skidding to a stop just before the pavement ran out and the car slammed into the trees ahead.

The car was still rocking on its shocks as both Flanagan and Curtis threw their doors open and dove out of the vehicle. It took Brannigan another second to follow, yanking his 1911 out of its holster as he plunged toward the brush on the side of the road.

The three pursuing vehicles were coming on fast, their headlights blazing in the early evening twilight. All three of them skidded to a stop not far on the other side of the turn, leaving their lights on.

Doors opened, and footsteps crunched and clattered on the crumbling pavement. Brannigan leveled his pistol at the blazing headlights that were concealing the men behind them, trying to flatten himself against the gravel at the side of the road. There wasn't any cover; even hiding in the brush wouldn't save them if their pursuers decided to hose down the vegetation.

A silhouette passed in front of one of the sedan's headlights. "Hey, *putos!*" an accented voice called out. "You should have gone home! Now it's too late!"

More figures were appearing, though they were little more than dark, blurry shapes, back-lit by the headlights. Brannigan squinted against the glare, as his finger tightened on the 1911's trigger. He couldn't see much, but the shotguns and pistols dangling from hands weren't hard to make out.

A moment later, all hell broke loose.

Gunfire thundered from the left, muzzle flashes strobing from the brush alongside the road. Bullets smashed headlights, blew out windows, and knocked dark, shadowy figures off their feet.

Brannigan saw a shotgun come up, and squeezed off a shot at the man holding it. The gangbangers hadn't stopped far away from the rental car, so it wasn't a long shot. The figure staggered, and Brannigan brought the pistol down from recoil, centering the glowing tritium sights high on the man's chest before firing again. That time, the gangbanger fell down on his ass, then toppled backward, the shotgun clattering to the asphalt beside him.

Almost as suddenly as it had begun, the shooting stopped. Brannigan stayed where he was for a moment, just in case any of their attackers were playing possum. He could hear groans coming from a few of the huddled forms on the road; not every one of their enemies had been killed.

Good. He got carefully to his feet, reloading as he did so. The 1911 was a top-of-the-line custom job, but it still was only a single-stack, which was why he had made sure he had newer, eight-round magazines. He knew younger guys who would insist that it still wasn't enough ammo, but there were some things that Brannigan was wedded to, and John Moses Browning's classic pistol was one of them.

Keeping the pistol indexed at his sternum, ready to punch it out and fire, he advanced on the gangbangers' bullet-riddled cars. Curtis and Flanagan flanked him, their own pistols held in similar attitudes.

The rest of the team was coming out of the trees and brush alongside the road, rifles held at the ready. None of them were wearing chest rigs; those hadn't come in yet. Extra magazines were shoved into pockets or belts.

Brannigan advanced on the guy with the shotgun, who was twitching and gasping on the pavement in front of the dark-colored sedan, blood bubbling from his lips. He'd been lung-shot, by the looks of it.

Looming over him, pistol still held ready, Brannigan kicked the shotgun away from his hand, though it looked like the guy was past even thinking about the weapon. "You ain't got long, son," he said quietly. "Tell me who sent you and I'll call an ambulance."

The dying gangster gurgled. There wasn't any defiance or insolence left in his dark eyes. He was dying, he knew it, and the fear was plastered all over his face. This wasn't the way it was supposed to have gone.

That's what happens when thugs go up against professionals. Brannigan didn't feel much pity. He didn't know what this kid had done to earn his place in the criminal underworld, but he doubted that it involved a lot of charity work. *Practice being a bully long enough, and you're helpless against somebody who knows what they're doing and fights back.*

The kid tried to say something, but choked on his own blood. Holstering his pistol, aware of Flanagan and Curtis flanking him, Brannigan crouched down and heaved the kid off the pavement, pulling him up into a sitting position so that he could breathe. A little, anyway. He wasn't just choking on his own blood; the bullet had clearly punctured the lung and collapsed it. If he didn't get medical attention soon, the growing air pressure in his chest cavity would kill him.

The gangster was trying to fight him, but Brannigan's grip was like an iron vise on his shoulder. He didn't want the kid to die, yet. He wanted answers.

"Yeah, that's not looking good," he said, still gripping the gangbanger's clavicle, hard enough that it would have hurt, even past the pain of the bullet hole in his chest. He wasn't trying to torture the kid, but he was sending a message. He was entirely in control of the situation, and the dying thug's feeble struggles were only going to cause him more pain. "Talk to me, kid."

But the gangster only rasped horribly and passed out. Brannigan put a pair of fingers to the kid's throat. He was alive; there was a fast, thready pulse there. But not for long.

"Got another live one over here, boss," Childress called out.

Brannigan lowered the dying gangster to the pavement, turning him over into a hasty version of the recovery position, and stood up, drawing his pistol again as he moved around the side of the wrecked sedan to join the younger man.

Childress, his dark hair sticking out from under his ball cap in tufts, was standing over another gangster, a short, skinny man wearing a black t-shirt and jeans. The t-shirt was sopping wet, the blood blending in with the black cloth in the dim light of the few unbroken headlights reflecting off the pavement.

Brannigan squatted down next to the man. He'd been shot at least three times, but was still breathing. "Who sent you?" he asked.

"*Chinga tu madre*," the man sputtered.

"What's that, asshole?" Wade snarled, stepping forward, a boot cocked to kick the man in the ribs. But Childress intercepted him.

"Let the Colonel handle him," Childress drawled.

Brannigan made a show of examining the gangster's wounds. "I'd say you've got even less time than the guy I shot in the lung back there," he said. "Make the most of it."

The man panted hard, blood seeping from the holes in his chest and arm. That was when Brannigan noticed that it looked like a bullet had broken his humerus and severed his brachial artery; there was blood pumping from his armpit. He had less time than he thought.

That fact seemed to suddenly sink in for the wounded man, as well. His eyes widened as he started to shiver. "We just got the money and the target, man," he said.

"No direct contact?" Brannigan asked. The gangster shook his head spasmodically.

"It was an email," he gasped. "And cash in a safe deposit box."

Brannigan stood. "I'd put some pressure on that arm of yours if you want to live," he said grimly. "Otherwise you might not last long enough for an ambulance to get here. We're a good way out, out here."

He started back toward the car. "Somebody call 911 once we're clear," he said. "I'm sure not all of these punks will make it, but maybe some of them will."

"What if they describe us to the cops?" Jenkins asked from where he was standing by the side of the road, his LWRC cradled in his hands, watching the dead and wounded gangsters.

Brannigan's chuckle was dry and utterly humorless. "You think these types will talk to the cops?" he asked. "Don't bet on it. And we'll be far away by then, anyway."

He looked the rental car over. There were a couple of bullet holes in it; that could be a problem. But they didn't have time to worry about patching it up. They'd just have to keep it out of sight as best they could until it was go time.

It started up fine, though. Flanagan and Curtis were still outside, holding security. "Get in," he called out. "We've still got a meeting to keep. No time to push it back."

The two men got in, Brannigan put the car in gear, and then they were heading down the road, back east toward the coast, passing the vehicles the others had brought to the ambush. Santelli and Hancock were already getting the rest of the team mounted up and ready to move.

Somebody sure as hell doesn't want us getting involved. Somebody who isn't *out on that GOPLAT, and somebody who has a* lot *of resources.*

He chewed on the problem as he drove. He didn't have any answers. There had been enough global tension over the last few years that the list of suspects could be a long one. And he wasn't plugged in deeply enough anymore to be able to venture even a semi-educated guess.

It bothered him, this informational vacuum where the opposition was concerned. The job should have been relatively simple; go to the GOPLAT, board it, rescue the hostages, kill all the terrorists, and go home. But there was obviously something more going on, and the terrorists had contacts and backers at large inside the United States, who were making a concerted effort to go after his team, before they'd even stepped off.

What the hell have we gotten ourselves into this time?

Behind them, wailing sirens and flashing lights began to converge on the site of the ambush, as local law enforcement and ambulances responded to the sounds of gunfire and the locals' emergency calls.

CHAPTER 6

Ciela International's headquarters wasn't in Corpus Christi; it was in Bonn, Germany. It wasn't a German company, either. It was a transnational conglomerate with an Esperanto name, which to Brannigan made it just that much more pretentious. And suspicious.

He didn't know for certain why Chavez had hooked them up with Ciela, but he somehow doubted it was because the company was a fine, upstanding exemplar of ethical global trade.

The Ciela office in Corpus Christi wasn't fancy, either. It was an ugly, off-white, corrugated steel building in an industrial park on the western edge of town. The parking lot, bordered by a deep drainage ditch alongside the edge of the road, was lit by stark, orange sodium lights and surrounded by palm trees. There were a handful of cars in the lot as they pulled up just before ten o'clock at night, but no lights were on in the building, and no one was moving around outside. It looked like they were closed up tight.

Brannigan combat-parked, backing into the outermost parking spot, facing the building, and shut off the car. He watched as the rest of the team's vehicles moved into vague overwatch positions in the surrounding lots. There wasn't any high ground, so they couldn't get much standoff, but they would be close if he and Flanagan had to holler for help.

He watched the building for a moment, as he rummaged in the small go bag under his seat for another magazine to replace the spare he'd reloaded with. Maybe somebody at Ciela had tipped off the gangbangers after Chavez had made contact. Maybe whoever was supporting the terrorists out on the GOPLAT simply had lookouts along the coast, watching for anything out of the ordinary. A quick glance through the lot didn't turn up any likely vehicles, but that didn't necessarily mean anything. Brannigan knew that there were plenty of unmanned vehicles out there for surveillance use, and if the Ciela building was using some kind of off-site servers for the surveillance cameras set up on the corners of the building and several of the light posts, then they were vulnerable to cyber attacks.

That gave him pause, and he squinted at one of the cameras, even as he stayed well back in the shadows, avoiding the sodium lights' illumination. Some of the later information he'd gotten from Chavez and Van Zandt had included the use of the drone to attack the El Paso border crossing. Cyber stuff was usually outside of his wheelhouse; he wasn't a Luddite, but he also wasn't much of a computer guy. But he knew enough to know that it was a threat, and that the more the tech companies tried to encourage people to use their "cloud" services, the more often reports seemed to come out about massive amounts of information being stolen by hackers.

But after a few minutes, he didn't see any sign of another ambush. "You see anything?" he asked Flanagan and Curtis.

"An ugly-ass building and some cheap rice-burner cars," Curtis replied. He was holding up his phone like he was taking pictures. "I don't see anybody lurking around in the landscaping. Place looks dead."

Brannigan looked back at him, a faint frown creasing his face. "How can you tell?" he asked.

Curtis grinned, his teeth flashing white in the darkness. He tapped a small, rectangular attachment plugged into the base of the phone. "Thermal imager for a smartphone," he said. "Cost me about three hundred fifty bucks."

"That thing actually works?" Flanagan asked.

"Sure it does," Curtis replied. "They wouldn't have started selling it if it didn't. Saw something about it at SHOT Show a couple years back."

Brannigan could almost *hear* Flanagan rolling his eyes. "Because nothing that's a worthless waste of hundreds of dollars *ever* shows up at SHOT Show," he said.

"Hey, it works, okay?" Curtis retorted. "I can even see Santelli's engine with this thing."

"Well, then," Brannigan said, pushing the door open and swinging his boots out of the car. "Let's go see what Ciela has to offer, shall we?"

The other two men followed, their weapons secreted under their shirts. "This isn't unusual at all, showing up in an industrial park after ten at night," Flanagan said.

"Time's wasting," Brannigan replied, as he led the way across the parking lot. "We can't afford to wait until normal business hours. And I doubt that they'd want to do this kind of business during normal business hours, anyway."

"Which makes me wonder just what it is these people really do," Flanagan wondered darkly.

"You and me both, brother," Brannigan replied.

They neared the glass double doors, adorned with simple, white block letters spelling out "Ciela International" and a street address in Bonn. The lobby beyond was dark, but small enough that Brannigan could see the wall when he peered through the glass. There was another door off to the right, and a camera in the upper left corner.

He tried the doors, wondering if he wasn't summoning the Corpus Christi Police Department by doing so. No alarms sounded. The door swung open as he pulled; it was unlocked.

Curtis was glancing back and forth, as if watching for a trap. "Just be casual," Brannigan said. "Act like we belong here." It was best, he figured, to act as if they were under surveillance, either by law enforcement or their mysterious and deadly earnest rivals.

He walked into the tiny anteroom; it was too small and barren to call it a "lobby." Curtis and Flanagan followed, keeping their gun hands free without being obvious about it.

A small speaker next to the camera in the corner crackled. "The inner door is unlocked, Mr. Zebrowski," a voice said. It was artificially deep and distorted, the kind of voice that villains in movies usually used over the phone.

Brannigan kept his expression neutral. He hadn't specified, but apparently Chavez had decided to re-use his alias from the Khadarkh job. Considering how that had gone, he probably needed to talk to Hector about changing that up a bit.

The door was heavier than the glass exterior doors; he was pretty sure it was reinforced steel, and would probably stand up to all but one hell of a torch or breaching charge. Ciela clearly took their security seriously.

Beyond, the short hallway leading into a larger room full of cubicles was dark, though there was enough light coming in the windows from the parking lot to illuminate a typical, cookie-cutter industrial office space, all the way down to the fake motivational posters on the walls. He had a sudden memory of meeting Van Zandt in a very similar place, one that he was sure had been abandoned shortly after their meeting.

If every one of these jobs involved going to one of these soulless cubicle farms set up in random rental office spaces, it was going to get really old, really fast.

He moved down the hall, his hand unconsciously slightly closer to where he could snatch his shirt out of the way and get to his pistol. This didn't feel right. There were no lights on at all that he could see, doors to side offices and closets forming dark holes in the orange-illuminated white walls.

Curtis was close behind him, holding a position just off to one side. Brannigan made for the main cubicle farm space ahead, though he was careful to glance into the two side doors as he passed them, moving at such an angle that he could draw and fire into the door in a heartbeat if a threat appeared inside. Curtis was moving up to take each space over from him, moving in the classic dance of Close Quarters Battle, even if they were moving more slowly and deliberately, without the kind of kinetic intensity that they'd have displayed on an actual hit. This was just caution.

Brannigan slowed as he neared the corner leading into the main room. Easing around the corner in such a way that he could draw and fire without exposing too much of his body, he took in the main room.

It looked just as dark and empty as the hallway. Darkened cubicles filled most of the space, with a narrow corridor along one wall leading toward the back offices. It was a very familiar view; the place might have been a carbon copy of Van Zandt's temporary headquarters before Burma. He was beginning to suspect that there were only one or two floor plans for industrial rental office spaces, and everyone used the same one.

The room was dimly lit by orange light coming through cheap, bent venetian blinds in the windows along the far wall. That was the only illumination, except for the line of light spilling from the partially open door of one of the offices at the far end.

"Nobody hiding in the cubicles," Curtis whispered. When Brannigan looked over at him, he had his phone with that thermal camera attachment out again.

"As if that thing could see through the cubicle walls," Flanagan hissed.

"It can see thermal blooms," Curtis protested. "Come on, I'm not an amateur."

"Put it away and keep your gun hand ready," was all Brannigan said, as he advanced on the open office, his boots rolling soundlessly on the cheap carpet.

He paused just outside the door. It was only cracked a few inches, so he couldn't see much of the inside, just a handspan worth of white wall.

"You might as well come in," a throaty, very female voice said. "It's not like I didn't already see you come in the front door."

He pushed the door open and stepped inside.

It took a second for his eyes to adjust to the light. He squinted, his hand still hovering near his pistol, ready to draw, but when he could focus, he let it hang.

The woman standing up from behind the desk and coming around to greet them could have been anywhere between twenty-five and fifty. Her features were nearly flawless; if she had lines on her slightly angular face, they were well-hidden. Her dark hair was swept back to a clip behind her head, except for a couple of strands that fell down in front of her ears, framing her face. She was wearing an off-white blouse and knee-length skirt; it was business attire, but somehow this woman managed to make it look far more...risqué.

She came around the desk and held out her hand. There was a faint smile on her red lips as she looked up at Brannigan with glittering green eyes. "You must be John Brannigan," she said. Her English was faintly accented, and Brannigan had to admit that it was sexy as hell.

The frontal assault of sex appeal did not mean that he wasn't entirely aware of the warning in her words. *She knows my real name, not the alias that Chavez gave her.* He didn't dare take his eyes off her long enough to glance at Flanagan or Curtis, but he was pretty sure Joe would have picked it up.

Kevin was probably staring and drooling.

"Come in, sit down, make yourselves comfortable," the woman said. She hadn't let go of Brannigan's hand, but was gently pulling him into the room. "Coffee?" she offered, waving to the Keurig machine on the table against the wall. Her smile got slightly wider, and a mischievous glint came into her eye as she said, "Or maybe something stronger? I think that you could probably use a good drink, after what you've already been through tonight." She smiled at him over her shoulder as she rounded the desk again and sat down. She produced a bottle of Pierre Ferrand and a pair of glasses and put them on the desktop.

Brannigan took the offered chair, across the desk from the blond woman who was pouring a generous glass of cognac, and leaned back, watching her with narrowed eyes. *Tread carefully. This woman knows* way *too much.*

"What makes you say that?" he asked, as she pushed the glass across the desk toward him and started pouring another. There were easily three fingers of liquor in the glass; more than he was willing to even look at under the circumstances. He knew he wasn't a lightweight when it came to booze; he wasn't the raging alcoholic that many Marines he'd known were, but a Marine leader had needed to be able to at least show he wasn't afraid of the stuff. But this was clearly a situation where he'd need all his wits.

She smiled again, her eyes smoldering with amusement, as she finished pouring, set the bottle down on the desk, and picked up the glass. "Oh, come on John," she said teasingly. "You know as well as I do that those poor *sicarios* down by the river didn't shoot themselves."

He watched her with narrowed eyes. "You had us under surveillance?"

"Of course I did," she said, sipping at her drink. He noticed that she didn't drink very much. The level of the cognac in the glass barely went down at all. "Knowing things is part of my business. Knowing *more* than the competition is vital to my business."

"Who's the competition?" Flanagan asked from where he was leaning against the doorframe, behind Brannigan. Curtis was out of sight; Flanagan must have pushed him out on rear security, probably because he didn't trust his friend's judgement in the same room with this bombshell of a femme fatale.

Smart move, Joe.

She looked up at him, that same seductive look of amusement on her face. "Why, it could be just about anyone," she replied, taking another sip. "Ciela International works in *so* many fields."

"Just who are you?" Brannigan asked. "You seem to have us at a disadvantage."

She did a convincing job of looking mortified. "Of course, where are my manners?" She put the glass down and leaned across the desk, holding her hand out again. In the process, Brannigan got a rather graphic reminder of just how low-cut her blouse was. "I am Erika Dalca. CEO of Ciela International."

"I thought Ciela International was based in Bonn," Brannigan said, pointedly focusing on her eyes. He wasn't sure that was much better than staring down her blouse. Her eyes were mesmerizing. "What is the CEO of that kind of transnational conglomerate doing in Corpus Christi?"

"This is one of our transshipment hubs into the United States," she explained. Something about the way she said it filled in the blanks for Brannigan. Not everything that Ciela International dealt in was necessarily legal and aboveboard. "I just so happened to be out here for a meeting with some of our American shareholders when the terrible string of incidents happened."

Brannigan nodded, though he watched her with narrowed eyes. He didn't know if he believed her or not. She returned his gaze, that little smile on her lips, as if knowing he distrusted her and enjoying it.

Hell with it. It wouldn't do any harm to follow up, and as he'd stressed to Curtis and Flanagan, time was pressing. "We've got a little shipment that we need to get to Matamoros, soonest," he said. "And it needs to be discreet."

Her smile only widened. It made her only more devastatingly attractive, at least until he looked closer. She hid it

76

well, but there was a lot of cold calculation going on in those glittering green eyes. "At Ciela International," she said, putting on like she was reciting a corporate advertisement, "we live and breathe discretion." She took another sip of her drink, watching him languidly. "How big is this shipment?" she asked.

"Passengers," he replied. "Twelve men, and probably about a hundred fifty pounds of equipment per man." He honestly didn't want to tell this woman any more than he absolutely had to, but he had a painful certainty in his mind that she already knew exactly who he was, and what the mission was.

She nodded, her lips pursed slightly in thought. "I think we can arrange something," she said. She sat up and pulled a notepad to her, scribbling something down with a very expensive-looking, gold-chased pen. She tore the page off and passed it to him. In delicate, almost flowery handwriting, there was a set of coordinates and a sum with an awful lot of zeroes after it. "Be at these coordinates by…six thirty AM. Presuming that you *are* in a terrible hurry?"

Brannigan nodded, as he took the paper and stuffed it in his shirt pocket. She made a moue. "I was afraid of that," she said disappointedly. "You have hardly touched your drink."

"I need to keep a clear head," he said calmly, only realizing once the words were out that they had more than one meaning. And Dalca had clearly picked up on that same meaning, because she smiled again, stretching a little in her chair like a satisfied cat.

"I'm afraid that the price tag is due to how quickly this is having to be put together, as well," she said. She looked at him from under her eyelashes. "You *will* be able to pay it, no?"

Brannigan reached across the desk and took the pad and the gold-chased pen. He quickly wrote down Van Zandt's current contact information, information that would doubtless change within hours of this operation coming to a close. "Reach out to this man," he said. "He'll arrange for all the financial necessities to be taken care of."

She made a point of touching his hand as she took the paper from him. "I'll certainly do that," she said. She sighed. "It's too bad this is all in such a rush. We might be able to arrange some sort of...personal discount."

Brannigan felt a hot flush rising from his collar. This wasn't exactly what he'd been expecting. This Dalca woman was a far cry from the Suleiman Syndicate thugs who had tried to murder them, or the man known to the Blackhearts only as "Dmitri," who had finally supplied the weapons and the dhow to get to Khadarkh.

He suddenly suspected that she was far more dangerous than either of them.

He looked at his watch. "Well, we don't have much time, do we?" He stood up. "If we're going to meet that time hack, we're going to have to hurry up and do some serious packing."

"Of course," Dalca replied, standing as he did. "Though I really wish we had more time to get to know one another. Personal relationships are so important in this kind of business." She tapped the paper he'd handed to her. "I will, of course, contact this Mr. Van Zandt," she said. Brannigan hadn't written Van Zandt's name down, or mentioned it. She was entirely too knowledgeable about this operation for comfort. "At least partial payment *will* be necessary before final arrangements can be made."

Brannigan nodded. "I'm sure it will be no problem," he said. "We're all in a bit of a hurry here." He held out his hand and she shook it, holding on for just a little bit longer than politeness demanded. "Thank you, Ms. Dalca."

"Erika, please," she said.

"Thank you, Erika," he said. She beamed at him.

Then he, Curtis, and Flanagan were beating a hasty retreat. Flanagan blew a deep breath out with a faint whistle. "She's a piece of work, ain't she?"

"She's dangerous as hell," Brannigan said, as they headed back out into the parking lot. "We're going to have to stay on our toes, or this could turn way nastier than Dubai did."

But, hopefully, they had an insert platform. And with time being as short as it was, beggars couldn't afford to be choosers.

CHAPTER 7

Huerta stood near the shore, his face stony. The platoon of Naval Infantry was almost completely loaded up on the RHIBs, the Rigid-Hulled Inflatable Boats floating off the pier in Punta de Piedra. They were a bit better equipped than the first assault team; they'd had slightly longer to prepare. Each man was armored and wearing an inflatable horse collar, with a P90 5.7mm submachinegun on a single point sling and two hundred fifty rounds of ammunition. Night vision was still scarce for the Marines, so they were going to have to make do with the high-intensity lights mounted to their weapons.

Salinas was standing beside him, wearing a windbreaker, her face as severe as his. Huerta glanced over at her and suppressed a sneer. Her tough act did not impress him. He knew what she was; she was a political appointee, who had gained that appointment by spreading her legs for every man in higher office who might advance her career, all while presenting the image of a strong, independent woman that the *Norteamericano* press loved so much. The fact that he had to defer to her demands irked him to no end. He wasn't some ball-less *maricòn* who simply took shit from a woman because he liked it.

But his instructions from his own commanding officer were clear. For whatever reason, Salinas had overall discretion on this operation, so he had to facilitate her demands. And she was determined to make sure he knew it, every step of the way.

He was looking forward to this being over. He'd put her in her place then. Or so he told himself, as he fantasized about it on the rare occasions he got to sleep.

Teniente Oquendo waved from the lead RHIB. Everyone was aboard and ready to go. Huerta returned the wave, signaling that they were clear. The *Teniente* nodded and stepped back down off the gunwale, tapping the coxswain on the shoulder. A moment later, the dark water churned around the RHIB's rubber hull as it backed water and pulled away from the pier.

Huerta didn't like this. One platoon was the absolute bare minimum for this kind of assault, but it was still doable, especially considering how thinly spread the Naval Infantry were, with *Los Zetas* stirring up more trouble in Tamaulipas lately. It still bothered him, especially considering the level of training his men had. Against most of the *narcos*, they were more than adequate. Against whoever had hit the meeting in Matamoros and shot down the four helicopters on the first assault, he found he was less sure.

But Salinas had insisted that the situation had to be resolved as quickly as possible. It was bad enough that Mexico couldn't bring the cartels to heel. This small group of terrorists, holed up on an easily-located oil platform, *had* to be eliminated.

Huerta didn't disagree. He just disagreed with the rushed nature of the operation. He'd watched four helicopters filled with his own men get shot down and fall into the Gulf. He feared that he was sending *Teniente* Oquendo and his men to their deaths, as well.

On the other hand, there was the chance that, on the surface, they would be able to get close enough to board the platform before being detected.

And if they succeed, then I won't have to bring those gringo mercenaries into this.

***

Oquendo squinted into the salt spray as the lead RHIB cleared the narrow passage across the narrow levee that divided the

Laguna Madre from the Gulf of Mexico. He was young, but had already seen combat against *Los Zetas* and the Gulf Cartel. He was no green novice.

But he was still nervous. He knew what had happened to the first assault force. And while he was a trained and hardened soldier in the Mexican Naval Infantry, most of his combat experience had been inland. As the only force that was generally considered incorruptible, the Naval Infantry were often tasked with hitting the truly high-value targets, and that often took them far from the ocean. He had been through all the training, but never on a real, live maritime mission.

"Señor, look," the coxswain pointed. "I thought all the fishing boats should have been cleared away from here by now."

Oquendo had to look hard to see what the coxswain, a young man named Robledo, was pointing at. After a moment, he could just make out the dim silhouette of what did indeed look like a fishing boat, floating just off the banks of the levee, only a few hundred meters to the south.

He frowned. The Navy had been broadcasting warnings to keep out of the waters around the Tourmaline-Delta platform for the last thirty hours, but apparently someone hadn't gotten the message. Or else, a local fisherman had decided to simply ignore the warnings. It wasn't unknown for such people to hold the government's warnings in contempt. If he was being honest, not entirely without cause.

That didn't make the fisherman any less of an idiot.

"Get them out of here," Oquendo ordered.

The Mexican Marines weren't particularly gentle, or concerned with the niceties that their neighbors to the north were. There were credible stories of the Naval Infantry firing on gringos across the border, and even executing three Americans outside Matamoros, not far away, in 2014.

So, they didn't flash lights or even pull closer to the fishing boat to use loudspeakers to warn them off. Instead, two of the

Marines near the bow of the RHIB leaned on the gunwale, levelling their P90s, and opened fire on the dim shape of the boat.

They weren't especially trying to hit anything. They were "warning shots." Just warning shots that also weren't necessarily aimed to miss, either.

The P90s stuttered, muzzles spitting flame into the dark. A few shots visibly sparked off the metal gunwales of the fishing boat.

At first, there was no response. The boat didn't veer away. Then flame blossomed from the dark shape, amidships.

Oquendo thought something flammable had been hit, at first. Then the first bullets *snapped* past his head, and he realized that whoever was on that boat was shooting back at them.

Machinegun fire roared in the dark, and bullets tore through the night air and *spanged* off the metal shelter over the RHIB's helm station. All of the Naval Infantrymen instinctively ducked for the rigid deck. Only Ochoa was too slow. Even over the crackling roar and the thumping of gunfire, Oquendo heard the meaty *thumps* as he caught several bullets, and sprawled lifelessly to the deck, bouncing off the rubber gunwale in the process.

The Marines returned fire, spraying 5.7mm gunfire toward the boat. Oquendo followed suit, lifting his submachinegun to his shoulder and squeezing off a long burst before ducking back down, himself, wondering why he was bothering. It wasn't like the RHIB's inflated rubber hull was going to stop machinegun bullets.

The machinegun fire from the boat didn't seem to be especially accurate; the rounds were going high and wild. One or two bullets in just the right place could end the operation, though. Oquendo heaved himself up, fighting the slickness of the salt-water-drenched gunwale and the weight of his own gear, and fired off another long burst, just over the gunwale. He knew a lot of his rounds weren't going anywhere near the machinegunner, but if he just made him flinch away just a little bit, it might save some of his men.

As he let off the trigger, he peered through the darkness. He'd been nearly blinded by his own muzzle flash, but after a moment, he thought that it looked like the boat was turning away from the Mexican RHIBs, though the machinegun was still firing, its muzzle blast flickering in the dark.

He ducked back down and reloaded. They needed to save some ammunition for the assault on the oil platform, but none of them wanted to get shot to pieces just past the levee.

Slapping the fresh magazine in place over the top of the bullpup submachinegun, he worked the charging handle and shoved himself up again, though this time he took a second to evaluate his surroundings and the situation before firing.

The boat was definitely pulling away, and fast. He still couldn't see much more than a vague shape, but it looked like maybe they'd been wrong; that didn't look like a commercial fishing boat. It looked more like a high-speed yacht. It was certainly heading back out to sea faster than the RHIBs could probably pursue, and they weren't slow boats.

A few last, desultory bursts of machinegun fire ripped and crackled overhead again, and then the boat was gone, vanishing into the darkness of the Gulf.

"Report," Oquendo snapped. "Anyone hit?"

"Ochoa's dead."

"Villar is hit, but he'll live."

Cabo Jimenez crawled over to Oquendo after a few moments. "On average, the men each expended a magazine against the boat, Señor," he said. "We should still have enough ammunition to assault the platform, but we weren't counting on an engagement before we reached the target."

"We will adapt," Oquendo said. "We have no choice."

The RHIBs sped toward the distant Tourmaline-Delta platform. Oquendo was glad for the darkness; he didn't have to see Ochoa's blood sloshing against his boots on the deck.

***

85

"Hey, Flint?" Dingo called, sticking his head in the door.

Flint cracked one eye with a growl. He'd been having a good dream, with five of the hottest bimbos in South Carolina. Or wherever he'd been in the dream. "What?"

"We just got a message," Dingo said. "No sub tonight."

"What the fuck?" Flint heaved himself up to a sitting position. "We've been sitting here for two damn days."

"No idea," Dingo said with a shrug. "Something must have gone wrong. But they didn't include any details."

"Of course they didn't." Flint ran a hand over his face. His stubble was getting long. Oh, well, he didn't really care. Maybe he'd grow a beard again. "Did they have an ETA at all?"

"Nah, just a 'stand by,'" Dingo said, shaking his head. "My guess? The sub got too close to one of those ships out there, and the skipper panicked."

"Didn't ask for your guess," Flint said, as he heaved himself to his feet. He wanted to go back to sleep, but realized that he really needed to piss. It was warm on the Gulf, so he was wearing just his skivvies. He was medium height, tanned, and hairy. His shock of dirty-blond hair was long and untamed, and he had a lot of tattoos crawling across his arms, chest, and back. Some of them had been blacked out.

He wasn't too worried about security, though his kit was close at hand, and his Field Pistol was never far from him, in this case underneath the pillow he'd raided from the platform's crew quarters. "Was that it?"

"Yeah, that was all." Dingo wasn't especially deferential, but Flint knew that the rest of the team was a little afraid of him. Whacking that Switchblade punk during the train-up had made sure of that. That was the way Flint liked it. A combat leader should make his men a little afraid. He'd just never been able to really cultivate that fear the way he would have liked before joining up with this outfit.

"Fine. I gotta piss." Ignoring his fellow team leader, he lurched toward the hatch. There was a head not far away.

He was about halfway there when he heard the radio crackling loudly behind him. It had to be Dingo's radio; his own was still on his gear.

"We've got incoming," Villain called out. "That lookout boat engaged some boats coming toward us. Looks like four RHIBs, coming fast from the southwest."

"Motherfuck," Flint snarled, turning back to his cabin. Leave it to the idiot spics to decide to spring this just when his bladder was full.

He hurriedly threw on a shirt and his plate carrier, swinging his gunbelt around his hips and holstering his Field Pistol. He loved that gun. And he sure as hell wasn't going to take the chance that another one of these lowlifes might try to steal it. Then, after shoving his feet into his boots, he was pounding up the ladder toward the control room, where they'd set up their little operations center.

"What have we got?" he asked, as he came through the hatch.

"Like I said," Villain replied, "four RHIBs, about ten nautical miles off, coming in at about thirty knots."

"Mexican Marines?" he asked.

"Looks like it," Villain answered. "They're coming from the mainland, so they're probably not American. The SEALs or the Marines would be coming from the sea."

"Provided that our friends had failed to keep them off our backs," Flint agreed. He stared at the darkness to the southwest. The boats were invisible to the naked eye, but he knew that Scrap and Gibbet had spotted them with the powerful thermals they had up top.

Slowly, a grin started to grow on his face. It was not a pleasant expression, though if they were given to such observations, his teammates would probably say that few, if any, of Flint's facial expressions could ever be said to be "pleasant."

"I think this is an opportunity," he said. "Let's break out the new toys."

"Do we have time?" Villain asked. Flint snorted.

"We've got plenty, if you fumble-fucks don't take forever getting the cases open." He started for the hatch and the ladder leading up to the top decks. "Get 'em up top with a quickness."

***

The "new toys" came in big black storm cases, that were a pain to haul up the steep metal ladderwells to the top decks. That was why Flint was in charge; he stayed up top, watching the oncoming boats with the thermals that he'd taken from Scrap. Let the peons do the heavy lifting.

With a lot of grunting, cursing, and banging as cases smacked against hatchways, railings, and various bits of anatomy, the team got the four sturdy plastic boxes up onto the top deck and started undoing the latches. Flint handed the thermals back to Scrap and went over to the first one that had been opened.

Inside the case was what looked like a standard, commercial, quad-rotor drone. It appeared to have been painted a flat gray, with any lights painted over, until a closer inspection revealed that it had not been built with lights. There was a camera mounted beneath the hump of its central fuselage, and a sophisticated transmission antenna above.

If it differed from the more common commercial drones in that the central fuselage was bigger, protruding fore and aft more than most, especially at a time when drones tended to be getting more and more miniaturized. It also had lines that made it look stealthy, not unlike an F-22 or F-35 fighter.

It was; if a modern stealth aircraft had the radar signature of a sparrow, this thing had the radar signature of a dust mote. And that was even with the extra ten pounds of explosive and ceramic fragmentation stowed inside the hump of the fuselage.

Psycho was pulling the drone out, having already taken the control unit out and laid it on the deck. Flint bent down, snatched the control unit, and powered it up as he stood again. He was going to get the first shot. It was a privilege of being the guy in charge. The alpha.

The control unit looked not unlike an X-box controller, only bigger, with more controls, and with a small but high-definition screen in the center. Flint quickly ran it through its boot-up sequence, the screen clearing and showing him Psycho's face, only a few inches away. With an ugly grin, he started the rotors.

"Fuck!" Psycho jumped back to avoid getting a digit cut off by the spinning props. Flint just grinned at him.

Applying power, he flew the drone up off the deck and out into the night.

It took some doing to get the feel of the thing. He wasn't a pilot, and almost lost control of the drone several times. Once he almost overcorrected enough to send it flipping over and into the ocean. Tight-lipped and angry, he slowed down and got down to it. He knew that Psycho and probably a couple of the others were surreptitiously looking at the screen over his shoulder. He had to do this right. It was part of being the Big Dog.

A distant part of him might have understood that the way he was running this team was less than ideal. Good, disciplined forces, professionals, don't work like the Lord of the Flies model he was following. But he didn't care. This wasn't the military, and he'd run his team the way he damned well pleased.

He finally got the drone flying straight and level, about fifty feet off the water, even as the other three dipped down off the platform to join it. The camera had limited night vision capabilities, and he still couldn't see the targets yet, not from that altitude. But at a closure rate of well over a hundred knots, that should change soon.

There. He almost overshot; the RHIBs were closer than he'd expected. He banked the drone hard to bring it in toward his target, nearly overcorrecting and losing control again. But with some struggling, and some particularly vile curses under his breath, he got the drone lined up and started its dive.

***

Oquendo never heard it coming. The drone's motors were extremely quiet, and further muffled for stealth. It's dark, flat coloring made it little more than a silhouette against the sky, and a tiny one, at that. Without night vision, Oquendo couldn't see enough of the contrast to pick it out. He wasn't looking at the sky, anyway; he was trying to pick out the Tourmaline-Delta platform from among the various lights of ships and other oil platforms in the Gulf.

The drone dropped out of the night and came to a hover right behind the coxswain. One of the Naval Infantry looked up and yelled. Oquendo turned, just in time to see a dark bulk buzzing faintly, the sound of its rotors still almost drowned out by the rumble of the RHIB's own motors.

A split-second later, Flint mashed a button on the controller, still most of a nautical mile away, and the drone detonated.

The ten pounds of Composition B was the equivalent of twenty M67 hand grenades going off at once, all in the same spot. Tightly packed in ceramic ball bearings, it was an enormous, three-hundred-sixty-degree claymore. It went off with a blinding flash, spewing its fragmentation in all directions, to flay already-pulverized flesh from shattered bones, smash metal fittings, and shred the rubber gunwales.

All of the Marines aboard were killed instantly. The RHIB stopped almost dead in the water, as the holes punched in its hull immediately started the boat sinking. With the inflatable hull shredded, it was about as buoyant as any random debris.

The other four boats died the same way, all within the next thirty seconds. Bright flashes were followed by rolling *booms* that echoed out across the water. Sound travels far over the ocean at night, and heads came up on watch miles away as the sound rippled across the Gulf.

Moments later, all that was left of the second Mexican Naval Infantry assault on the Tourmaline-Delta platform was some debris, oil, blood, and hammered meat floating in the water.

The sharks were already starting to circle. Fortunately for the Mexican Marines, they were already dead.

CHAPTER 8

The meeting with Erika Dalca at the Ciela International offices was not the end of the night for Brannigan's Blackhearts. Time was slipping away, and they could sleep when the op was over.

Or when they were dead.

David Aziz was not happy about it. He wasn't happy about any of this. Deep down, he understood that he'd had a choice; he could have simply refused to come along, even after the dressing-down he'd gotten from Santelli. *Especially* after that. It chafed, even over a day later. He was still happy that Jenkins had borne the brunt of it.

He also knew that Santelli was right, as much as he might have hated to admit it, even to himself. The whole tattoo thing had been dumb. He still thought the emblem was cool, and it was something that he would know the meaning of, that set him another notch above the spoiled brats he taught at the college, when he wasn't taking leaves of absence to go play mercenary. But it was still bad OPSEC.

He should have walked away after Burma. That shit-show had nearly gotten them all killed, and had destroyed the good thing he'd had going with Sanda. So far, none of the others had commented on her conspicuous absence when he'd showed up for the little get-together that Jenkins had started. But he'd seen the looks, especially from Wade.

She'd started to withdraw before they'd even gotten out of Burma, and eventually stopped returning his calls altogether. She'd never told him what she was unhappy about, but the one time they'd met up and he'd tried to re-kindle things after they'd gotten back Stateside hadn't gone well.

"You don't get it, David," she'd said. And he didn't. He hadn't forced her to go. It had been a job, and he'd counted himself lucky to have pulled off a caper like taking his lover at the time along. She didn't seem to have found that little coup as impressive as he had; not that he'd been so stupid as to phrase it that way.

What the hell am I still doing this for? He struggled with the Hollis Explorer Rebreather on the bench in front of him. *I'm no diver. And these guys don't really want me around much.* Not that he necessarily wanted to be a part of them with all his heart, either. *But I'm good enough that I belong here, whether they like it or not.*

How much of that was self-delusion was something Aziz would never ask himself. Pride was pretty much his primary motivator in life, and his association with Brannigan's Blackhearts was no different.

"Come on, Aziz, it ain't rocket surgery," Santelli called. The stout, balding fireplug was standing there with his own rebreather already on his back, his regulator dangling in front of his chin by its retaining strap and oxygen hoses. "Get the damned thing on, we're wasting time."

Aziz grimaced as he heaved the rebreather pack up and around and strapped it on. It was still white; they hadn't had time to paint them, and they probably wouldn't get the time, either. They'd probably have to ditch the rebreathers while still underwater, hopefully deep enough that they couldn't be seen easily from the surface, and then free ascend to the platform.

"All right," Santelli bellowed. "Everybody to the edge of the pool. Start your purge."

A rebreather didn't work like a Scuba tank. Running on pure oxygen, it was a closed system, and therefore the diver had to cleanse his lungs of any outside air before daring to go underwater with it. Nitrogen and other trace gases could slowly overtake the oxygen in the system, making the diver suffocate even while breathing deeply. The lime in the rebreather's scrubber didn't take nitrogen out, only carbon dioxide.

The Blackhearts, dressed in fatigues from a nearby Army surplus store, London Bridge Trading Company chest rigs, and the Hollis rebreathers, lined the sides of the pool and started their purge.

***

Hancock was most of the way through his own purge, making sure his lungs and his mask were full of pure oxygen, when he noticed that Tanaka seemed to be having trouble.

It didn't especially surprise him; Tanaka had been a regular infantryman in the Army, and hadn't ever trained for combat diving, or any other specialized insert method. The train-up and insert into Burma had been his first experiences jumping out of an airplane. He was game, but he wasn't on the same level of training and experience as the rest of the Blackhearts.

Right at the moment, he seemed to be hyperventilating a little, struggling with the unfamiliar feeling of having a regulator in his teeth and being unable to breathe through his nose. That was something that usually got dealt with in dive school by having the students fill their masks with water and do flutter kicks on the side of the pool.

When breathing through your nose just fills your sinuses with pool water, you learn really quick to breathe through your mouth.

But they didn't have time for a full dive school, or even a pre-dive course. Tanaka was going to have to keep up as best he could. He'd demonstrated that he had the guts for it with high-altitude jumping, but, if anything, diving involved even more ways to die horribly.

Hancock stopped his purge and pulled his regulator out of his mouth. "Alex, look at me," he said loudly.

Tanaka turned to meet his eyes through his mask. The man's eyes were a little wide. *Yeah, he's having trouble.*

"It's pure oxygen, Alex," Hancock said. "I know it feels like you can't breathe, but trust me, you can. And you won't need as much of a breath, either. Just concentrate on in and out, in and out. You'll get used to the back-pressure soon enough." One of the hard parts about diving on a rebreather was also the fact that, due to it's being a closed system, it took more effort to breathe out than it did to breathe in.

Tanaka nodded, and seemed to calm. His chest rose and fell more deeply, as he tried to get used to the altered breathing.

Hancock clapped him on the shoulder and re-inserted his own regulator. Taking a deep breath, he pressed a palm to the top of his mask and blew out hard through his nose, re-starting his purge.

You know, this whole 'being John's 2IC' thing isn't as bad as I was worried it would be. Sure, he had had to scale back some of his own more adventurous activities; he tended to be an adrenaline junkie, both in and out of combat. In fact, the longer he'd been away from the battlefield, the more extreme his hobbies had gotten. He'd kept it up until just before the Burma job, when Brannigan had dressed him down for risking his neck unnecessarily, and revealed that if the Colonel ever went down, Roger Hancock was going to be his successor.

It had been a shock, and one that he'd slightly resented. He'd retired, just like Santelli and Brannigan—though willingly, unlike Brannigan—and he'd been fine with just being another hired gun, leaving much of the responsibilities that he'd held in the military behind him. Having to put that hat back on hadn't been all that welcome.

But it had been Brannigan. So, he'd agreed. And now he was finding that it was a good thing.

Being the second in command meant that he had to look after the boys when they were on a mission. Sometimes, it meant looking after them, when he could, in between missions. Hart worried him. He'd known that the man had had some issues with depression and substance abuse since being medically separated after losing his leg. Having found him drooling drunk with Tanaka was a problem.

The fact was, having to keep an eye on the boys helped quell his own restlessness. It gave him an outlet, something to focus on.

He knew that it still wasn't a cure-all. He knew that his wife and daughters deserved more of his attention. He knew that he'd been running from the "mundanity" of his home life by surfing, skydiving, racing cars, and all the other stuff that he'd been doing. And he was still doing some of it, coming out to jump into gunfights as a mercenary.

But this is different. This is at least serving a purpose.

He put the thoughts aside as he scanned the group. Santelli was already in the pool, his buoyancy compensator inflated enough to keep him on the surface without having to kick too hard, his own regulator in his mouth, his purge complete. Brannigan was beside him, watching the Blackhearts through his own mask.

Tanaka was calming down. Hart was sitting stiffly, his prosthetic jutting out over the pool. Hancock glanced at the replacement leg, thinking briefly that they were going to have to treat it much the same way they were going to have to treat their rifles. Hart's prosthetic was mostly aluminum and carbon fiber, but sea salt and corrosion could still bind it up at the worst possible time.

Jenkins appeared calm; he should, he'd been a SEAL. The water should be second-nature to him. Hancock knew that that wasn't necessarily always the case; a lot of the SEAL teams, like a lot of Recon units, had spent a lot more time in land-locked Afghanistan than at sea in recent years. But Jenkins appeared to be all right.

It's just his attitude I wonder about.

Wade seemed to be struggling a little with the back-pressure. The big man had been a Ranger. He wasn't nearly as amphibious as the predominately Recon background made much of the rest of the team. But he wasn't freaking out, so that was good.

Childress was next to Wade, and was finishing his own purge; he must have done the same thing for Wade that Hancock had just done for Tanaka; dropped his regulator to coach him through. The thought of Childress' coaching almost made Hancock crack a smile; the younger man could only be described as "blunt." His lack of tact had gotten him into trouble more than once in the Marine Corps.

Gomez was as silent and still as ever. Hancock had seen the Recon Jack tattooed on the inside of Gomez' arm; he didn't worry much about him. Except to occasionally wonder just what all was going on behind those deep-set, black eyes.

Flanagan, Bianco, and Curtis were just sitting there, waiting, their purges complete, eyes on Santelli. All three men had been Recon Marines, and knew what they were about.

Hancock was momentarily glad that they were on oxygen. As amusing as it could be, the constant bickering between the Curtis and Flanagan occasionally got tiresome. It seemed to get that way to Flanagan sometimes, too. Curtis, however, never seemed to run out of energy.

Santelli had his hand up in the "OK" sign, and was looking at Tanaka. Hancock nudged the other man, and pointed toward Santelli. Tanaka started a little as he figured it out, then nodded and held up the same sign.

Santelli went down the line, checking with each man, and getting the same sign. Good. Everybody seemed to be doing all right, which hopefully meant no bad purges or malfunctions in the rebreathers. There were dozens of ways that closed-circuit diving could go wrong, even more than open-circuit.

He waited a few more minutes. Some diving-related illnesses could take some time to manifest. When nobody started vomiting into their regulator or doing the "funky chicken," he was apparently satisfied, and held up two fingers. With regulators in, they may as well already be underwater, which meant that hand and arm signals would have to do for communications.

At that signal, the Blackhearts came off the wall, careful to avoid hitting the rebreathers on the edge, and sank into the water.

Hancock kept a close eye on Tanaka. Learning to take that first breath underwater could be a bit harrowing for some people. The former infantryman seemed to get a hitch in his breathing for a moment, but then relaxed a little and gave Hancock an "OK" sign. He wasn't comfortable, but he was making do.

The water is the great equalizer. He looked around, focusing a little more on the "Common Air Breathers" in their midst. Aziz was looking a little twitchy; fortunately, they weren't on compressed air, so the risks of getting the bends if one of them shot to the surface were minimal. Of course, there were other potential problems, like going too deep and getting Oxygen Toxicity...

Aziz didn't shoot for the surface, but as Hancock neared him, he could see something close to panic in the other man's eyes. Aziz wasn't made for the water. Frankly, Hancock didn't know exactly *what* Aziz was made for, aside from stroking his own ego.

He didn't like the guy, but he was detached enough to know that Aziz had, despite his attitude, put himself way out in the line of fire more than once. He'd gone into Khadarkh City on his own, to lay the groundwork for the diversion that had gotten the rest of the team into the Citadel. That had taken balls.

Then he'd basically sat most of the fight in the Citadel out, though only *after* he saved Flanagan's and Curtis' butts by blowing up an AMX-10 with an RPG. The man was hardly consistent, and Hancock realized that that was the main reason he didn't like him. For all his own wild nature, Hancock was a man of constancy. You either had balls or you didn't. In that way, he knew he was a lot like Santelli, if perhaps slightly more given to nuance. Santelli was a blunt instrument in many ways.

Aziz might be scared shitless, but his ego was keeping him underwater. Hancock could see that much, even as the man gave him an "OK" sign. *I guess that massive self-regard of yours has some use, after all, Aziz.*

Childress was next to Hart, and Wade seemed to be handling himself. The others were moving with the deliberate but practiced movements of men knocking the rust off a skill long unused.

Flanagan was already kicking out to start his laps around the pool, even before Santelli signaled to do so. Hancock knew why. A rebreather wasn't comfortable when stationary. The slight positive pressure in the breathing loop tended to overpower the diver's lung capacity to some extent, leading to the condition known as "chipmunk cheeks," as oxygen was forced into the diver's mouth faster than they could breathe it in. So, to be comfortable, the rig needed to be worked. And worked hard.

With one more look around, assuring himself that they didn't have anyone about to explode, he turned and followed.

***

The team did four laps around the Olympic sized pool before Santelli stopped, sitting on the bottom in the deep end. He reached up, closed his regulator, then unbuckled his rebreather, pulled it off, and stowed it under his weight belt on the bottom of the pool. Then he looked around at the rest of the team and held up four fingers, signaling them to surface. Without waiting for the rest of them, he kicked upward.

The rest of the team followed suit. It wasn't much of a train-up, but it was all they had time for, and neither Brannigan nor

Hancock had been comfortable launching into the insert without making sure everyone knew how to handle their rig. It was dangerous; in its own way, it was even more dangerous than the jump into Burma. But there simply was no time.

Once they had all surfaced, Brannigan hauled himself up to sit on the edge of the pool. "All right, get your breath, then head down and retrieve your gear. Post-dive, then head back to the hotel and get a couple of hours' rest. We've got four hours from right now until we need to leave for the rendezvous with Dalca's people." He waited a moment, then slipped back into the water and dove for the bottom.

Time was a-wasting. They needed to move.

***

He, Curtis, and Flanagan were almost back to the hotel when the phone rang. He pointed, and Flanagan fished it out of the cup holder in the center console.

"It's our favorite former General," Flanagan said dryly.

"Answer it," Brannigan said.

"You're on speaker, Van Zandt," Flanagan said. Flanagan had never had any direct dealings with Van Zandt. His dislike stemmed from a combination of the enlisted man's perpetual distrust of the brass, the nagging suspicion that, as mercenaries, they were eventually going to be sold out by their employer, and his own loyalty to Brannigan. Van Zandt had presided over Brannigan's forced retirement for doing what had been necessary to save hostages. Flanagan disliked such people on principle.

"The Mexicans gave it another shot," Van Zandt said, without comment on Flanagan's greeting. "An amphib insert this time. Nobody knows exactly what happened, but not a single boat got closer than a nautical mile."

"No idea at all?" Brannigan asked.

"There were reports of explosions out on the water," Van Zandt said. "That's it. Huerta lost all contact with Lieutenant Oquendo at that time, and was never able to reestablish it."

101

"When was this?" Flanagan asked.

If Van Zandt was irritated about answering questions from anyone but Brannigan, he didn't show it in his voice. "Contact was lost about ninety minutes ago. Thirty minutes ago, a message, apparently from the hijackers, was uploaded to the internet."

"Have you got a link?" Brannigan asked, pulling the car over.

"Sending it now," Van Zandt replied.

Flanagan handed him the phone, as a text message with a link popped up. Brannigan tapped it, wondering what he was getting into. Propaganda messages from terrorists were rarely what he would call "good, clean, family entertainment."

The video was surprisingly crisp, but it didn't show much detail for all that. Part of it was because the majority of the frame was taken up by a face wearing a balaclava and sunglasses. There was no way to even identify whether the face belonged to a man or a woman.

"We are *Los Valientes*," the heavily distorted voice announced. "We control the oil platform Tourmaline-Delta. The revolution begins now! We have struck twice against the corrupt puppets of the Americans, the hopeless sheep who call themselves defenders of Mexico. I warn you, gringo puppets, do not attempt to approach this platform again. If you do, the consequences will be more terrible than you can bear."

The video ended.

Brannigan frowned down at the phone. "That's peculiar," he said.

"Yeah," Curtis ventured from the back seat. "Don't these assholes usually have a more, I dunno, *long-winded* manifesto? That sounded like a kid playing at being a terrorist."

"Whoever these bastards are," Van Zandt said over the phone, "they're not kids. They're far too sophisticated. And I don't know of any group called *Los Valientes*, much less one well-established enough to be able to summon up the resources these clowns have."

"*Los Valientes* is Spanish for 'The Valiant Ones,'" Flanagan said quietly. "It's the nickname for the narcos among some of the locals, particularly in Sinaloa, who look at them more as Robin Hoods than bloodthirsty savages."

"I think it's a blind, Mark," Brannigan said. "Like Curtis said, it's too pat, and too amateurish. They're trying to throw us off the scent."

"But why bother?" Van Zandt asked. His frustration was clear in his voice; this wasn't a new question. "What's their endgame? Who are they? And if they're not going to make any demands, why the hell are they still sitting out there?"

"Stealing oil, maybe?" Flanagan suggested. "That's turned into big money for the cartels, lately."

"Maybe," Brannigan mused, "but somehow this doesn't feel like that. Any ship that was going to take the oil off would have to get past the blockade that the Mexican Navy has put around the platform." He shook his head. "No, there's got to be something else going on here. You don't launch simultaneous mass-casualty attacks across the borderlands just to cover for an oil robbery."

He straightened and began to pull back out onto the road. It was utterly deserted at that time of night. "Doesn't matter," he said. "The mission's still on. Maybe if any of these punks survive, we can ask them what the point of the whole show was."

CHAPTER 9

None of the Blackhearts looked particularly chipper. The sun was just rising, and if any of them had gotten a full three hours of sleep, it would have been a miracle. Brannigan knew that his own eyes felt gritty and aching as he drove across the bridge toward the rendezvous.

They were still in civilian clothes, at least for the moment. The gear and weapons were in duffel bags in the backs of the vehicles. They weren't worried about checkpoints; the advantage to staging in Texas was that nothing they were carrying was illegal. Questionable, maybe. A cop might wonder why they were rolling with chest rigs, combat loads, dive gear, and Broco torches. But not illegal.

Of course, that meant they didn't have the kind of explosives and pyrotechnics they might otherwise have wanted to bring along. No frags, no flashbangs, no breaching charges. Van Zandt might have managed to find some for them and run top cover with law enforcement, but there simply hadn't been time.

Most of Portland, Texas was still asleep as they rolled through. There was enough traffic on the streets that they didn't stand out, but there weren't going to be many eyes on them.

He had to wonder about that as he drove. He glanced in the rearview mirror, ignoring Curtis' snoring in the back seat. So far, there had been signs aplenty that the enemy, as yet unidentified, had spotters everywhere. Was somebody making note of traffic, and sending possible target profiles to strike teams even then?

Who are these guys? Who has the kind of resources that this operation would need? He was reminded of the cartels, again, and their networks of *halcones*, usually young kids paid to spot for the *sicarios* and smugglers. But this didn't feel like a cartel op. The cartels were businesses and tribal political movements. Even cults. This was something else. So far, it appeared to be terror and destruction for the sake of terror and destruction.

They hit the interchange on the outskirts of Gregory, and turned southeast, on Highway 361. He watched the mirrors and watched the surrounding traffic, as thin as it was. His eyes sought out the drivers, taking note of who might be watching them a little too intently.

Am I being too paranoid? He dismissed the thought. Especially on an op like this, there was no such thing as *too* paranoid. Not when the enemy had already tried hitting them once.

Cars, SUVs, vans, and more pickups than the other three types of vehicles combined passed them in both directions as they headed toward Inglewood. Nobody seemed to pay them much mind. At one point, there was a big, red dually pulling up behind them, closing fast. Brannigan kept a close eye on the truck as it got closer and closer.

"Joe," he said quietly. "Red Ford, on the left."

Flanagan was sitting in the right seat, his STI in his lap under a jacket, being just as watchful as Brannigan. He carefully turned around to look behind them, sizing up the approaching truck.

After a moment, the black-bearded man shook his head fractionally. "I doubt it. Big-haired blond behind the wheel. No sign of passengers. Unless they're being *really* clever, and they're all lying down in the cab, I don't think we've got much to worry about aside from the fact that she's driving and talking on her phone."

Brannigan nodded. Fair enough. He'd take Flanagan's word for it.

They were entering Ingleside, passing through on the way to Ingleside on the Bay. The town wasn't large, and wasn't particularly impressive. Brannigan would have initially expected Dalca to have wanted to be in more sumptuous surroundings, but then remembered the industrial office space she had been using. Dalca was cunning, and wouldn't have picked someplace predictable, particularly not for a meet like this.

The sun was fully over the horizon, a sullen red and orange ball floating above the waters of the Gulf of Mexico, when the Blackhearts' vehicles stopped with a crunch of gravel in the parking lot at the end of the long pier reaching out into the bay.

Brannigan got out, stretching his back and stifling a yawn. *I'm getting too old for this.* He looked around them.

He would have expected a place with a pretentious name like "Ingleside On The Bay" to be fancier than their current surroundings. But none of the houses looked particularly expensive; they were mostly double-decker stick houses with various pastel shades of siding. Aside from the really weather-beaten ones that had apparently been through a hurricane or two without a fresh coat of paint.

There was a yacht tied up at the far end of the pier, and even at that distance, and silhouetted against the sunrise, he recognized Dalca. She was a striking enough woman that he'd have a hard time missing her, even at a distance.

And that's intentional. That femme fatale *act in the office wasn't an accident or a quirk of her personality.* He had to admit that he was tired enough that he had to remind himself of that fact. Dalca was calculating and dangerous.

That he needed the reminder was a testimony to just how long Rebecca had been gone. He didn't want to think about that part.

He pulled the back door open. "Come on, Kevin, rise and shine." Curtis picked his head up off the headrest and squinted blearily at him. "Come on, or I'll let Joe help you out."

Curtis grumbled vaguely, but started levering himself out of the car. "He'd enjoy it too much."

"Which is the point," Brannigan said, as he looked around and confirmed that everyone was there. They had arrived at roughly the same time, along the same route, but they hadn't exactly convoyed there, for obvious reasons. "He wouldn't take it easy on you." He straightened and looked around the parking lot.

"Everybody grab your gear and head down to the boat," he said, just loudly enough to make himself heard over by the farthest vehicle. There were some people stirring around the nearby houses, and he'd already seen cars and trucks apparently leaving for work, but there was no reason to broadcast their presence or purpose to the locals any more than necessary.

He suited actions to words, pulling the car's trunk open, noticing that the bullet holes in the metal were already showing rust. It was humid on the Gulf Coast, and bare metal wouldn't last that way for long.

With a grunt, he hauled his duffel out and slid it over his shoulder. The camouflage utilities, booties, fins, dive gear, rifle, pistol, and ammunition all made for a heavy, clumsy load in one bag. It would be better once he was wearing it, but for the moment, it was like carrying a dead body.

Trying not to notice how much his back creaked under the load, he headed for the pier.

Dalca was indeed standing by the gangplank, dressed in shorts and a loose, puffy blouse that for all its apparent shapelessness only seemed to accentuate her own shape with every gust of breeze. She was standing there with her hands on her hips, which were slightly shot out to one side. Huge-lensed dark glasses covered her eyes.

She looked like she was going for a cruise, not meeting mercenaries for a covert infiltration.

"Good morning," she said cheerfully. "Is everyone ready to go?"

Brannigan just grunted as he shifted the load on his shoulder and started up the gangplank. The others followed, most of them avoiding looking at Dalca, who watched them board with a faint smile on her ruby lips. Once Santelli had started up the gangplank, she turned to follow him.

Brannigan had already deposited his duffel on the deck and was counting the team aboard. He looked at Dalca as she followed Santelli up.

"You're coming with us?" he asked.

"At least part of the way," she answered easily. "It *is* my yacht." She breezed past him and ducked into the pilothouse. "Why should I give up the chance to spend a morning on the water?"

Brannigan and Hancock traded a glance, even as the muscular young man in khakis and a polo shirt with "Ciela International" embroidered on the front started to pull the gangplank in. Once it was stowed, he started casting off the lines.

"Once we're out on the bay, start having the boys get ready," Brannigan said quietly to Hancock. "I'm going to go discuss the approach with our hostess."

"You think this is gonna work?" Hancock asked. "I mean, sure, the bad guys are probably looking for military boats, like those Mexicans that got smoked last night, but it's broad daylight. They won't be able to miss us."

"I'll bring it up," Brannigan said. He wasn't looking forward to that conversation, either.

Truth be told, as he turned toward the pilot house, he realized that he wasn't looking forward to *any* sort of conversation with Dalca. Something about her bothered him. He suspected it was the easy, manipulative way she acted, as if she knew the effect of her every word and gesture, and used them with a calculated strategy.

But he had to get this straightened out, so he followed her into the pilot house.

He found himself in a luxurious lounge. The cabinets and walls were paneled in what looked like mahogany, and the deck was covered in deep, beige, pile carpet. Cream-colored couches sat against the starboard side, with a sizeable wet bar on the port side. A table that looked like it was probably solid mahogany sat in the center, with chairs of the same wood pulled up around it. Dalca, her sunglasses now on the table beside her, was sitting at the table, facing the steps down from the main deck, buttering a croissant and watching him. Her eyes seemed to glitter in the overhead lights as she smiled.

"I'm glad you decided to join me, John," she said, motioning toward the chair next to her. "Breakfast just isn't the same, alone."

He stood at the end of the table and shook his head. "I don't have time to play socialite, Ms. Dalca," he said grimly.

She pouted a little. "Well, that is a shame. Especially since you must have gotten up so very early."

"What exactly is your plan, here?" Brannigan asked. "A luxury yacht is not exactly what I'd had in mind when I mentioned 'discreet.'"

She cocked her head slightly to one side. "Have a little faith, John," she said. "I have no intention of taking you gentlemen to Matamoros aboard my lovely *Desiree*. Of course not."

When she finished buttering the croissant and took a delicate bite instead of continuing, Brannigan's eyes narrowed.

"So, then," he said as she swallowed, still smiling at him with her eyes. "When were you going to tell us what you *do* plan on doing?"

"When we get to the second rendezvous, of course," she replied. "Come on, John, you people came to me for a reason. Do you really think that I'm so air-headed that I don't know how to do 'discreet?' I've been in this business a long time. I know what I'm about. Be patient. All will be made clear in time." She smiled again, and patted the table next to her. "Now, are you *sure* you don't want to have a bite with me?"

Brannigan just turned and headed back up the short ladderwell to the main deck. It wasn't his best display of manners, and a part of him rebelled at it, but he wanted to get far away from this woman for some reason. "I've got prep work to do. And so do my men."

That's it. The boys don't get to eat luxury foods in a fancy lounge, so I don't get to, either. Has nothing to do with her.

Keep telling yourself that.

***

Erika Dalca's apparent lack of hurry notwithstanding, the yacht's pilot didn't dawdle. As soon as they were clear of the pier and out into the bay, he was pouring on the throttle. It was a smooth ride, but it wasn't a slow one. They were heading north, up the coast, twisting between the islands that lined the bays and lagoons along the east Texas coastline. They rounded the point where Ingleside On The Bay sat, ran underneath the Highway 361 bridge, passed Stedman Island, and kept going.

They passed barges, fishing boats, sailing boats, and yachts. The coasts and bayous slid by to either side, the yacht's wake forming a wide, white vee on the water.

The Blackhearts didn't talk much on the trip. They were busy, getting their gear ready and changing from civilian clothes into the camouflage fatigues they'd be wearing for the op. They weren't going to blend in with anything on the platform, but they were better for fighting in than civvies.

The weapons were hauled out, disassembled, and carefully sprayed down with lube and silicone spray. They were going to be spending a good amount of time submerged in salt water, and none of them wanted a rifle to seize up or even start to rust on a CQB mission. Which a platform boarding most definitely was.

Even the ammo got the silicone treatment. It would hopefully help reduce stoppages, as well.

Santelli was going around, checking gear and passing out earplugs. They were going to be in close quarters, with metal walls all around them, and none of their weapons were suppressed. If any of them wanted to hear anything after the op, they were going to have to take precautions, even if it cut down on one of their senses. They'd just have to be extra watchful, and communicate by hand and arm signals where possible.

"Boss," Gomez called quietly. Gomez had been one of the first ones with his gear ready, and had moved up toward the bow to post up as a lookout. When Brannigan looked up at him, he pointed.

Brannigan followed his finger. They were sliding past a group of barges anchored off the west shore of the long island to their starboard. But Gomez was pointing to a small, densely-overgrown island directly ahead of them.

He nodded to indicate he understood. It had been less than an hour; the yacht had to be doing close to thirty knots. It was possible that the island ahead was just a waypoint, but it certainly looked like it was their destination.

A moment later, he got his confirmation, as Dalca stepped up onto the deck from the pilot house. She'd changed; she was now wearing a no-nonsense coverall, though a bit of gauzy white cloth sticking up out of the collar suggested that she'd just pulled it on over her other clothes. It would probably be quickly shucked and tossed into a locker when this phase was over with.

"Is this our 'second rendezvous?'" Brannigan asked.

She nodded. "Indeed it is," she said, glancing over the Blackhearts, taking in the sight of them.

Brannigan saw what she saw. Twelve hard-faced men, of various sizes and builds, dressed in fatigues, rigged for diving, festooned with weapons and ammunition. Pistols were affixed to their gear in various places, and rifles that glistened with protective lubrication were held easily in their gloved hands. All were still and watchful, with the coiled-spring tension about them that often could be seen in men readying themselves for combat.

He saw the appreciative glint in her eyes. He wasn't sure what to make of it. Was she just showing a woman's appreciation for the warrior, or was she showing a kingpin's appreciation for their capacity for violence?

He didn't know her well enough to say. And he wasn't sure if he wanted to.

She didn't say anything more as the yacht chugged around toward the north side of the island. They seemed to be in the middle of nowhere; the shores to their west and east were abandoned, covered in thick, swampy growth.

As the yacht cleared the north side of the island, they saw a shape lying low in the water, waiting for them.

At first, it looked almost like another yacht, only nearly awash. The hull was dark and dingy, with spots of rust where the dark blue paint had been worn away. The pilothouse barely rose a few feet above the blank, featureless top deck.

"That's a fucking narco-sub," Childress said. The gawky-looking man was frowning as he looked at the strange craft. He turned to Brannigan. "I've seen pictures of other ones like it."

Brannigan turned to Dalca, a tightness growing in his gut. He'd known that they were going to be operating somewhat on the dark side for this; hell, they already had in Dubai. And he knew that the hostages on that GOPLAT needed their help. But he knew too much about the *narcos* down in Mexico, and to see that their new ally apparently had dealings with them...

"There are other things besides drugs that need smuggling," Dalca said airily. "Some of my people picked this up when a deal went bad between the traffickers and their contacts on this side of the line. There was a shootout; when it was over, only

113

one of the contacts was still alive, so my people swooped in and took the whole thing off their hands." She looked at Brannigan levelly. "We took the sub, and dumped the drugs. I've had a successful enterprise for this long without getting on the cartels' radar, and I have no intention of changing that anytime soon. So, you can relax. Yes, it was a narco sub. But *I* didn't sell the drugs aboard it, and given the time constraints you are under, I hardly think that beggars can afford to be choosers. Don't you, John?"

He had to admit that she had a point. Time was short, and a submarine was probably their best bet to get close enough without the terrorists detecting them and sending them the way of the Mexican Marines. It just felt wrong, somehow, getting into a narco sub.

And do you think that Dmitri's Russians had any qualms about getting into the drug trade? Or human trafficking, for that matter?

"If you look forward," Dalca continued, "You'll see that there's a hatch. We've done a few modifications, so that the entire cargo hold can be used as a lock. You can exit out that way. You'll never need to surface until you get where you're going."

All eyes turned to her. Brannigan watched her with a frown. She seemed completely unconcerned with their scrutiny, but the fact that she had apparently divined their target didn't escape any of them. And they *knew* that none of them had told her.

"Just what did Hector tell you?" Brannigan asked quietly.

"Very little," she said, stepping closer to him. "But it doesn't take a rocket scientist to figure it out. Terrorists kill hundreds, maybe thousands of people, on both sides of the border. Other terrorists kidnap a number of VIPs in Matamoros, and seize an oil platform. Not many hours later, a group of what can only be some kind of special operations soldiers shows up, looking for 'discreet' transport to Matamoros." She was standing very close now, looking up into his eyes. "What else *could* you be doing, except trying to go liberate the Tourmaline-Delta platform? Hmm? I'm not an idiot."

She suddenly lifted up on her tip-toes and kissed Brannigan on the cheek. "Good luck," she said quietly. "Now, you'd better get moving."

Brannigan wasn't going to argue, especially not when he was getting looks and raised eyebrows from Hancock, Curtis, and Flanagan. Santelli was pointedly ignoring the little interplay, but he knew that the squat, pudgy Italian was going to have some pithy remarks about it later.

As for him, he didn't know what was going on with this gal. And he couldn't afford the time or the mental energy to think about it.

"You heard the lady," he said, hefting his M6. "Let's go."

The yacht's young crewman, who had hauled in the gangplank, was now lowering it to the deck of the submarine, as the pilot brought the boat in close. Once it touched, the pilot backed water slightly, then held the yacht steady, apparently by engine power alone. The guy was good.

Brannigan led the way down the gangplank, which swayed alarmingly as the yacht and the sub both rocked on the gentle waves of Dunham Bay. He had to step carefully to keep from getting dumped in the drink.

The hatch opened easily; it looked like a rusty hunk of junk, but had clearly been carefully oiled and greased. Below, the former cargo hold was a dark pit in the hull. A rickety-looking aluminum ladder had been welded to the inside of the hatchway, leading down into the darkness.

Brannigan shone his rifle light down into the hold. Moisture and greenish algae glinted back at him. The smell coming from the hold wasn't especially pleasant, either. But he didn't see any white powder down there, or smell any strong chemicals, so it seemed unlikely that they'd get high riding in a compartment that had been used for transporting large quantities of cocaine and heroin.

The same young crewman who had deployed the gangplank was now following him down it to the sub. "I will be piloting the sub," he said. He was light-skinned and light-haired, but he spoke with a decided Mexican accent. He had a chart in his hand.

Brannigan looked from the chart to the young man. "You know where we're going?" he asked.

"How close to the platform do you need to be?" the crewman asked, pointing to the marked location of the Tourmaline-Delta GOPLAT.

"No more than two thousand meters," Brannigan said. Especially with the experience level of a few of the Blackhearts, much more than that would tax their endurance underwater. And they still had to fight once they came up. "The closer you can get me, the better. Is there a way to communicate between the control room and the hold?"

"There is an intercom," the young man said. "I will update you when we are close." Without another word, he headed for the short pilothouse, pried open another hatch, and disappeared inside. A moment later, a faint rumble through the hull announced that he'd started the sub's engines.

Brannigan ushered the rest of the Blackhearts off the gangplank and down into the hold-turned-lock. He'd be the last one inside, because, as was his wont, he was going to be the first one out.

John Brannigan had always led from the front where possible, and leading the Blackhearts had made it a necessity, if only due to their numbers. It was what made men willing and even eager to follow him. It was also an element of leadership that he had long felt was dying out.

Finally, he clambered down the ladder, pulling the hatch closed over his head and dogging it. A few moments later, he felt the deck heave slightly as the sub lurched into motion.

They were on their way.

CHAPTER 10

The rocking and swaying eased as the sounds of rushing water against the hull closed in overhead. They were submerging as the sub moved away from the island and toward deeper water.

A few minutes later, as the hull started to creak and pop under the mounting water pressure, most of the Blackhearts looked around in the hold, dark except for Santelli's and Brannigan's weapon lights, as if wondering if this was really such a good idea. It wasn't as if the narco sub was the product of a professional shipyard. It appeared to have been built by simply welding a pressure hull around a speedboat.

It wasn't confidence-inducing. Nor was the slapdash way the whole thing had been laid on, with a helmsman they didn't know, and had never seen before about an hour previously.

There wasn't much conversation. The men were absorbed in their own thoughts, mostly sitting on the deck, against the dark, rusty wall, lit only by one or two weapon lights, staring at nothing as they either tried to let their minds go blank, shutting out the fear and nervousness of impending action—or even the fear of being in an ad-hoc sort of submersible, that might decide to start leaking at any moment, with a helmsman who was an unknown quantity.

Curtis leaned over to Flanagan and said something. But the taller man only answered with a monosyllable, his eyes closed, and Curtis subsided.

Time seemed to slow down as the trip proceeded. The only sounds were the thrumming of the engines through the hull, and the faint swish of water outside, except when someone shifted positions. They weren't actually too worried about the bad guys having sonar, but for some reason they all seemed to feel that quiet was called for.

The sounds changed, and a faint rocking began to be felt. Eyes opened, and the men looked up, fingers tightening slightly on weapons.

But soon they were moving again, the rocking fading away, and the hull creaked and popped again as the pressure changed.

"Tac peek?" Jenkins wondered, in a whisper.

"Must have been," Hancock replied, in the same tone.

"Unless the helmsman got off, and we're heading for the bottom," Wade said, with a bleak half-smile.

Curtis shot him a glare, but the big man was unaffected. Brannigan got the dark humor. The thought had occurred to him, too.

Time resumed its crawl. There was no impact, and while the hull continued to make its odd noises, the creaking had stabilized, suggesting that they'd reached a set depth. So, Wade's surmise hadn't been accurate. They weren't being "consigned to the briny deep."

At least, not yet.

The sound of the engines slowed, and they felt a faint push as the sub decelerated. A moment later, a waterproof box bolted to the bulkhead aft lit up, and the young crewman's voice called out. "We are here. Are you ready?"

It sounded deafeningly loud in the hold after the quiet. More than one of the Blackhearts flinched a little at the noise; if there *was* anyone out there listening, they'd just made enough noise to be heard almost to Corpus Christi.

"Lower the volume," Brannigan said quietly, after he'd found the push to talk switch. "And tell us where 'here' is."

There was a pause. When the helmsman's voice came back, it was noticeably quieter. "We are one and a half kilometers north of the platform," he said. "The platform itself is due south, bearing one eighty magnetic."

It sounded like he knew his stuff, at least. Provided he was telling the truth.

"Good copy," Brannigan said. "We'll start our purge. When I break squelch on this intercom again, it means we are ready, and you can start to flood the hold."

"Okay," was the reply.

Brannigan turned. The Blackhearts were getting up, fitting their masks to their faces and tightening the straps on their regulators. They were pros, all of them. They knew what had to happen. And none of them wanted to still be sucking air when the hold started to fill with water.

He followed suit, clamping the regulator in his mouth and tightening the straps before opening the valve and starting to purge the system. Once he was done, he checked that he had everything else; the retention on his pistol was tight, his rifle sling was cranked down so that the weapon wouldn't flap against his body as he swam, and shouldn't catch on the hatchway as he went through it. The others were conducting their own checks.

Once he got "Okay" signals from all twelve of the others, he pushed the PTT on the intercom. For a long moment, he thought that it hadn't been heard. There was no response. But then water started to pour into the hold from valves against the bulkhead, and he realized that the helmsman simply hadn't bothered to answer otherwise.

The water flowed in relatively quickly, and in moments they were up to their waists. Brannigan had a sudden, nightmarish question pop into his head. *Did he bring us up to twenty feet first?* If he hadn't, they could very well all be dead soon. Oxygen toxicity wasn't an instant killer, but they wouldn't last long, especially once the convulsions started.

He kept an eye on the other Blackhearts, watching for the telltale twitching or altered behavior. None of them seemed to be acting abnormally, and they were steady. He would have breathed out a sigh if he hadn't been on a rebreather.

The hold finally filled all the way, and, pulling his fins on, he reached up and undogged the hatch.

Light flooded into the hold; the water was clear, and it was nearing midday. That could end up being a problem. They might very well be spotted on approach, if the terrorists were keeping an eye out. But time was pressing; they couldn't afford to wait until nightfall. The hostages probably didn't have that much time.

They haven't threatened the hostages in any of their videos. In fact, that jackass crowing over killing those Mexican Marines never even mentioned them. As if he didn't already have enough worries about the job, that thought gave Brannigan a new sense of foreboding. One that he had to ignore, as he swam up over the sub.

A quick look revealed that they were probably about fifteen feet down; either they'd gotten lucky, or the helmsman hadn't wanted to take chances. Minor excursions below twenty feet on pure oxygen weren't necessarily game-stoppers, but they sharply limited the time on oxygen that the divers could afford.

He hovered in the water, adjusting his buoyancy compensator to make sure he was neutral, neither floating nor sinking, as the rest of the team swam up out of the sub's hatch. Jenkins had the nav board and the "Budweiser line," a one-inch rope with clevises studding it at regular intervals. It was a good way to keep the team together and make sure nobody got lost.

One by one, the Blackhearts clipped into the Budweiser line. Brannigan stationed himself right behind Jenkins, who was already looking for the one-eighty bearing. Brannigan kept watching as the rest checked their buddy lines, and then tapped Jenkins. When the former SEAL turned his mask back to look at him, he gave him an "Okay."

It was time to go.

Jenkins put his head down, bracing the nav board between his forearms, and started kicking out. Slowly, the rest of the team followed.

It had been a long time since Brannigan had been underwater, and he soon found that his shins were screaming in pain as they kicked out. He had to ignore it. Jenkins wasn't towing the rest; they were all kicking strongly, if only to keep the rebreathers working smoothly, absorbing enough oxygen into their tissues to keep the positive pressure of the closed system from overwhelming their lungs. The Budweiser line was slack, for the most part.

After about a klick though, the line started to tighten slightly. Brannigan half-turned, looking back, to see that Hart was having a hard time keeping up. He realized that the man's prosthetic might be giving him a hard time; he knew of amputees who could run faster than ever with prosthetics, but he'd never heard of how they performed while finning.

And, as much as he hated to think of it, Hart might have kept up in Burma, but he wasn't in the best of shape. And finning shape was different from running or rucking shape.

He let it go. It was too late to change anything, and this part should be over soon, anyway. They should only have about another five hundred meters to swim.

Jenkins was slowing, coming vertical in the water. Brannigan frowned behind his mask; maybe he was off in his own calculations, but he didn't think they were that close yet. There wasn't any sign of the platform's pilings ahead of them. But Jenkins signaled that he was going to do a tac peek, to check on their position.

Brannigan just nodded, giving him an "Okay." Jenkins was the one navigating. If he needed to get his bearings, better that he did it, rather than try to gut it out and get them lost.

Slowly, Jenkins rose toward the surface, breaking it just before Brannigan did.

Careful to keep his mask halfway submerged, Brannigan looked around, taking stock. He hadn't been off. The stacked boxes on stilts of the Tourmaline-Delta platform loomed ahead, less than five hundred meters away. They were right on course, and right about where he'd figured they'd be. Jenkins had just second-guessed himself.

He stared briefly at the back of the other man's head. He knew how easy it was, underwater, with few landmarks, to get disoriented. He'd just expected the SEAL, of all people, to have been a bit more on the ball.

Jenkins started back down, using the nav board as a paddle to thrust himself under the water. Brannigan followed, ducking beneath the surface to see Bianco behind him, hovering upright in the water, leaning back and holding onto the Budweiser line, pulling down to help them submerge with a minimum of surface ripples.

Jenkins looked back at him, and he just pointed. *Let's go.*

The other man nodded, rolled back to the nav board, and started kicking again.

After a few more minutes, the massive steel towers, sitting atop the even more massive storage tanks that the oil platform rested on began to loom out of the water ahead of them. Visibility under the water was definitely shorter than on the surface, but it was still very clear.

The bottom was a long way below them; they weren't going to be able to swim down and stash their gear. They'd have to either keep the rebreathers on until they could establish a foothold on the platform itself, or drop them and forget about them. Which would mean finding another way off the platform.

As always, Brannigan wasn't counting on the people who hired them to expend much effort to extract them. He'd been proven wrong in Burma, but it was something that was always a possibility. They were hired guns for a reason.

They were deniable. And "deniable" often meant "expendable."

After a moment's deliberation, he decided to take a chance. As they floated near one of the pilings, slowly working their way around toward the boat deck, he unlimbered his M6 and pointed it up. They were going to take their chances surfacing on their rebreathers. He didn't want to ditch the equipment until he knew they weren't going to need it.

They did unclip from the Budweiser line and let it fall away, twisting down into the darker waters below them. That was just going to limit them in a way they really didn't need in a firefight.

Slowly, their weapons held ready, Brannigan's Blackhearts rose toward the light of the surface.

***

Brannigan, Jenkins, Hancock, and Flanagan surfaced at almost the same time, bringing their weapons up with them, pointed toward the boat deck. The deck itself was empty except for what looked like a couple of orange lifeboats.

Brannigan tilted his M6's muzzle toward the water and carefully drew back the bolt, breaking the seal and helping the water flow out of the bore. Firing with water in the barrel wouldn't *necessarily* be catastrophic, but it didn't pay to take chances with the weapon you were depending on for your life.

Jenkins had already drained his own, and was treading water, his rifle pointed up at the platform above them, scanning. Brannigan followed suit, even as the rest surfaced, and Flanagan and Hancock dropped their regulators out of their mouths and began to grab hold of the ladder extending down from the boat deck.

***

125

Joe Flanagan was happy enough to be getting out of the water, even if it involved an awkward clamber under the renewed weight of his soaked gear, trying to keep his fins, which were now looped around his wrists, from getting in the way. He'd always been a competent swimmer—he could never have been a Recon Marine otherwise—but he wasn't one of those who were always entirely comfortable in the water. He was, in his own words, a "land mammal."

He and Hancock had picked a spot shadowed by one of the lifeboats; they hadn't seen any bad guys yet, but that didn't mean they weren't there. The platform's superstructure towered eight stories above them, the stairs and framework making a maze of girders that could be hiding a platoon. They didn't have any information that suggested the bad guys had quite that kind of strength, but at the same time, they didn't know that they didn't, either.

There wasn't enough information about the opposition, period.

Crouched behind the lifeboat, his regulator hanging from its straps beneath his chin, he peered out and around the boat, scanning the gray-and-yellow-painted steel around them. Nothing.

Then a bullet skipped off the top of the lifeboat, less than a foot from his head.

"There's somebody up there," he said, as he ducked back and ripped his mask off. He could see better without it.

A moment later, a storm of fire smashed into the boat, bullets hitting the fiberglass with loud *thumps*, muffled by the saltwater-soaked earplugs he already had in. Both men dropped flat, as Bianco and Childress, who were starting to climb up onto the deck, ducked back down below the lip of the boat deck.

Hancock had shed his own mask, water dripping from his shaved head, and ducked around the lifeboat's bow, where he cranked off a fast five shots. The incoming fire slackened, and

Flanagan turned, leaning back to make sure his muzzle cleared the top of the lifeboat.

He wasn't entirely sure where the shooter was; he needed to get a better look. He had a general idea, but hadn't actually seen him. He scanned the superstructure above, his finger hovering near the trigger, his eye just above the small red-dot sight.

There. A figure in some kind of blue-gray camouflage was on one of the landings of the zig-zag stairwell leading up to the heli-deck. Steadying the rifle, pulling it back into his shoulder, Flanagan put the red dot on what he could see of the terrorist shooter, and fired.

Flanagan didn't have a great deal of faith in the 5.56x45mm NATO round. He'd been in enough firefights where it simply hadn't done the trick without five to ten rounds that he wasn't even going to think about only shooting once. Tightly controlling the recoil, he dumped five rounds up at the semi-obscured figure as fast as he could pull the trigger.

Steam puffed from the LWRC's barrel as the saltwater was boiled off by the shots. The figure vanished.

Flanagan didn't move from his spot, keeping his rifle pointed and his eyes open. Maybe he'd gotten him, maybe he hadn't.

Either way, they were definitely made.

There was a lot of splashing and grunting as the rest of the team clambered up onto the boat deck. They had to move quickly.

"I've got you," Bianco said, moving up next to Flanagan and taking up his sector. The enormous, weight-lifting gamer had shed his dive rig and was now wearing just his cammies and chest rig. "Drop your stuff."

Flanagan didn't say anything. There was, in his mind, no need. He simply lowered his rifle, unslung it, and put it on the deck while he started to unfasten the Hollis Explorer's straps, pulling the regulator's straps over his head. His fins went on the deck, and the rebreather went on top of them. Then he had his rifle in his hands again.

Joe Flanagan didn't like to talk if he didn't have to. And the middle of a firefight was pretty much his definition of "talking is unnecessary."

But the firefight had died away, apparently. The figure he'd shot at hadn't reappeared, and nobody else had a target. There seemed to have only been one sentry on the boat deck.

That was bound to change.

Brannigan was suddenly there next to them, having dropped his own rebreather. "All right," he said, just loudly enough to be heard with earplugs in, "Wade and Tanaka have security on the far ladderwell. Let's move up, finish securing the deck, and get at least a couple of guns high."

"I'll go up," Flanagan said.

"With you," Bianco answered.

Getting up from a knee, keeping his eyes and his muzzle moving, watching the hatch leading into the superstructure ahead, the ladderwell above, and the handful of portholes in the superstructure across the boat deck, Flanagan started for the base of the steps. Water squelched from his canvas shoes; he would have preferred boots, but the shoes fit the fins better, and held up out of the water better than the neoprene fin booties that he had often used in the Marine Corps.

No more shots sounded as he crossed the boat deck and pivoted, putting his back to the steel wall behind him as he aimed up the stairs. The empty landing was all he saw. He scanned around one more time before starting up the steps, Bianco a half a step behind him.

It was eerie. The bad guys were definitely there, but aside from the first few shots, they weren't showing themselves. Why not? They'd massacred the Mexican Marines who had tried to assault the platform; what game were they playing now?

He kept climbing, his legs burning a little. It had been a while since he'd been finning, and now he was climbing eight flights of stairs after his leg muscles had had time to cool a little. But he kept his movements smooth, pivoting his muzzle to cover wherever Bianco wasn't.

The helipad at the top was empty. The helos that the terrorists had used to get out there were long gone. And there didn't appear to be any lookouts up there, either.

Where was everybody? He was pretty sure they hadn't bugged out already; otherwise that sentry shouldn't have shot at them.

And if they weren't fighting back, what other nasty surprises were they prepping in the bowels of the platform?

CHAPTER 11

Wade knelt on the deck, silently cursing the diamond texturing that was digging into his knee, dripping saltwater onto the steel and blinking it out of his eyes. *I was definitely not made for this amphibious shit.* Still, he had to admit that it was something different.

He and Tanaka were barricaded on the corner of a part of the superstructure, watching the catwalk leading back behind it to where their imagery had said there was another stairwell, as well as the second boat deck. He knew that the squids and Marines called them "ladderwells," but Wade had never used that kind of nautical terminology, and wasn't about to start. He was a Ranger, not a sailor.

"Hey, Wade?" Tanaka ventured. The younger man was slightly farther out, crouched behind some gray-painted piece of equipment that Wade couldn't identify. He had a slightly different angle. "Can you see this?"

"Since I don't know what 'this' is, I guess I can't, can I, Tanaka?" he asked, trying not to roll his eyes. Tanaka was a tough kid; tougher than some of the former special operations guys on the team. But there were times that he really needed to think a little more before he opened his mouth.

Of course, Wade would have to admit that he was an impatient son of a bitch. Something which every other Ranger who'd known him in his twenty years in the Army could attest to.

"I've got movement, just around the corner," Tanaka said, sounding a little chastened. "I can't see anything that clearly, but there might be somebody back there, by the base of the stairs."

At least he didn't say "ladder."

"Well, I can't see the stairs at all from here, so no, I can't see it," Wade said. Getting to his feet, once again silently cursing the rubbery feeling in his legs that seemed to come from being back on solid…well, a solid surface, if not solid ground, after being in the water for so long, he lifted his rifle to the ready, and started forward.

His move seemed to have surprised Tanaka, who stayed behind cover for a long moment before getting up to follow. He had to remind himself to give the kid some slack; he'd done all right in Burma. Wade bit back the impulse to yell at him to get moving.

He didn't want to go around that corner by himself, especially not if there were bad guys there. Wade might live for a firefight, but he was as averse to getting his head blown off as the next guy.

He slowed as he neared the corner. He thought he could hear something by then, but couldn't be sure, past the pulse thumping in his ears, along with the rasp of his own breathing. He almost ripped the earplugs out, but forced himself to leave them in. Surrounded by that much steel, things were gonna get *loud.*

Tanaka's own muzzle came into his peripheral vision, and then he moved.

Stepping out carefully, his rifle up and ready, he eased around the corner, the red dot just below his line of sight. The skeletal, gray-painted girders of the stairwell came into view, and then he could see just what Tanaka had been talking about.

A figure moved between the girders, and a voice spoke, pitched low, the words just outside of the threshold where he could understand them, especially with the earplugs in. Lifting his rifle fractionally, he continued moving forward.

There was a yell, immediately followed by a flash and a sharp report. The bullet hit one of the girders around the stairs and ricocheted, flying out over the water with an angry whine. Wade returned fire, snapping two shots back at the muzzle flash while he dove for the nearest cover, which appeared to be the stairway itself. The shots' concussions rang and reverberated painfully through the structure of the platform.

Tanaka was moving, dashing for the rack where a lifeboat hung above the blue water below, firing quick snap-shots at the enemy as he went. Bullets *cracked* through the air, reaching for him, but he got to the minimal shelter of the steel rack and threw himself behind it, dumping the rest of his magazine toward the unknown hostiles as fast as he could pull the trigger.

Wade got his feet under him and lunged out, pivoting to bring his own rifle to bear as he came around the corner of the stairs. He could see a little bit through the steel mesh of the steps and the interweaving, zig-zag pattern of the steel supports, but there was just too much crap in the way to get a clear shot.

Three men were crouched near the stairs, all dressed in what looked like Kryptek Poseidon camouflage, with matching chest rigs and gunbelts. Two of them were facing him and Tanaka, their bullpup rifles in their shoulders.

The first one saw Wade at the same time he came around, and was already aiming in. Wade snapped his rifle up, painfully aware that he was off-balance and out of a good shooting stance, and snapped a shot at him.

In that single instant, he was aware of the face of the man facing him, clean-shaven, either Hispanic or deeply tanned, wearing expensive Gator sunglasses, looking at him through a red dot almost identical to his own. The muzzle flash from the bullpup rifle wasn't bright, not in the sunshine, but he saw just about every detail of it, anyway.

The man in the blue-gray Kryptek missed. Wade didn't.

His bullet smacked into the man's shoulder, throwing him to one side as it blew a chunk of meat out of his deltoid with a spatter of blood. The rifle went off-line just long enough for Wade to line up the man's head, cursing that he'd missed it with the first shot, and blow a good portion of his brains out a quarter-sized hole in the back of his head.

The second man was already down, shaking violently and screaming as he bled out from half a dozen of Tanaka's bullets. The third had ducked behind the fifty-five-gallon drum behind them, drawing a pistol and firing unaimed shots over the top of the barrel, cussing loudly.

And he was cursing in English. With a noticeably American accent.

What the fuck? Nobody had said anything about these assholes being Americans. Of course, Wade remembered that nobody really knew *anything* about them, so it shouldn't have come as a surprise. At least no more a surprise than anything else about this op. But it still pissed him off.

Of course, Wade being Wade, he wasn't going to let it stop him from killing as many of them as he could. Because if there was one thing Wade thought was worthwhile, it was killing assholes, regardless of what kind of assholes they were.

He wasn't especially outraged that Americans were the assholes this time. Wade had few ideological hangups. To him, there were His Guys, and Everyone Else. And any time some of Everyone Else crossed His Guys, or managed to get on his target deck, then he was fine with killing them dead, regardless of who the hell they were.

He stepped out from the stairway, even as a pistol round hissed passed his head, returning fire with a pair that smacked into the steel wall above the hiding man's head. He didn't have a clear shot, but the guy was shooting at him and Tanaka, and that pissed him off.

The pistoleer stopped shooting, and suddenly scrambled away, ducking through a hatch a few feet behind the barrel. Tanaka chased him with a trio of shots, but they smacked into the coaming and the hatch itself. Then the guy was gone.

"Come on, Tanaka," Wade snapped, as he stepped over to the man he'd killed. "That was *maybe* a fifteen-yard shot. You should have hit him."

"You didn't hit him when you shot at him," Tanaka replied, getting up and moving forward, his rifle still held at the ready.

Wade kicked the bullpup rifle away from the grasping hands of the man he'd shot in the head. "I wasn't trying to hit him, I was just trying to get him to stop shooting so that I could move to get a clear shot," he said. "Different animal." He looked down at the corpse. "What do we have here?" The guy looked American, all right. And that was a Desert Tech MDR bullpup, or he wasn't a gun nerd. And if there was one thing Wade liked above and beyond his comics collecting, it was guns.

"Uh, Wade?" Tanaka sounded like he was suddenly very reluctant to be anywhere near the corpses.

"What now, Tanaka?" he asked. But as he lifted his eyes, he suddenly didn't need to hear Tanaka's explanation anymore. He could see it with his own two eyes.

There were wires coming off the fifty-five-gallon drum that the three dead terrorists had been gathered around. And that looked an awful lot like an electrical initiation system on top, with shock tube going down inside the top of the drum.

"Don't move," he said. Contrary to every screaming nerve in his body, he stepped forward, closer to the barrel. *I'm dead anyway if this thing is set to go off. May as well make sure.*

To his relief, it didn't look like everything was entirely set up. The initiation system was there, but there were loose wires, and the remote receiver didn't look like it was entirely connected.

"Cover me," he said shortly. Tanaka moved up next to him, rifle raised and scanning the nearby hatch, up the stairs, and up toward all of the handful of hatches and portholes on the quarterdecks above them that were in view. It was a lot to cover, but Wade had business.

Slinging his own rifle, he gingerly picked up the remote receiver and pulled the wires out. Then he carefully started dismantling the initiation system, pulling the shock tube out of the igniter and tossing the igniter toward the ocean.

Finally, though he couldn't be absolutely sure that he'd gotten everything, he'd torn apart every bit of the initiation system that he could find. There might be a backup down inside the drum, in which case he and Tanaka were probably screwed, but he'd done what he could.

"Let's go back," he said, bringing his rifle back up. "Brannigan needs to know about this."

***

Brannigan was crouched behind a lifeboat, looking up at the surrounding superstructure. The platform was huge; clearing the entire thing was going to be a long, laborious process, and fraught with risk. Not least for the hostages. But they wouldn't do the hostages any good by getting shot to pieces rushing it. Not for the first time, he wished he had the kind of resources that he'd had as a MEU commander.

He briefly thought back to that last op, in East Africa. He'd taken a good chunk of the Ground Combat Element ashore, after sending his Recon teams ahead to clear the air defenses. Three companies of Marines had stormed the terrorist village, secured the hostages, and been out within minutes.

The Blackhearts were more than competent. There was no doubt about that. And they had a certain, nearly-surgical effectiveness that the bad guys often weren't expecting. They'd proved it on Khadarkh, and they'd proved it in Burma. But he still wanted a Battalion of Marines to do this job.

There was a hiss, barely audible through his earplugs, and then Wade was kneeling next to him, having come around the lifeboat's bow. The big man took a knee beside him, his pale blue eyes still scanning the platform's superstructure around them.

"Tanaka and I found three bad guys back by the other stairs," Wade said without preamble. "They were setting up charges; looked like a fifty-five-gallon oil drum full of explosives. We killed two, and I tore out the initiation system, but there are probably more."

Brannigan grimaced. "Probably a lot more," he agreed. "Hell." He thought he understood, now, why they'd encountered so little resistance. The enemy must have an escape route, and be planning on drawing them deeper inside, where they could go down with the platform when it blew sky-high, coincidentally creating another disaster on the Gulf Coast. "Carlo!" he hissed. "Roger!"

Looking a bit like Mutt and Jeff, the squat Santelli and lean, hatchet-faced Hancock hurried over. Brannigan let them wait for a second while the plan formed in his mind.

"Tell 'em what you told me, Wade," he said. He needed a moment.

Wade repeated his report. Hancock took it in, stony-faced, his dark eyes never still, flicking from danger area to danger area. They were still in a bad spot, tactically speaking, and Hancock knew it. They had a tiny foothold, but they were still holding on by their fingernails. Santelli shook his head and swore under his breath.

"All right, here's the plan," Brannigan said. "Three elements; Carlo, Roger, and I will be element leaders. Carlo and Roger, you're on bomb-hunting detail. Start on the outside as best you can, and work your way in. Find the charges and disarm them, if you can't just kill the bomb-layers as you go. I'll take the third element, head up top, and start looking for the hostages." He figured that their best bet was going to be the crew quarters. That would be the largest open area on the platform, more than likely.

"Four men per element," he said. "Grab your guys and get moving. We don't have a lot of time. I'll grab Joe and Vincent." He looked around. "Aziz!" he snapped. "You're with me. Let's go."

Aziz might have grimaced, but he couldn't tell for sure. He also didn't have the time to worry about it. If the man thought that he could just hunker down on the boat deck and hold security, he was in the wrong job. Without waiting for him, Brannigan got to his feet and drove toward the ladderwell leading up to the helideck.

***

Flint looked up at the noise. He wasn't entirely sure if he'd heard anything or not; a lot of the platform's equipment was still running, despite the fact that it wasn't going to be pumping oil anywhere, and hadn't been for several days. And with his left ear being not quite up to snuff anymore, he couldn't be sure. But Scrap and Inmate looked up at the same time, so he figured he probably wasn't hearing things.

"What was that?" Inmate asked. Inmate's portrait could have been in the dictionary under "thug." His flat face, smashed nose that had clearly been broken repeatedly, small eyes, and distinct lack of a neck went right together with his shaved skull. He wasn't *quite* as dumb as he looked, but Flint still didn't think much of his brains. His Eastern European accent didn't help Flint's impression of his mental facilities, either. He just *sounded* thick.

"Unless I'm losing my mind," Flint said, pulling his radio out, "those were gunshots." He lifted the radio to his lips. "Crash, this is Flint."

There was no reply. He repeated the call. His eyes narrowed. Crash was a dumbass, a notch below Inmate, which was why he'd been put on security. Give him a sector to cover and tell him not to budge from it, and he couldn't screw up too badly. "Crash, Crash, this is Flint."

Still nothing. "This is Flint. Anybody got eyes on Crash?" *I bet the idiot shot himself.*

But then more shots reverberated faintly through the structure. *Maybe not. Even Crash wouldn't shoot himself a dozen times.*

"This is Gibbet," the breathless voice over the radio said. "We've got boarders. Crash, Carnage, and Viper are down."

Flint thought fast, even as he mentally cursed Gibbet for forgetting to specify just where the boarders were. Carnage, Viper, and Gibbet were supposed to be setting charges...down by the southeast lifeboat deck. That was right.

"Listen up," he said over the radio. "This is Flint. We have boarders down at the lifeboat decks. Report status on all charges."

One by one, the demo teams started checking in. It sounded like only half the bombs were set, and none of the really big ones, the ones that were supposed to go on the wells, were even in position yet.

Son of a bitch. "I want everybody not currently on an active bomb team to report to the main office, about thirty seconds ago," he snapped. Snatching up his MDR, he stormed out of the crew quarters and toward the stairs leading up to what had been the platform supervisor's office. It had become his impromptu command center since they'd taken the Tourmaline-Delta.

Dingo, Villain, Dogmeat, and Lizard were already there when he arrived, kitted out and ready. Dogmeat, Villain, and Lizard were wearing their Kryptek balaclavas, but Dingo was open-faced. He also looked pissed.

"What the fuck is going on?" Dingo asked. "I thought your guys were supposed to be on the ball, keeping a lookout? It was my team's down time."

Flint almost shot him right then and there. He could have sworn his palm itched as it twitched, ever so slightly, toward his Field Pistol. "I don't know," he admitted through clenched teeth. "Maybe they figured we'd spot any vehicles they used to insert, so they swam all fucking night. Your guess is as good as mine. Doesn't matter." Chopper and Funnyman ran up the ladderwell from below, Funnyman's plate carrier still unfastened. Flint did a quick count in his head. That was everybody who wasn't on explosives detail or dead.

"We've got to buy some time," he said. "The sub just came to periscope depth and made contact; it's less than an hour out. We need to contain these guys at least until we can get the rest of the bombs set and fall back to the sub. Once that's done, they can go up with the platform."

"They've had at least ten minutes already," Dingo said. "How the hell are we supposed to contain 'em?"

Flint glared at him. "They shouldn't be too hard to find. Yeah, it's a big platform, but they only have so many ways up. Head for the ladderwells and start pushing down. I'll take the west, you take the east. Once you've made contact, either barricade and hold 'em in place, or push 'em back to the boat decks." He spat on the deck. "We've got plenty of explosives and plenty of ammo. Use your imagination."

He looked around at the rest. Funnyman looked bored. Which, knowing him, meant he was *really* ready to play. He wasn't called Funnyman for his jokes.

"If there are no more stupid questions," Flint snarled, "let's get moving. We've got Mexican heroes to kill."

CHAPTER 12

Hancock made sure to double-check the charge that Wade had disarmed. It wasn't that he didn't trust Wade to have rendered the thing as safe as possible; it was just that they hadn't had eyes on it for some time, and it was entirely possible that some of the bad guys might have come back around and re-rigged it.

Roger Hancock hadn't survived multiple tours in Iraq and Afghanistan by playing around with IEDs.

Fortunately, it appeared that the barrel bomb hadn't been touched since Wade and Tanaka had dealt with it. The two corpses were still lying on the deck, the puddles of blood underneath them getting sticky. There were drops spattered around the hatch, too.

"See?" Tanaka said. "I didn't miss him."

"He's still breathing, isn't he?" Wade said coldly. "So you may as well have missed him."

Hancock might have said something to Wade, but let it go. Tanaka was one of the big boys now. He had to have a Rhino Liner for a skin. If he couldn't handle Wade ragging him for missing a kill shot, then he needed to reassess his position with the Blackhearts.

Of course, in the middle of a mission was probably not quite the best time to do that...

Gomez was as silent as ever, his M6 covering up the ladderwell. The man never seemed to have a comment about anything. He just watched, listened, and acted.

Which was fine with Hancock, at that point. Chatter wasn't what was needed.

"Let's make sure they can't set this thing off in our rear," Hancock said. "Tanaka, Gomez, hold security. Wade, you and I are gonna roll this drum of boom-boom into the drink."

Wade nodded, slinging his rifle around behind his back and cinching it down as Hancock did the same. Together, they put their gloved hands, still damp from the ocean, on the rim of the oil drum, and started to twist.

It was heavy; there had to be a *lot* of explosives inside. Hancock took a deep breath, as he and Wade tipped the drum up onto the edge of its lower rim and started to wheel it toward the rail.

Hancock wasn't having fun. He was an adrenaline junkie, an extreme-sports guy. But explosives were where he drew the line when it came to thrills. Roger Hancock didn't like playing with things that went boom. There were too many ways it could go wrong.

That didn't include things like grenades, or even breaching charges. Those were just a part of the job. But bombs that somebody else had made, usually somebody hostile? Those gave him the heebie-jeebies.

He knew that it wasn't likely that the barrel was going to explode. The initiation system had been ripped out, and the number of explosives in general use that detonated when shot was pretty small. Given the apparent sophistication of their enemy, he doubted that they were using anything that wasn't already pretty well-known and relatively safe.

That didn't make him feel any better. Enemy bombs were enemy bombs, and never to be trusted.

He and Wade got the drum to the nearest lifeboat and laid it down on its side. The gap in the deck below was designed to allow the lifeboat to drop into the water, and there wasn't a whole lot of room beside the orange fiberglass craft.

They'd have to make do.

Wade held onto the rim and stepped around to one side, while Hancock moved to the other end. Together, they shoved, hard, and the bomb rolled forward, coming to rest against the lifeboat's hull with a hollow *clunk*. They didn't stop, but kept pushing, finning shoes slipping on the deck, straining to shove the bomb hard enough to get through the gap.

The lifeboat didn't seem to be moving, but the barrel slipped, then slipped again. Then it went all the way through, disappearing into the blue water below with a splash, as Hancock caught himself on the side of the lifeboat's hull, reaching out to grab Wade before he could follow the drum into the depths.

He pulled his rifle back around in front of him, and was about to say something when a flurry of bullets hit the side of the lifeboat.

Tanaka was returning fire, huddled next to a big, blue-gray box of machinery. More rounds were scoring bright scars in the paint, but Tanaka didn't even flinch. He was blasting shots back at whoever was engaging them, rapping out fast hammer pairs at someone Hancock couldn't see. A moment later, Gomez had rolled away from the ladderwell and taken shelter behind the same blue-gray metal box.

Hancock could have gone to join them. Instead, he headed for the lifeboat's bow, keeping low and moving around the side instead of trying to pop over the top. Too many amateurs went over the top, where they were easier to target.

There were at least three of them. And they weren't exposed; they were shooting around the maze of pipes on the seaward side of the platform, underneath the gigantic tubes that returned seawater to the Gulf after it had been separated from the crude oil coming up the derricks. They were trading shots with Tanaka, but neither they nor he were going to get good hits.

Hancock, on the other hand, was better set. He could just see enough of one of them, who was easing his rifle and one eye around the corner, to get a shot. He put his red dot on the man's head and hammered three rounds at him, the dot bouncing ever so slightly with each shot. The head vanished, and the shooting stopped.

Wade was next to him, cursing steadily under his breath as he searched for a shot. All three of the bad guys had disappeared. *Wade really can't stand not getting a share, can he?* But Hancock didn't move immediately. He could never say exactly why, but something about the setup made the hackles rise on the back of his neck. He just knew that rushing in after those three was going to be a bad idea.

Not for the first time, he wished they had some grenades. *Even just some flashbangs.* They were extremely useful for this kind of clearing operation.

"Tanaka, Gomez, move up!" he hissed, just loud enough that he hoped they heard him. The earplugs were causing some communications problems, but he still acknowledged that they had been a good idea. The thunderous echoes rolling back and forth between the steel and concrete surfaces of the platform would have been deafening without them. They were plenty loud even with the earplugs in.

There wasn't a lot of maneuvering room. If anything, this platform was worse than the Citadel on Khadarkh. There were only so many places they could go, and a good defender would have most of them covered.

He just barely saw Tanaka and Gomez halt just short of the corner, Tanaka aimed in on the corner itself, and Gomez behind him, covering his back. "Moving," he said to Wade. As he'd expected, Wade was right with him as soon as he started advancing.

There was another blocky container, or bit of unfathomable machinery, standing on thick steel girders about a story over their heads. The girders hemmed them in, their crisscrossing pattern neither providing a clear way through nor offering much in the way of cover. The alternative was to just

144

boogie around the corner, though, so Hancock moved up next to the thicker, vertical girders, and took a knee.

"Get ready to pull me back if this turns out to be stupid," he muttered. Then he dropped down on his side, his rifle in his shoulder, and shoved himself out past the girder, along the deck.

Sure enough, there they were. He'd apparently hit his target; one of them was a corpse, lying where he'd been dragged by his fellows. The other two were back along the side of the platform about twenty yards, aimed in at the corner.

They hadn't been ready for somebody to try to slide out, flat on the deck, though. Their initial fusillade of fire went high, bullets smacking into steel with ringing *bangs* that echoed and reverberated, showering Hancock with stinging fragments. He returned fire, hammering half a magazine at them, though it wasn't the best-aimed. He saw one of them crumple with a scream as a bullet shattered his shin, but then Wade was hauling him out of the line of fire, even as the bullets began dropping lower, reaching for his life.

He was about to protest; there was only one left, but then Gomez yelled an alarm and opened fire on the ladderwell.

Wade was hauling him to his feet and rushing toward the cover of the blue-gray machinery. Hancock was barely able to get his feet under him, the barrel of his rifle glancing off the girders as he stumbled after Wade. Bullets hammered at the deck near their heads, but Gomez was putting enough fire down that the terrorists up on the ladderwell weren't able to get a good shot, even from such a short distance away.

He and Wade slammed into the side of the big metal box. Tanaka was, to his credit, still covered down on the corner; if they'd all focused on the ladderwell, they could very well have gotten shot in the back. And none of them were wearing plates; the requirements of time and the need to streamline and reduce weight for the dive insert had precluded them. That was something that Hancock, who had always detested wearing body armor, was finding he rather regretted. If ever there was a situation where body armor was called for, it was this kind of close-quarters nightmare.

Gomez ran dry and rolled back behind the machinery, dropping the mag out of his rifle. Wade then popped out around the side where he'd been, and fired a rapid trio of shots at the movement he could see on the ladderwell. It might have been better to back up and shoot over the top, but that risked exposure to the shooters around the corner.

Hancock used Wade for cover and leaned out farther. It looked like there were three or four men on the ladderwell above them, moving down in alternating bounds. One or two would post up on the landings, keeping as much steel as possible—even though none of it was solid—between themselves and the Blackhearts, and opening fire while their compadres bounded down another flight. They had the high ground, but they didn't have a lot of cover.

Taking a low knee, peeking his muzzle just past Wade's shoulder, Hancock zeroed in on one of the shooters on a landing. He rapped out two shots, and the fire slackened, either because he'd hit the guy, or because he'd gotten close enough to force him back from his firing position.

A moment later, the second shooter opened up with an even heavier volume of fire, bullets smacking into the decking and the metal casing of the unknown machinery that formed their cover. Both he and Wade had to duck back from the advancing impacts.

"We could wait until they're on the deck," Wade suggested, as he swapped mags. "Not much cover between here and the stairs."

"That's 'Gunfight at the OK Corral' time," Hancock countered, "presuming they don't leave one guy up top to keep our heads down." The incoming gunshots slowed again, and he popped out, just in time to get a snap shot at a figure hustling down the steps. He fired, the report reverberating against the metal, and the figure staggered. That hitch in the enemy shooter's step was all both Hancock and Wade needed. Leaning out, the two of them fired again, smashing the terrorist off his feet with a fusillade of six or seven rapid shots.

The echoes faded, rolling across the water, and then there wasn't any more movement on the ladderwell.

"You think we got all of 'em?" Wade asked.

"I doubt it," Hancock replied. "I think they ducked into the hatch after we shot that one. We can't stay here, though."

"No, we can't," Tanaka said over his shoulder. "I think I see another bomb."

"Hold on that ladderwell," Hancock said, before moving to join the younger man at the corner. Taking a knee to get his profile down, he eased an eye around.

He had to move farther than he'd anticipated; there were enough pipes on the outside of the platform that it was difficult to see without moving farther around the corner. But after a moment, he could see that Tanaka was right; there was another fifty-five-gallon drum about fifty feet down the rail, and it looked like the initiation system might be complete already.

Glancing back at Wade and Gomez, he pointed at the corner, then at Tanaka, then back toward the ladderwell. He hadn't seen any of their little friends on the far side, but that didn't mean they weren't there. There were a *lot* of places to hide on this rig.

Tanaka seemed to get the message, and just whispered, "With you."

Hancock went around the corner low and fast, his rifle up in his shoulder, the Aimpoint just fractionally below his eye. He saw the man in the blue-gray camouflage an instant before the faint flash of the shot. He threw himself flat, cranking off another snap shot that he knew was going to go high.

Tanaka was behind him, and put a bullet through the terrorist's skull. The blue-gray-clad man fell backward on the deck, spasmodically triggering another shot, that slammed into the steel wall above him.

As Hancock got himself sorted, getting up on a low knee behind his rifle, Tanaka held what he had. Once he was confident that Hancock owned the catwalk in front of them, he turned and pointed his rifle back around the corner.

"I've got you!" he yelled. Both Gomez and Wade had earplugs in, and were facing away from him. Yelling was probably the only way he was going to be heard at all. "Turn and go!"

Gomez was the first one to turn. He ducked to make sure he wasn't anywhere near Tanaka's line of fire, and dashed to the railing, where he took a knee and aimed back up at the ladderwell. He was exposed, but then, they all were.

Wade followed shortly behind him, and then they were all around the corner and closing on the barrel bomb that Tanaka had spotted. *Is that thing smoking already?* Hancock couldn't tell, but he had a very hollow, sick feeling in his stomach at the sight.

Wade suddenly grabbed him by the shoulder, bringing him up short. He almost barked at him, until the big, pale-eyed man pointed.

There was a small, black plastic box zip-tied to the railing only a couple of feet ahead of his legs. It looked like a sensor for a garage door opener.

It was also out of place. But Hancock recognized what it was almost as quickly as Wade had.

There was a booby trap between them and the barrel bomb.

***

Aziz could already hear shooting above them. Remembering the layout from the imagery, he tried not to cringe. There wasn't exactly a whole ton of cover up on that helideck, and they were pounding up the steps to run right out onto it, while somebody was shooting at them.

Why the hell did I come along this time? It was a question that Aziz had asked himself repeatedly, every job he'd joined the

Blackhearts on. And it was one that he never had a satisfactory answer to. Money was the one he usually settled on; his own egoism wasn't something he thought much about.

He slowed as he neared the top. He couldn't see anything past the landing just above them, but he could hear gunfire going in both directions; Flanagan and Bianco were apparently still alive, though for how long, exposed out on that helicopter landing pad, was anyone's guess. Bullets *snapped* past overhead, only a few feet above the landing, and Aziz decided that he *really* didn't want to go up there.

But Brannigan was right behind him. "With you," he growled.

Aziz realized that the Colonel had thought he was pausing just to make sure that there was another shooter behind him. *Yeah, that's what I was doing. Don't want to pop up there by myself. I was just taking a pause to make sure we weren't all spread out.* It sounded weak, even to him.

Leading with his muzzle, he popped over the landing, aiming toward the seaward side, where most of the fire was coming from.

Bianco and Flanagan were lying prone on the deck, as flat to the steel and non-skid as possible, firing back at several figures in and around the cranes and containers at the far side, off the edge of the helideck. It wasn't a long shot; there were no long shots on that platform, but the terrorists were keeping behind cover as much as possible, and Flanagan and Bianco were burning through ammunition to keep them back there.

Aziz scrambled clear of the landing and threw himself flat, as a burst ripped through the air overhead. His return fire was fast and wild; he didn't even have his eye anywhere near the sights. He just hammered half a dozen rounds in the general direction of the bad guys.

Trying to press himself down through the helideck, he kept firing, dumping the mag as fast as he could pull the trigger. *At least on Khadarkh, it was dark.* Here they were, exposed like bugs on a plate in broad daylight. He wanted to dig a hole in the deck and pull it in after him.

Flanagan was suddenly passing him, up and moving fast, not quite running, but with his rifle in his shoulder, firing at one of the terrorists who was leaning out from behind a container near the landing to the far stairs. *Is he nuts? Oh, shit, we're gonna attack, instead of getting low and picking them off.*

Brannigan was moving next, having jogged around behind Bianco so as not to cut off his line of fire. He and Flanagan were advancing on the terrorists at the stairs, firing as they went.

Then Bianco was getting up. Aziz delayed as long as he could, swearing in English and Arabic as he finally hauled himself up off the deck and followed. *I'm gonna die because of you damned heroes.*

***

Flanagan was moving fast, his feet rolling on the deck, trying to keep his rifle as steady as possible. They were in the open, but this was close quarters battle, nevertheless; whoever got on target fastest was going to win.

As near as he'd been able to tell, there were only three or four of the terrorists, and they weren't anxious to expose themselves, preferring to fire from cover, and that barely aimed. Somehow, he didn't think it was because they were booger-eaters who couldn't shoot.

It's like they're just trying to pin us down for a while. Which didn't make much sense, until one considered the barrel bomb that Wade had found.

Which just means we don't have a lot of time. Flanagan was sure the Colonel realized that. Not much got past him, especially in a combat environment.

He angled out to his left as he closed on the terrorist, who had ducked back as soon as he'd seen Flanagan advancing, disappearing behind the container before he could get a shot. A lot of the shooting had died down all of a sudden as the Blackhearts had gotten up and advanced; most of the rounds were going the other way now, as Bianco and Aziz laid down covering fire.

He slowed fractionally, trying to slow his heartbeat, and then stepped around the corner, his red dot already at his eye, looking for the terrorist he'd been trading shots with for the last couple of minutes of eternity.

All he saw was a faint flash of movement disappearing down the ladderwell.

Brannigan was behind him, checking the other containers and the crane. The shooting up there on the helipad had stopped, though the booming and hammering cacophony of gunfights lower down were still echoing up through the superstructure.

Flanagan barricaded himself on the container, keeping his rifle pointed at the ladderwell. If the bad guys had gone back down, there was nowhere else they could pop up again. "Did they all skedaddle?" he asked.

"Looks that way," Brannigan replied, as Bianco and Aziz joined them. "Looks like there might be a little bit of blood over there, so you and Vinnie might have winged one."

"We gonna follow 'em down?" Bianco asked.

"We've got to clear this sucker," Brannigan replied grimly. "Can't do that sitting up here." Suiting actions to words, he lifted his rifle and advanced on the ladderwell.

The three of them followed, Aziz and Bianco first, while Flanagan turned to check back behind them, just to make sure that there weren't more bad guys coming up from the ladderwell they'd ascended to get to the helideck. The platform was *big*, and they really had no clear idea of how many terrorists there might be. There could be a company crawling around the various passageways and ladderwells, and with eight stories of structure, there were a *lot* of places to hide and move around.

Satisfied that they weren't about to get shot in the back, Flanagan rose and followed the rest to the landing.

Brannigan and Aziz were already starting down. If Aziz was reluctant, he was keeping up and keeping his expression neutral. Flanagan spared a moment to study the man.

He'd never particularly liked Aziz. He knew that the guy had really stuck himself out there once, going into Khadarkh City alone and hobnobbing with the worst of the worst to arrange the distraction that had helped them get into the Citadel. But then the same guy, who had even climbed to the Citadel itself and covered them against the Iranians' commandeered AMX-10 APCs, had hung back and barely fired a shot after that.

Then he'd recruited a linguist for the Burma mission who had just so happened to be a tiny slip of a girl he was also banging.

Aziz had guts when he had to. The rest of the time, Flanagan thought he was a sniveling little weasel, who'd try to get one over on anyone and everyone, including his teammates, and try to get through a mission with as little effort as possible, so he could blow his paycheck later.

That was why Flanagan tried to keep an eye on him when he could. He didn't trust that Aziz wouldn't screw them over, possibly at the worst possible time, just out of either laziness or spite.

All of this flashed through his mind in a glance, as he followed the other three down the ladder.

Brannigan and Aziz only went down the first flight; there was a hatch leading off the first landing, and Brannigan didn't even slow down. Flanagan saw the last of the Colonel's back as he rolled through the hatch, rifle up and ready.

It made sense. They didn't have flashbangs or frags. They had to use speed and aggressiveness to keep the enemy off balance. Get in fast, shoot first, and shoot a lot.

He could hear the thunderous reports of gunshots reverberating off the steel walls inside the passageway, and he pushed to get in behind Bianco.

Brannigan and Aziz were on either side of the passageway, weapons aimed down toward a far hatch that looked like it was open. Bianco had taken up position just behind Brannigan, his own muzzle alongside the Colonel's shoulder. Bianco was a big man, but he was still half a head shorter than Brannigan; he'd never be able to get his rifle *over* the boss's shoulder.

Flanagan moved up behind Aziz. Whoever they'd been shooting at had disappeared. The passageway was momentarily empty and quiet.

There were a half a dozen hatches along the left-hand side of the passage; the right-hand side was blank, except for a few portholes letting bright, Gulf sunlight through.

Brannigan and Bianco were advancing carefully down the passageway, but Aziz wasn't moving. He was standing there, kind of pressed against the bulkhead, breathing hard.

Flanagan bumped him with a knee. "With you," he said. Aziz didn't move. He repeated it.

That time he got through. Aziz started moving, advancing down the passageway. Flanagan paced him, pausing once or twice to lift his muzzle and check over his shoulder. This platform was already making him paranoid, given how big it was.

Brannigan and Bianco posted up just short of the open hatch, continuing to cover down the passage. Aziz slowed again, seemingly reluctant to approach the open portal. But he was the man on the spot, and he stacked on the hatch.

But he didn't go in. He seemed to be psyching himself up for something. Flanagan started to get pissed. The middle of a passageway wasn't the time or the place; hallways and passageways were deathtraps. "*With you!*" he hissed.

Aziz started to go, stutter-stepped, as if unsure if he should commit all the way, and then almost tripped as he went through the hatch.

A storm of gunfire caught him in the side, bullets knocking him back against the hatch coaming. He hit the coaming and fell, leaving a smear of blood on the gray-painted steel.

The three remaining Blackhearts surged forward, trying to get through the hatch and kill the terrorists while they still had any momentum remaining at all. But the initiative had already been lost; someone inside had their weapons aimed in and ready.

More fire followed, bullets hitting the coaming with loud *bangs* that were painful even through the ear protection the Blackhearts were wearing, then zipping out into the passageway, as the shooter tracked around the edge of the hatch.

Brannigan got a step inside the hatch, got one shot off, and then his head snapped back with a spray of blood and he fell.

CHAPTER 13

Jenkins was on point as Santelli's element wove through the girders and pipes on the west side of the platform. They hadn't seen any more of the barrel bombs, but they were moving slowly and carefully, looking everywhere.

Santelli was right behind Jenkins, with Hart and Childress behind him, and Curtis taking up the rear. Childress was trying to look everywhere at once, knowing he probably looked like a gawking chicken, swiveling his head on his long, skinny neck, but he didn't care. Better to look a little bad than get blown up.

He spotted it at the same time Jenkins did. The blond former SEAL stopped dead, throwing up a fist, already way too close to the gray box zip-tied to a pipe. It looked kind of like an ammo can or a toolbox, but the IR sensor on the side belied its innocuous appearance. That was an improvised claymore, if Childress had ever seen one. And he'd played around with making some in his day.

Fortunately, the ATF had never found out.

Jenkins shied back and found some shelter behind another big block of machinery. Childress didn't know what it was; all of the various mechanisms that made the platform work may as well be inert blocks of metal to him. He'd never worked oil drilling, and didn't know the first thing about it. He just hoped that whatever it was stopped bullets and frag.

"Whatcha got, Jenkins?" Santelli asked quietly.

Jenkins pointed out the box, even as he scanned the catwalks and hatches above them. "Looks like a booby trap," he said. "Maybe an IED."

"Or a claymore in a box," Santelli finished. He looked up and around, sizing up their position. "No other way around," he mused. "They must have thought this through a bit." Slinging his rifle, he pulled a multitool out of his chest rig.

"You sure that's a good idea, Carlo?" Curtis asked. "There might be failsafes."

"I'm sure there probably are," Santelli said bluntly. "That don't change nothin'. We've got to get past it, so somebody's got to disarm it." That was Santelli's way. See the problem, fix the problem. Whatever it took. He wasn't a subtle man or a subtle thinker.

"What if I tried shooting it?" Hart suggested.

Santelli looked at him as if he was stupid. "We're a little close to try to SMUD it," he said. Standoff Munitions Disruption was usually done from a lot farther away, and with something a lot heavier than their 5.56mm rifles. It was usually done with a 40mm grenade launcher or a .50 caliber Barrett. "There's a chance that it won't blow up in my face. If you shoot it, either it won't do anything and we're right back where we started, or it blows up in all our faces." Turning back to the bomb, he looked up, searching for any enemy, and then started to cross the narrow walkway to the gray box.

He'd gotten about two steps when Childress saw movement up above.

Whipping his rifle to his shoulder, he yelled, "Contact, high!" just before his trigger broke. The LWRC bucked into his shoulder, and the movement vanished. He didn't know if he'd hit anything.

Then all hell broke loose.

Muzzle flashes were just puffs in the midday sunlight, but bullets were pounding the deck around Santelli, who scrambled

156

backward to get away from both the oncoming fire and the explosives. It was possible that a stray round might set the trap off, or the bad guys might have a remote. Either way, it was a bad idea to stay close to an enemy explosive device in the middle of a firefight.

Childress, Curtis, Jenkins, and Hart all opened fire at the same time, leaning out or moving back to shoot around the big, green-painted steel box they were sheltering behind. They didn't have much to shoot at; the bad guys were well barricaded and exposing as little of themselves as possible. Between that and the play of sunlight and shadows, especially as the Blackhearts had to squint up into the bright, clear sky, they may as well be next to invisible.

Childress hunkered down behind the steel box as bullets hammered into it, ringing the steel like bells, and dropped an empty mag. This wasn't good. He wasn't sure just what these guys were shooting, but it seemed to be hitting harder than the 5.56 rounds in his M6.

Of course, that could just be because they were shooting at him.

They were pinned. There was no way around it. Those assholes up ahead, and above, had a *lot* of ammo, and they weren't shy about spending it. If they could get inside the hatch, they might be able to break contact and get around to flank their adversaries, but that damned booby trap was in the way.

"Fuck it," he barely heard Hart say. Then the amputee was running out onto the walkway, heading straight for the bomb.

"Hart!" Santelli yelled, leaning out and dumping half a mag at the nearest muzzle blast he thought he could see. "Get your ass back here before it gets shot off!"

But Hart wasn't listening. He slammed up against the pipe where the bomb was affixed, fired a fast five shots toward the shooters on the catwalks up above, even though he probably couldn't see any of them, then slung his rifle and pulled out his knife.

Childress had to force himself not to stare, and to keep shooting back at their tormentors. He'd known Hart had some issues; he was prone to binge drinking and emotional outbursts. But this was nuts. If Hart just yanked that charge off, and broke the IR laser's beam in the process, he was going to blow himself— and quite possibly the rest of them—to bits.

But Hart wasn't quite that crazy. Hunkered down as best as he could get behind the pipe, he started prying carefully at the box's lid. A few bullets hitting the girders over his head didn't even make him flinch. He was in the zone, and Childress, between shooting back at the terrorists, hoped it was the right zone.

Getting the lid open, somehow without disturbing the IR sensor attached to it, Hart reached inside with his knife. A moment later, he was pulling a block of explosives, inside a black sheath that had to contain the fragmentation, out of the box. Hugging the explosive block to his chest, he dashed back toward the shelter of the green box.

"Don't bring that fucking thing back over here!" Curtis yelled, even as Hart ran behind him and into cover. "Are you out of your mind?"

"I'm not gonna keep it!" Hart yelled back, as he heaved the explosives over the railing to fall toward the Gulf waters below. "What do you think I am, crazy?"

"After that little stunt?" Curtis replied. "Yeah, I *do* think you're crazy!"

"Let's go!" Santelli snapped, leaning out beside the edge of the big metal box. "Get in that hatch! Go!" He opened fire, blasting three or four rounds at each muzzle blast he could see.

Childress took a deep breath, his prominent Adam's apple bobbing. There was nothing for it. He leaned out past Santelli, fired a few rounds in the general direction of the enemy, and then ran for it, his head down and his legs pumping.

He hit the wall next to the hatch with bruising impact, and gulped for air. He really, *really* wished for a flashbang. Because there was no way to disguise the fact that he was about to go through that hatch.

Curtis nearly collided with him, snapped, "With you," and then they were going through the hatch, Curtis' rifle only a few inches off to one side of Childress' upper arm.

The passageway was dark, and apparently empty. No gunfire met them coming in, and no movement drew their own fire. Childress honestly wasn't sure if he wouldn't have fired at anything that moved at that point. It was poor fire discipline, but this boarding operation was turning into an absolute nightmare.

Curtis suddenly grabbed him by the straps of his chest rig and hauled him back. Childress saw what the little man had spotted a moment later. There was another box in the hallway, barely ten feet ahead. It was just sitting there against the bulkhead, on the deck. In any other circumstances, it might have been perfectly innocuous. After what they'd just encountered, though, it was almost certainly another bomb.

"How much boom-boom did these fuckers *bring*?" Curtis hissed, even as Hart and Jenkins piled in through the hatch behind them. Santelli was last, barricading on the hatchway.

"What's the holdup?" Santelli asked, breathing hard. There was a lot of power in that stubby, slightly round frame of his, but he wasn't built for speed, and they all knew it.

"Another IED," Childress reported.

"I've got it," Hart said, pushing past him and Curtis. "Just make sure nobody pops out to shoot me."

"Dude, when did you become a demo expert?" Childress asked. He'd known Hart by reputation in the Corps, though really only after he'd lost his leg.

"I've got a farm, full disability, quite a bit of money put away, and a lot of spare time," Hart said, as he knelt by the box. "I might have spent some of that time building bombs just for the hell of it."

Childress was about to say something, then just shrugged. He'd done the same thing, from time to time.

This time, it took Hart less time. The bomb was set up along the same lines as the last one, and he got the box open, stripped out the initiation system, and then carefully pulled out the explosive block. "What do we want to do with these?" he asked. "Because I don't really want to go running back out there to toss it."

"Just set it away from the box and do what you can to wreck the initiation system," Santelli ordered. "And make it snappy; we don't have a lot of time."

Fortunately, the initiation system appeared to be exclusively keyed to the garage door opener. Hart stomped on the fragile electronic components with his good foot, and then unslung his rifle and pointed it down the hallway. "Set," he said.

"Good, let's move," Santelli said. "And watch your fire; Roger's element might be in here with us."

***

"What are we gonna do with that thing?" Tanaka asked. The four of them were frozen where they were, all too conscious of the proximity of both the barrel bomb and the booby trap. "I can't even see the explosives."

"Maybe it's linked to the barrel bomb," Wade suggested.

"Maybe," Hancock said. "Or maybe there's a claymore just out of sight, zip-tied to the rail."

"We don't exactly have a lot of time to debate the matter," Wade pointed out.

Hancock looked up and around, even as Tanaka pointed out that getting blown to smithereens was going to kind of defeat the purpose of moving quickly. There wasn't a hatch between them and the booby trap, as he'd expected. The enemy wasn't going to give them that easy an escape route, and even if they had, he'd be suspicious that there would be another trap inside. It was what he'd do.

"Does anyone think they can detach the sensor and keep it on the beam across to the rail?" he asked.

"Hell no," Wade replied. "I can't even get my garage door to close right without fiddling with the damned thing half a dozen times. I'd dip just far enough out of true without even knowing it that we'd probably never feel it. At least I wouldn't."

"What if we shot it?" Tanaka suggested.

"Supposing you're a good enough shot, that could just break the beam and blow the charge," Wade pointed out.

Gomez abruptly turned around, leaving his sector on the corner for a second, craned his neck out, then looked back around the corner. "Come on," he said. "On me."

Hancock didn't know what was in Gomez' head, but figured he'd probably spotted something. "With you," he said, falling in behind the dark, quiet man.

Gomez didn't take his eyes off his sector, but as soon as he knew that Hancock was behind him, he was moving, pushing back around the corner toward the ladderwell. A head appeared, two landings up, and Gomez' rifle snapped up and barked. The head jerked and disappeared.

Then he was flowing into the hatch just outside of the ladderwell, Hancock right behind him and to his left, both muzzles entering the passageway at almost the same time.

The passageway was dark and empty. There also didn't appear to be any booby traps in it. Hancock started to understand Gomez' thinking, though he figured it was probably still pretty likely that the enemy had defensive devices scattered all around the big bombs.

Then he remembered that the bomb that had been set up on the boat deck hadn't been so defended. So, maybe they had a chance. Of course, the terrorists hadn't had a chance to finish arming that one; it might have been one of the last charges set. If that was the case, they were in trouble.

Gomez stopped dead, peering into the dim interior, that seemed even darker after the glare of sunshine on the water outside. He held up a hand to halt, motioned for the rest to stay where they were, then crept forward soundlessly.

Hancock was impressed at Gomez' stealth. The man could give both of the team's designated woodsmen, Flanagan and Childress, a run for their money. His shoes rolled soundlessly on the deck, making hardly a sound.

Gomez moved about fifty feet ahead, keeping his rifle up and scanning every opening he passed, no matter how small. Hancock was about ready to go after him, before he got ambushed, when he stopped again and knelt. He studied something in front of him for a second, then crossed himself and bent down.

He fiddled with something in the shadows for a minute, then rose and ran back toward them. "Way's clear," he announced. "It needed a power supply." He tossed a battery pack out the hatch.

"That was risky," Hancock said.

Gomez just shrugged. "We had to get through. Either it worked, or it didn't."

"You've got more faith than I do, brother man," Hancock said. "Let's go."

***

Flanagan all but leapt over Aziz' and Brannigan's fallen bodies. He definitely stepped on Brannigan's leg, but pushed off as he swiveled to bring his rifle to bear, acutely aware that he was about to die. There was a beaten zone of fire through the hatch, and he was running right into the middle of it. But they were committed, had been committed as soon as Aziz had crossed the threshold, and to hesitate at that point meant to die. So he attacked instead.

A bullet burned past his ear with a painful *crack*, even as he opened fire, stitching five rounds from the blue-gray camouflaged figure's upper chest into his head. Or at least, that was what he intended to do. He was moving fast enough, and unsteadily enough, thanks to stepping on Brannigan's leg, that only the first two bullets hit; the other three went high and smacked into the overhead.

Then Bianco was through behind him, blasting a second man off his feet with a flurry of shots that were so fast they sounded like Bianco was shooting one of his beloved machineguns, rather than a semi-auto rifle.

Flanagan was already committed to his lunge, and couldn't quite stop himself. He dropped on his side on the deck, keeping his rifle up, and pumped three more bullets into the man he'd already shot. The guy had staggered, but was still on his feet, his bullpup rifle tracking toward Flanagan's head. The weapon fell from nerveless hands as Flanagan and Bianco both put bullets through his skull, the rounds crisscrossing through his brainstem to blow bloody chunks out of the back of his head. He fell to the deck like a puppet with its strings cut.

Those two had been the only ones in the room, which otherwise looked like a bunkroom, fitted out for four people. Two stacks of bunks, a small sink, and an even smaller head took up a good deal of the space.

Aching from his impact with the deck, Flanagan levered himself back up, still keeping his rifle trained on the two fallen terrorists. But Bianco moved quickly to check the one he'd shot first. The man was dead, one eye staring sightlessly at the overhead, blood running from his ruined throat and a hole just beneath his other eye, which was bulged out and staring at the bulkhead.

"On the door," Flanagan rasped. Bianco didn't need to hear it twice, but barricaded himself on the hatch, covering down the passageway. Flanagan slung his rifle and started hauling the two fallen Blackhearts inside.

Brannigan was still breathing. That was a relief. He was unconscious, and bleeding freely from a head wound, but a brief examination showed Flanagan that it hadn't gone through; it had been a glancing hit that had just knocked him out.

The bloody holes in his leg and chest were another matter.

Getting Brannigan's bulk inside the hatch, he looked over at Aziz. Their former interpreter and designated pain-in-the-ass was still alive, but it didn't look like he would be for much longer. He was shaking, bloody froth at his mouth, and he was audibly choking on his own blood. He'd been hit at least three times through the vitals; it was a miracle one of the bullets hadn't blown his heart out of his back.

Flanagan might not like Aziz, but he wasn't going to leave a teammate to die in a hatchway, not if he could help it. He left Brannigan on the deck and moved to Aziz.

He'd just grabbed the other man's vest and started to pull when it happened. Aziz shuddered, then went very, very still. Flanagan thought he felt a sudden chill in the air, even though it was sweltering on the Gulf Coast.

Aziz was gone.

He hauled the body back inside anyway, then turned to Brannigan.

The hole in the Colonel's leg wasn't spurting blood, so it probably wasn't an arterial bleed, but he ripped a tourniquet out of Brannigan's kit and threw it around the leg anyway. As soon as it was cinched down, he pulled Brannigan's chest rig over his head, tore open his camouflage blouse, and looked for the bullet hole in his chest.

It was low down, and off to one side, and the exit wound was, thankfully, not far away. It might not have gone through his guts. It was high enough, though, between navel and clavicle, that he ripped a pair of chest seals out of the Colonel's first aid kit and slapped the adhesive dressings over both holes. Only then did he take the time to carefully wind some gauze and an ACE wrap around the bleeding head wound.

There was no way they were diving out now, not with Brannigan a casualty. And with just him and Bianco still in the fight, their element wasn't going anywhere.

The fate of the platform, and the hostages, was going to have to depend on the other two elements. And neither one was necessarily looking for hostages; they were looking for bombs.

They hadn't used the radios much, so far. They didn't have headsets for the little black Motorolas, for one thing, and none of them had been sure how far they'd reach through the structure. But Flanagan pulled his out of its waterproof pouch, stuffed into his chest rig.

"Surfer, this is Woodsrunner," he called. "Kodiak and Professor are down. Kodiak is alive, but Professor's dead. Nerd and I are strongpointed just below the helipad. Need support."

He let off the push-to-talk button, staying on a knee next to Brannigan, his rifle pointed toward the hatch, one hand on the pistol grip. He glanced down at their big commander. He was still out, but still breathing, and didn't seem to be choking on his tongue. He was just bleeding a whole lot.

Flanagan was starting to wonder if any of them were going to get off the Tourmaline-Delta platform alive.

CHAPTER 14

Hancock couldn't hear Flanagan's radio call. There was too much steel on the platform for the radios to reach very far. So he, Wade, Tanaka, and Gomez continued to push deeper into the structure, hunting terrorists and bombs.

The deeper they got into the bowels of the platform, the fewer traps they found. There were more barrel bombs, though, all of them placed near machinery or electronics. The entire platform appeared to be wired to blow. However they had initially boarded the platform, the terrorists had brought a lot with them.

They moved carefully, systematically, even as haste gnawed at them. Maybe not at Gomez, Hancock thought, even as he glanced at the dark man's impassive face. Gomez was the model of taciturn focus, alert and ready to kill, efficiently and emotionlessly.

Wade paused at another hatch, waiting just a moment as Tanaka moved up behind him and Gomez covered down the passage they were following. Hancock took up the rear.

True dynamic entries had become impossible. There had been too many booby traps. To simply flow into a room was asking to trip an improvised claymore and get them all shredded by flying ball bearings.

So, Wade paused longer than usual at the hatch, scanning the coaming for tripwires, pressure plates, or more of the glorified garage door openers. So far, the IR lasers and sensors had been the only initiation systems they'd found, which made disarming the traps a bit more difficult. You could always cut a tripwire.

The hatch appeared clear, so Wade stepped through, pivoting through the opening to cover the near corner with his weapon, while Tanaka followed half a step behind. Hancock turned as he felt them move, and flowed in behind them, tapping Gomez with an elbow as he went.

They were in a large engine room, lined with diesels, most of them idling. The power was still on, but the well machinery wasn't operating, so the engine room wasn't at full capacity. Hancock suddenly wondered just what sort of imminent catastrophe was in the offing, just from failing to maintain the equipment for the last few days.

They hadn't seen any of the crew so far, or the hostages. Which didn't bode well for either group.

A quick scan confirmed the worst. There were more bombs set up near each engine. They'd turn the engine room into a nightmare of fire and flying metal in a heartbeat.

"Where the hell did all this crap come from?" Tanaka hissed.

"I'm betting that most of the drums are full of crude," Wade replied. "With just enough PETN or whatever dropped in to make it go boom." He looked at Tanaka with an icy smile. "It's what I'd do. Why pack in more explosives, when there should be plenty of raw materials on-site?"

"Let's get to it," Hancock said. "Hopefully before some asshole pushes a button somewhere and *we* all go boom."

With Tanaka and Gomez providing security, Hancock and Wade started at the nearest engine. They were getting it down to a science. Yank the shock tube out of the black plastic box that had to be the timer/detonator, then pull it out of the barrel, making sure to separate it from the blasting caps. It was careful, nerve-wracking work. None of them were Explosives Ordnance Disposal techs, and Hancock could almost hear his EOD friends losing their minds over the slapdash, ham-fisted way they were disarming the bombs. By all rights, they should all have been blown to pieces already.

He glanced down inside the hole in the top of the drum as he pulled gingerly on the shock tube. It looked like Wade had been right; two blocks of explosive were floating in what looked like a slurry of crude oil and something else. Possibly something they'd dumped in to act as a plasticizer.

Hancock's mind was working, even as he focused on trying not to explode. So far, the bombs had been set to sow a lot of fire and destruction, but nothing truly catastrophic. They'd been apparently placed to cause maximum casualties among an attacking force, but these were placed to put the rig out of action. Which led him to wonder just what else they were going to find, deeper in.

He came to the last bomb on the last diesel. He looked up at Wade as he finished up, hoping that they weren't just wasting their time, that the terrorists hadn't wired the bombs with backup initiation systems inside the barrels that would detonate them anyway.

"We've got to think," he said. All three of the other Blackhearts were close enough to hear; they'd been moving together along the engine room as he and Wade had worked. There was still no sign of anyone else around. No opposition, no crew, no hostages. "If they're setting up to destroy the rig, this isn't going to be the big one. They'd do a lot of damage by destroying this room, but I doubt it would necessarily destroy the whole platform."

Wade shook his head. "It might, once the fire took hold. But I think you're right. The wells themselves are going to be the prime targets."

Gomez was nodding, without taking his eyes or his muzzle off the nearest hatch. "That's how the big ones usually start," he said. "Like the *Deepwater Horizon*."

"So, we make for the wells?" Tanaka asked. He sounded a little nervous at the idea of driving straight toward the center of the platform, bypassing the spaces in between. There were a lot of ambush sites in a structure that size. Charging through and bypassing adjacent spaces was a good way to get shot in the back.

"I don't think we've got any choice," Hancock said. He wasn't any more thrilled with it than Tanaka; he might be a bit of an adrenaline junkie, but that didn't mean he had no sense of self-preservation. "If we can head off the main threat, then we can start clearing more methodically, without worrying about getting turned in to pink mist."

"Except by the booby traps," Wade pointed out.

"Yes, thank you for the reminder, Wade," Hancock said sarcastically. "I'm sure we all needed it." He looked around the room, then glanced out at the passageway. "Where the hell are all the bad guys?"

"Maybe we killed enough of them that they only have enough left to guard the hostages," Tanaka suggested.

"Maybe," Hancock mused, unconvinced. "Well, guns up and heads on a swivel. Let's go."

With Gomez in the lead, the four of them rolled out of the engine room and turned inward, toward the center of the platform and the massive oil derricks that dominated it.

***

Santelli was getting pissed. They'd encountered three more of the improvised claymores affixed to the bulkheads on their way inside, and it was giving him flashbacks to the roads in Iraq. He was pretty sure these assholes weren't Islamic terrorists; they were too sophisticated, and hadn't made any of the usual pronouncements. But they'd certainly learned from them. And that pissed him off even more.

The truth was that terror is terror, and a lot of the tools and techniques have never been unique to Islamists. Santelli even knew that. But he was a simple man, and when he got mad, the

170

nearest parallels sufficed to his way of thinking. These murdering bastards were using the same techniques as the jihadi terrorists who had tried to kill him and his boys in Iraq and Afghanistan, and therefore they had to have gotten the same ideas from the same jihadi assholes.

He and his element had made it to the far side of the tower of living and control spaces just short of the twin oil derricks that formed the basis of the Tourmaline-Delta platform, and had just gone up another level. Most of the lower spaces had been devoted to machinery and storage; this level seemed to be the same.

Childress and Curtis were on point; positions in their little formation were constantly changing and shifting as they worked their way through the structure. None of them were particularly married to a spot in the stack; they all had enough training that they could move around from task to task seamlessly. Granted, they hadn't trained all that much together, but there was enough commonality of experience and training to make up for that shortfall.

Childress moved quickly to a corner, paused, and then popped around it as Curtis moved up next to him. A moment later, he reared back as a long burst of automatic fire hammered the bulkhead past him.

"Barricade," he announced, barely audible over the thunder of the gunfire and bullet impacts in the confined space. "Looks like a bunch of barrels set up with a shooter behind them, firing through a loophole."

Santelli had to hand it to Childress; he'd gotten a pretty good look and cataloged it in his head in the split-second he'd been exposed. The kid could seem like a bit of a yokel, the kind of simple-minded trigger-puller often found in the infantry, but he had a good head on his shoulders and a keen eye.

He looked around at their surroundings. They were at a T-intersection of sorts; there was another hatch, that might be partially open, across from them, and then there was the passage around the corner where the barricade was set up.

"I can run the rabbit, maybe get in that hatch," Jenkins suggested. "Then somebody nail him when he tries to shoot me."

"The rabbit gets shot trying that, more often than not," Hart said.

"I don't see another option," Jenkins replied defensively, looking back at the big, bearded amputee. Hart's bushy brown beard was still dripping, partially from seawater, partially from sweat.

"Of course there's another option," Curtis said. "We go up a level and come down behind these shitheads."

Jenkins looked nonplused for a moment; he apparently hadn't thought of that. Santelli kept his own pugnacious face impassive; he hadn't either.

"All right, back to the ladderwell," he said. "And let's make it snappy, before these punks figure out what we're doing."

With Hart taking the lead, since he'd been covering their six, they started retracing their steps. Hart popped out onto the landing first, his rifle trained upward, while Santelli followed, covering the lower landing, just in case the terrorists had circled around.

Both ways were clear. Hart started up, while Santelli held his place, letting the rest of the stack flow past him to climb to the next level. Only when Childress murmured, "Last man," did Santelli abandon his post and fall in behind.

Hart got to the next landing up and pointed his muzzle at the hatch. Jenkins was about to open the hatch when it swung inward on its own.

Two men in blue-gray camouflage, wearing skull balaclavas and carrying bullpup rifles, were right in the hatchway.

Hart didn't hesitate. He pulled the trigger as soon as the first silhouette registered in his mind. The M6 barked, muzzle blast almost close enough to punch a ragged hole in the terrorist's magazine pouches.

But Hart's reflexes weren't quite what they had been. And they were definitely slower than the terrorists'. Both rifles hammered at each other from a couple of feet away, seemingly right at the same time. But the terrorist was slightly faster.

Hart staggered backward, blood spouting from his shoulder, even as the terrorist staggered. Then Jenkins put a hammer pair into each terrorists' head from less than three feet, his own muzzle blast scorching and tearing even as the bullets tracked through their skulls, punching bloody holes out through their balaclavas. He kept shooting even as they tumbled to the deck, tracking them all the way down and putting two more bullets apiece into their ruined heads.

Curtis had shouldered in front of Hart and shoved the hatch the rest of the way open, driving inside the passageway over the pair of corpses. Santelli took a hand off his rifle to grab Hart, and propelled the wounded man inside with him. They had to get out of the fatal funnel of that hatchway, not to mention the exposed landing, with its gridded steel mesh in the place of solid decking. Once they had hardpointed, he could see about treating Hart's wounds.

Provided he survived. At that range, it seemed impossible that the terrorist could have missed putting a bullet through the man's vitals.

Jenkins and Curtis were driving ahead, Childress taking up the rear as Santelli moved Hart along. The big man hadn't said anything, and seemed to be in some shock. His arm was awash in blood, but that was all Santelli could tell right at the moment.

Curtis drove to the nearest hatch, holding on it until Jenkins was right behind him, ready to go in. Driving the hatch open, they plunged inside. Santelli, his rifle up, followed with Hart in tow. It was less than ideal to go through a door with a casualty, but he didn't want to hang out in the deathtrap of a passageway, either. The room was potentially safer, anyway.

He almost forgot about Hart as he cleared the threshold and entered the room.

There were no terrorists inside. Jenkins and Curtis had nothing to shoot. Which was why nobody objected to the fact that Jenkins had his rifle dangling by its sling as he puked his guts out on the deck.

The room was a big one; it had once been a rec room or meeting room. The walls had been white, with beige leather couches, a TV, a row of phones, and several vending machines.

The walls were spattered with dried blood, and the couches were black with it. Where they weren't covered by rapidly decomposing corpses.

It was hard to pick out individual bodies; the dead had been piled together in the middle of the room after they'd been gunned down. Some were wearing the orange coveralls and hard hats of oil rig workers. Others were in suits or business casual. Or what was left of it.

From the stench, and the state of several of the bodies he could see, it was pretty clear to Santelli that this mass murder had happened several days ago.

Possibly even before the Mexican Marines had first tried to assault the platform.

Feeling his own gorge rise, Santelli tried to hold his breath. "Everybody out," he gasped. He wasn't going to try to treat Hart in there. Hopefully they could find a different strongpoint before the man bled to death. Hell, he'd take his chances in the passageway.

They didn't so much flow out as stagger out of the hatch and into the hall. Only long-ingrained discipline drove them toward the next hatch, weapons ready, hoping they weren't about to stumble into a similar charnel house as the one they'd just left.

The clinical part of Santelli's mind was pretty sure they wouldn't. He hadn't had time to make a count, but he was pretty sure that all the people they were there to rescue were lying dead and rotting in that break room.

Childress stacked on the next door, Curtis joined him, and they went in. The rest followed, still choking, still smelling the sick stink of death in their nostrils, even though the next room was the dining hall, apparently untouched by the violence across the hall.

That stench wasn't going to go away anytime soon. Santelli knew he'd wake up smelling it for weeks hence. Maybe even years.

He had already compartmentalized the horror, putting it aside as he turned to Hart, who was looking pale and shaky. He quickly moved the man to a table, pulling out his knife and cutting away his cammies around the wound in his shoulder.

It wasn't good, but it wasn't as bad as he'd feared, either. The bullet had just missed the clavicle and torn through most of the deltoid, punching out the far side. Hart's chest cavity seemed to be intact, and his artery hadn't been touched. There was just a lot of blood, and a good-sized chunk of meat missing.

He quickly checked Hart over for any other holes or bleeds, pulling his chest rig clear and getting under his camouflage blouse. "You're a lucky bastard, Hart," he said. "Your arm's gonna be fucked up for a while, but you don't seem to have any fatal holes in you." The terrorist must have just mashed the trigger as soon as he'd seen Hart, while his rifle was still off-line.

Of course, he'd seen enough to know that Hart had done the same. It had taken him a bit longer to register that there was an enemy in front of him. He'd just gotten lucky, in that his rifle had been on target when he'd done it.

That was going to have to be addressed. Tanaka and Hancock hadn't mentioned finding Hart falling-down drunk, but Santelli had seen enough when they'd shown up to suspect it. If the booze was slowing the big man down too much, he was going to have to get cut away.

Provided they survived and got off the platform.

He had a moment to take stock, even as he packed the entry and exit wounds with gauze and wrapped a bandage tightly around Hart's shoulder. The man was still ambulatory, and could even still shoot. His support hand would be stiff, with the bandage in place, and it would hurt, but he could fight. At least, Santelli hoped that he could. He peered into Hart's eyes, bleary and glazed with pain and shock.

"Hart," he said, lightly clapping the man on the cheek. "You with me? You good? I need you all here, buddy."

Hart blinked, flexed his shoulder, winced, and picked up his rifle. "Yeah," he said hoarsely. "Yeah, I'm good."

Santelli was skeptical. But they couldn't afford to take him out of the fight, not in the situation they were in. He looked around at the rest. Jenkins, Curtis, and Childress were all posted up on the doorways, holding security on the passageway beyond.

"All right, plan's changed," he said. "Clearly, this is no longer a rescue mission. The hostages are dead, and apparently have been since before we boarded this thing. So, it is now a *retribution* mission. I want these miserable, murdering fucks dead, and I want 'em *all* dead."

"How the hell are we going to hunt them all down?" Childress asked. "There are only a few of us, and it's a big platform."

"We head up top, see if we can link up with Brannigan, and start to clear it from top to bottom, one compartment at a time," Santelli bit out. "Unless they've got a boat down below, which I didn't see, they've got no way off this thing. It's us or the sharks."

He hauled Hart to his feet. "Tac reload if you have to. Time to move."

***

Flanagan checked Brannigan's tourniquet and bandages for what felt like the fifteenth time in the last few minutes. Bianco was still on the door, but hadn't seen anything. They had heard the distant thunder of gunfire reverberating through the structure, but there had been no other sign of either the terrorists or any of the other Blackhearts.

"Surfer, this is Woodsrunner," he tried again.

"I don't think they can hear us, man," Bianco said.

Before Flanagan could answer, Brannigan groaned. Bianco's head twitched to look over at him, but he corrected himself and stayed trained on the doorway.

"Don't try to move, Boss," Flanagan said. "You got hit pretty bad."

Brannigan opened his eyes, but they were glazed and not quite focusing. "Where am I?" he asked thickly.

"You're in a room just inside the top level of the Tourmaline-Delta platform," Flanagan answered. "Do you remember how we got here?"

Brannigan, despite Flanagan's warning, shoved himself up on an elbow, then groaned again, his face going gray with pain. "Yeah," he whispered, his eyes shut tight. "I remember everything up to getting a bat to the head."

"You were lucky," Flanagan told him. "It creased your scalp, but it doesn't look like it cracked your skull. You've got a through-and-through just below your ribs, though; I don't know how bad it is."

Brannigan slowly opened his eyes again and squinted down at his leg and the tourniquet cinched down just below his pelvis. Then he sagged back against the deck. "Guess I'm not going anywhere anytime soon." He looked over at the still form lying just inside the hatch. "What about Aziz?"

"He's gone, Boss," Bianco said quietly.

"I was afraid of that," Brannigan said, closing his eyes again. He just breathed slowly for a long moment. "What's our status?"

"I can't get either of the other elements on the radio," Flanagan answered. "But we're pretty much stuck here."

"Haven't seen any bad guys in the last ten, fifteen minutes," Bianco reported. "We've heard some shooting, but that's it."

After another long moment, Brannigan started to heave himself to a sitting position. "Take it easy, John," Flanagan said.

"Teach your grandpa to suck eggs, Joe," Brannigan replied. The response actually reassured Flanagan somewhat. If Brannigan had that much fire left, maybe he'd make it. "I'm breathing all right," he continued. "I want to see the hole in my leg." He pulled aside the tattered cammies. "Doesn't look like it hit the artery. Help me pack it so I can get this tourniquet off."

"Not sure that's such a good idea," Flanagan began, but Brannigan cut him off.

"We ain't out of the woods yet, Joe, and I can't walk right with that damned thing cutting off my circulation. I already can't feel my foot, and the sonofabitch hurts. As long as I'm not going to bleed to death, let's try and get me as mobile as possible. Unless you know of some second rescue force that's on its way here?"

Flanagan shook his head. The Colonel was right. They were on their own. Pulling another package of gauze out, he started helping Brannigan put a pressure dressing on the wound.

CHAPTER 15

"What the fuck is this bullshit?" Flint snarled, barely restraining himself from throwing his radio across the room. "Here I thought I'd gotten a crew of hardened killers, but instead I got the fucking Short Bus crew of retards! *Fuck!*"

Several of Dingo's team were watching him, and he knew that he was sending the wrong message. Let them think that he was losing it, and he'd lose some of the sense of fear that he'd so carefully cultivated. Then he'd probably have to pop one of them, and he'd rather save the ammunition to deal with whoever these boarders were.

He leaned over Psycho's shoulder. "Have we got any idea where they are right now?"

"There might be two groups," Psycho said. He was leaning over a printout of the platform's layout, holding a map pen. "There's the bunch that managed to break contact on the seaward side." Psycho must have known on how thin a thread Flint's patience was hanging, because he didn't mention that that group had broken contact from *Flint's* team, who hadn't been able to pin them back down. "And somebody tore the shit out of Dingo's group over on the coastal side. I think they're moving up, too; there's been no contact from Reaper or Gravedigger in about fifteen minutes."

Flint snarled silently, then forced himself to calm down. It wasn't consideration for his men that prompted his anger; he couldn't care less about any of these guys. Just like any of them would probably watch him get his head blown off without batting an eye. They'd been well-paid to do this, and that was all that mattered.

But he was still pissed at these bastards who were fucking up a perfect op. Everything had gone without a hitch, until they'd somehow managed to board the platform, and in broad daylight, no less. He still remembered Dingo's accusatory tone as he'd pointed out that it had been Flint's team on lookout, and was momentarily viciously glad the fucking Aussie was dead.

"What's the status on the main charges?" he asked.

"Shank says they're ready," Psycho answered. "He's just waiting on the evac order."

Flint nodded, chewing his lip. The sub was due any minute, but hadn't surfaced yet. They couldn't make their escape until it did, and he didn't want the final destruction of the Tourmaline-Delta to get headed off because they left the charges unattended. He'd never gotten to blow something the size of an offshore drilling platform up before, and he wanted to make sure this went off. He was even planning on making the sub's skipper hold at periscope depth so he could watch.

Assuming he didn't kill the man for being late. There had better be a damned good excuse for *that* particular part of the plan going awry.

Maybe I'll shoot him once we get to the dispersal point. The bosses might not like it, but they need me.

Then he had an idea. He grinned. "Hey, there's a PA system on this rig, isn't there?"

Psycho looked up at him, a puzzled look on his dark face. "Yeah, I think so. Should be up in the main office."

"Good," Flint said, still grinning. "Get everybody back to the derricks and set in. I've got an idea."

If this doesn't work, at least they'll all be nice and close when this fucker goes boom.

***

"Hey!" a voice crackled over the loudspeakers in the passageways. Hancock and his element didn't stop. They were moving fast, but not rushing, careful to scan every doorway and adjacent space as they proceeded. None of them wanted to get caught unawares.

Tanaka jerked a little at the sound of the voice; he hadn't been expecting it. Hancock half-expected Wade to give him shit about it, but the big former Ranger held his peace.

They were all keyed up; Tanaka was just a little more keyed up and tense than the rest of them. His experiences were different.

"Listen up, you fucksticks, whoever you are," the voice continued. It sounded clearly American, vaguely Midwestern. "In case you haven't found 'em yet, I'll tell you where the precious hostages you're probably looking for are. They're in the west break room. Been there for a while. They're not going to go with you, though. They're a little the worse for wear, if you know what I'm saying.

"I thought about keeping them alive for this part, but they were just too much trouble. So, you'll be the only ones to stick around when I finally push the button on this rig. Yeah, that's right. I've got about two hundred pounds of PETN very carefully placed on the two oil wells. They're still working, at minimum capacity, which means that there's plenty of drilling mud, gasses, and crude oil down there. Hell, they're probably about ready to pop on their own, but I'm just going to make sure, and give 'em that little extra *oomph*, if you take my meaning.

"I'm telling you this out of professional courtesy, you understand. If you don't want to go up in a nice, big fireball, you might want to go see if you can disarm the charges. Of course, I might already have made sure that that'll blow up in your faces, but I'm a sick man that way." The man laughed. "You might jump overboard, but I don't know. That might just get you covered in burning oil. I don't know just how big a boom this thing is going to make. I'm hoping it's big enough to put the last few oil rig fires here on the Gulf to shame. Professional pride, you know?"

Gomez hadn't said anything, but picked up the pace. It sounded like Hancock's suspicions were correct; the terrorists were going for the complete destruction of the platform.

"Keep your heads up and your eyes open," Hancock warned. *Why else would this bastard taunt us like that, unless he's got an ambush set in?* "Let's kill them before they can get to us."

Gomez slowed. He didn't look back, but said over his shoulder, "If they've got an ambush set in, it'll probably be high. We should go up, link up with the Colonel, and see if we can get the drop on them from above."

"He's right," Wade said. "There should be a good shot from the helideck, at both derricks."

"Good thinking. Up it is."

The four men turned in the passageway and headed back the way they'd come, making for the ladderwell off the boat deck.

***

Santelli had reached the same conclusion. "If they're all gathered around the wells to try to ambush us," he said, "then we'll have 'em all in the same firesack."

He was looking forward to killing these assholes, especially that gloating son of a bitch on the PA. He didn't know what their deal was, and he didn't care. The motivations of terrorists had never entered into Santelli's thinking. To him, it was a non-issue. They were terrorists, therefore they were Bad Guys, and Bad Guys needed to get dead.

Some people might criticize him for simplistic thinking. He figured those people needed to think more clearly.

Getting back to the ladderwell, they started up. Better to attack from high ground and work down.

***

As they neared the top of the ladderwell, Hancock pulled his radio out of its pouch. He'd never been a fan of the black plastic radios; they were less than reliable, particularly compared to the military "green gear" radios they'd used in their past lives. Their arrangement with Van Zandt had gotten them the use of the green SINCGARS radios in Burma, but this op had been laid on too fast, with too many shortcuts.

"Kodiak, Surfer," he called. There hadn't been any contact with either Brannigan's or Santelli's elements since they'd split up, and it was bothering him. He didn't know where Brannigan was; only that he'd gone up top. Which meant that they were nearing the area where the Colonel was probably working, and if they didn't coordinate their linkup, there was a risk of a blue-on-blue shooting.

There might have been a reply, but it was broken and filled with static. Hancock cursed. "Kodiak, Surfer," he repeated, as he pounded up the metal steps. Wade was in the lead, slowing as he neared the top landing, his rifle trained up to cover the opening above them.

Finally, broken and static-laced, a voice came across the radio.

"Surfer, Woodsrunner," Flanagan's voice said. "Kodiak is down. Professor is out. We are strongpointed on the second deck down."

That almost gave them pause. "Down" meant severely wounded and combat ineffective. "Out" meant dead. None of them were necessarily going to mourn Aziz that much, but it meant that the main element that had been hunting for the hostages was out of action.

"Roger, Woodsrunner," he replied. "We're moving to link up." He looked up at Wade. "Second deck," he hissed.

Wade didn't reply; he didn't even nod. But he cut his climb short, instead stacking on the hatch leading inside the superstructure just long enough for Hancock to get behind him and give him the go-ahead. Together, they flowed into the passageway.

The target hatch wasn't hard to spot; the bullet holes and blood splatter on the coaming were all that was really needed. "Friendly!" Wade called out. It wasn't quite a shout, but not a whisper, either.

"Come ahead," Bianco's voice replied from the bloodstained hatch.

The four of them flowed into the room, to find Flanagan kneeling over the Colonel, who was sitting up against the wall, cinching down a pressure bandage around his leg. There was another bandage around Brannigan's head, and he was covered in blood.

Pausing just long enough to make sure the door was sufficiently covered, and that there were no more entrances, Hancock knelt next to the two of them. "What the hell happened?" he asked.

Flanagan glanced ever so briefly at Aziz' body, but then simply said, "Bad entry. They were already aimed in at the door when we came in."

Hancock had caught the glance. He peered briefly at Aziz' corpse, but decided not to pursue it. There was no point in badgering the dead. "How are you doing, Boss?" he asked Brannigan.

Brannigan looked pale under the drying blood, and his eyes were a little glazed. "I should be able to move," he said hoarsely, "but I'm not doing too hot." Hancock could only imagine what kind of pain he was in, as the initial shock wore off. Even bandaged up as he was, he wasn't going to be much good in a fight.

"Did you hear the PA?" he asked.

Flanagan nodded. "Sounded like a call-out to me," he said.

Hancock agreed. "I think so, too. But it's a lose-lose situation. Either we spring the ambush, or we sit tight and wait to get blown to hell. There's a chance we could kill our way through the ambush. I'm not keen on the idea of sitting here when this thing goes *Deepwater Horizon*."

Brannigan nodded. "I can still handle a gun," he said. "Let me get strongpointed in here. Roger, you're in charge. Take these bastards down, then come get me when the platform's clear."

But Hancock shook his head. "I'm not leaving you here by yourself," he said. "If you pass out and they circle around on us, you'll be a sitting duck. Tanaka!"

With a faint grimace, quickly hidden, Tanaka backed away from the hatch and joined them. "Yeah?"

"You're gonna stay here with Brannigan," Hancock told him. Tanaka tried to control it, but Hancock caught the sudden disappointed, crestfallen look in his eyes. He snapped a finger at the younger man. "Don't start," he said. "*Somebody*'s got to stay here. And the rest of us have more CQB training and experience than you do. This isn't a reflection on you." He clapped Tanaka on the shoulder, gripping it hard and shaking him a little. "Your time will come. This is just how it fell out this time."

Tanaka nodded, though he still looked a little like a beaten puppy. But Hancock didn't have any more time to reassure him. "Everybody else, on me. Vinnie, grab Aziz' mags and hand 'em out. He ain't gonna need 'em anymore." If it seemed cold, that was something else he didn't have time to worry about.

"Surfer, Goodfella," Santelli's staticky voice came over the radio.

"Go for Surfer," Hancock replied.

"Hey, I can't raise Kodiak," Santelli said.

"Kodiak's been hit," Hancock told him. "We've linked up, and I'm moving the element to deal with the bad guys on the derricks. What's your location?"

"Moving up to do the same, on the coastal side," Santelli replied. "Be advised; we found the hostages. They're all dead. Looks like they have been for days, too."

Wade started cursing, a low, hissed stream of vicious invective that was made all the nastier by the tone of his voice. It wasn't even that emotional. It just promised horrible death to any of the terrorists who crossed his path.

"Acknowledged," Hancock said coldly. As if they needed another reason to kill all of these bastards. "You take the west derrick, we'll take the east. Assume that they've rigged both, and watch your shots."

"Roger that," Santelli replied.

Hancock shoved the radio back in his chest rig and accepted the pair of magazines that Bianco was holding out for him. He found an empty mag pouch for one, and shoved the other into a cargo pocket. "Let's go, before they set this thing off."

***

"*Contralmirante?*" the young Naval Infantryman called. "We think something is happening on the platform."

Huerta had been outside the command post, smoking a cigarette. He had no idea what the count was for that day. He'd smoked a lot. He dropped the butt in the dirt, ground it out with his boot, and turned to go inside.

The command post wasn't the most advanced; it would look shabby and low-tech compared to even the most expeditionary of American CPs. Two folding tables were set up in a tent, with maps scattered over them, a few tablets with commercially-available imagery on them, and a bank of radios. The radios were crackling with voices reporting in Spanish, both from the lookouts on the coastline and the bridge of the ARM *Hermenegildo Galeana*, the formerly American *Bronstein*-class frigate that was holding station to seaward of the Tourmaline-Delta platform. The coastal watchers couldn't see the platform; it was too far out. Even with the powerful telescopes they were equipped with, the platform was a speck on the horizon. But the *Hermenegildo Galeana* had a better view.

Huerta went to the radios and seized the handset from the young man talking to the frigate. "Report," he said, as he keyed the mic.

"There appears to be shooting on the platform, *Contralmirante*," *Capitàn* Cantu replied. "We are too far out to say for sure what is happening. Perhaps the terrorists have turned on each other."

No, that's definitely not what's happening. But he wasn't going to say that. He didn't dare let *anyone* know what he'd done. Let it get back to Mexico City that he'd hired gringo mercenaries to clear the terrorists off the Tourmaline-Delta platform, and he was finished.

"It is possible," he conceded. "We do not know enough about the group to say. It seems somewhat improbable, though."

"What other explanation is there, *Contralmirante*?" Cantu asked. "This could be our opening. I do not have sufficient Naval Infantry to launch an assault, but if there is another platoon ashore…"

Which there was. The Tourmaline-Delta standoff was of prime importance to Mexico City. Even as *Los Zetas* and *Cartel Jalisco Nuevo Generaciòn* started running even more rampant, resources were quietly being moved to Matamoros. Three more Mi-17s and nearly a company of Naval Infantry had arrived in the last hour, and were assembled and ready to launch. And with the firefight on board the platform, they just might make it all the way without being shot down.

Huerta made his decision. There was a great deal of risk, but if that Brannigan gringo and his men got in the line of fire, that would just mean that he had little left to explain.

Have you really fallen so far, Diego? He thought of what his mother and *Padre* Esparza would say. Yes, most of the authorities of his country were corrupt, and the worst gangsters lived in palaces in Mexico City. They were every bit as bad, in his mind, as the *capos*, but they wrapped themselves in the Mexican Flag, even as their people's lifeblood was sucked out by corruption and the *bandidos* ran wild. But Diego Huerta had been raised a good Catholic, and he knew that to betray the men who had taken his pay to fix his problem was deeply wrong. *They are mercenaries.* He ignored the thought and keyed the mic again. "Agreed, *Capitàn.* Move your ship closer to provide support, especially if we need medevac." He handed the handset back to the young enlisted man, and turned on his heel.

If I go, maybe I can keep this from getting out of hand. He knew his Naval Infantry were not like the gringos. The *Norteamericanos* could be counted on to watch their shots, most of the time. His men would more than likely kill anyone with a gun, or near a gun, and then maybe ask questions later.

It was a short walk to the tarmac, where the helicopters were staged, and the Naval Infantry were sitting next to their gear in the hangars. "*Teniente* Medina!" he barked.

The Naval Infantry lieutenant came running. The younger man was a hard-case; Huerta had heard that he'd been a *sicario* himself, once, then had gotten out, killed a lot of people to do it, and joined the Navy. Exactly how he'd gotten a commission was a little bit of a mystery. It usually required connections to get into one of the service academies, but to the best of Huerta's knowledge, the shark-eyed killer in front of him had no such connections, *especially* not after the string of horribly mutilated bodies he'd reportedly left behind him when he'd cut ties with the cartel.

There was, of course, the distinct possibility that Medina's entire back story was bullshit, made up to explain his hard-charging viciousness in combat. That part, at least, Huerta knew was true.

"Start getting the men loaded up and ready to move," he ordered. "We are going to assault the platform."

"*Sì, Contralmirante,*" Medina answered with a salute. "So, their air defenses have been suppressed somehow?"

The kid was smart; that could be a problem. "We will get to the platform," he confirmed. "Now get your men moving."

He was a *Contralmirante*, he didn't need to answer a *Teniente*'s questions.

Leaving Medina in his wake, he headed for the back part of the hangar that had become his temporary living quarters. His own P90 and body armor were waiting there, hanging on a gear tree made of 2x4s.

***

Less than fifteen minutes later, the Mi-17s were thumping into the sky, their rotors beating the afternoon air as they drove toward the platform on the horizon.

CHAPTER 16

Flanagan eased around the container set between the ladderwell and the helideck, his rifle leveled, and wished for a scope.

It wasn't that the distances were that long; the longest shot on the entire platform might have been two hundred yards. That was easy with a red dot. No, Flanagan didn't want the magnification of a scope for accuracy's sake; he wanted it so that he could look more closely into some of the nooks and crannies around the platform.

There were a *lot* of places to hide, if you were a shooter setting up an ambush. It might not have seemed that way at first, but the north side of the platform, aside from the bulk of the structure of the derricks themselves, was a maze of girders, pipes, cranes, and support structures. The blue-gray of the enemy camouflage actually worked pretty well in the shadows, and he wanted to be able to zoom in when he was looking through smaller gaps in the obstructing structures.

You can wish in one hand and take a dump in the other, and see which one fills up first. Flanagan wasn't much of one for spending time and mental energy bitching about stuff he couldn't change. So, he kept his gripes to himself and scanned.

The charges that were presumably planted on the wells beneath the derricks weren't visible from up there; they were probably down below, in the workings of the wells themselves.

But given the challenge they'd been issued from the terrorist leader, he doubted that they were going to find an easy route inside.

Hancock, Wade, Gomez, and Bianco were spreading out among the piles of equipment, containers, and various other detritus that was placed around the edge of the helideck. Out of the corner of his eye, he could see Santelli's element coming up on the edge of the helideck itself.

For a long time, the platform was eerily still. There was the sound of the breeze in the girders and cables, the distant rumble of the generators that were still keeping the power on, and the swish of the waves against the pilings holding the platform up. But no gunshots sounded, and no one seemed to move.

"Shit," Hancock muttered. He was on the other side of the small container, peering around that corner. "Somebody's gonna have to move first."

"If they're set in, they're going to wait for us to make the first move," Flanagan pointed out quietly.

"Unless they've already got the charges smoking," Hancock countered. "Still," he admitted, "these guys don't seem quite like real die-hards. I don't think they want to go down with the ship any more than we do."

Flanagan didn't take his eyes off his sector, but kept scanning. There had to be bad guys out there, possibly watching them right then. But they were being disciplined and holding still.

Then a shot cracked out. Flanagan didn't hear the *snap* of the bullet's passage, so he knew that it wasn't anywhere near him. But he saw Santelli and the rest drop flat on the helideck, keeping back from the edge.

He widened his search, his eyes unblinking as he scanned for the muzzle blast. It was about midday, so the contrast between light and shadow was pretty intense. A shooter huddled in the darkness had a pretty good chance of going relatively unnoticed.

He wished he had a hat. It was an old trick, lifting an empty hat to draw fire, but he knew that it had worked in the past.

He'd never tried it, but it would be worth a shot. Except that he didn't have a hat, and he wasn't going to stick his bare head up to see if one of these assholes took a shot at it.

More shots echoed across the platform, coming from off to his left. A glance showed him that Jenkins had crawled up to the edge and was shooting at something, off to one side of the western derrick. Maybe he'd gotten a glimpse of the guy who'd shot at him.

Or maybe he was doing a little recon by fire. It seemed like something Jenkins would do.

Flanagan preferred not to give his position away if he could help it. He was a hunter; he preferred to let the enemy move first, expose himself first. Recon by fire occasionally flushed someone out, but it could also draw more fire from elsewhere.

Which promptly happened, as a storm of fire erupted from a nearby crane, sending bullets ripping through the air around Jenkins, punching into the metal and surfacing of the helideck, and forcing him back from the edge.

But while it might not have worked out that well for Jenkins, Flanagan now had a target. As did the rest of Hancock's element.

Leaning out just a little bit, Flanagan put his red dot just above the spot where he'd seen the muzzle blast and squeezed the trigger. The bark of his shot was drowned out by a ragged, rattling roar as the others opened fire on the same shooter.

Bullets hammered at the crane's control cab, shattering the plexiglass and punching holes through the sheet metal walls and door. There was a hint of movement inside, then the crane was still. No more gunfire came from the cab.

But more return fire started to come from the higher decks of the skeletal structures on the far side of the derricks. There had been terrorists up there, too, watching for just that to happen. Flanagan ducked back as a bullet smacked a shiny hole in the yellow-painted side of the container, only a few inches from where his head had been.

He snapped off a few shots in the general direction that the round had come from, but he really couldn't see much. The shooter must have had a nice, small loophole to shoot through. Flanagan had a sudden flashback to firefights in Afghanistan, trading bullets with Taliban fighters who had been dug into compounds with thick mud walls, shooting through tiny murder holes where the Americans couldn't touch them.

"We could be up here all day trading shots with these bastards," Hancock snarled, echoing Flanagan's thoughts. "Joe, John, get back down below and see if you can get in close and deal with them. We'll cover you from up here."

Flanagan didn't argue. He didn't even comment. Wade just uttered a monosyllabic grunt and rolled away from the corner where he'd taken cover, making eye contact with Flanagan before they both headed for the ladderwell, sprinting to get through the gap before they could get shot.

Bullets *snap*ped and *crack*ed past them as they pounded down the steps.

Payback's coming, assholes.

***

They could still hear gunfire from above them, dimly echoing hammering that reverberated through the steel fabric of the platform. Neither man flinched. They'd trained together only a little, but they soon fell into a rhythm. It was an old dance for both of them, even though Wade had been a Ranger and Flanagan a Recon Marine. The principles were the same; move smoothly, watch the corners, get eyes and a gun muzzle on any opening or angle where you might get shot.

Of course, on the Tourmaline-Delta platform, bullets were hardly the only worry.

Flanagan was in the lead when he stopped dead, holding up a fist. They were down in the bowels of the lower decks, having just come out of the main superstructure near the base of the eastern derrick. And, just as Flanagan had expected, there was a trap waiting for them.

"How much crap did these fuckers bring with them?" Wade whispered. He'd just turned from checking their six o'clock to almost run into Flanagan, the other man's fist right in front of his face.

"A lot," Flanagan said. He was wondering the same thing. It was apparent that there had been a great deal of preparation for this op, but how they'd seized the platform without anyone finding out about it prior to the attacks was still a mystery. *Maybe they hijacked a supply shipment.* It was about the only thing that made sense.

Slinging his rifle on his back, Flanagan bent down and advanced slowly on the charge, while Wade moved forward with him, eyes and rifle tracking up and around through the hatch, looking for the shooter that they were both pretty sure was waiting for them to stick their heads out.

The trap was pretty much exactly the same as the others they'd encountered; a block of plastic explosive, wrapped in a fragmentation sleeve, inside a weatherproof plastic box and wired up with IR sensors. Flanagan grimaced behind his dark beard; as familiar as the traps were getting, it wasn't getting any less hazardous to disarm them. And the longer they messed with them, the more likely one of them would make a mistake.

Fortunately, they hadn't yet found a trap with a failsafe. They were fairly straightforward. At least, they had been.

"Hell." He looked down at the setup and knew this one wasn't going to be as easy. The laser was affixed to the plastic box's lid, instead of the side or the nearby wall. Which meant that opening the box was going to interrupt the beam and blow them both to kingdom come.

He briefly thought of finding something to throw through the beam, backing off, and setting the trap off that way. But he quickly reconsidered. *Any* explosion that close to the wells had the potential to be disastrous. Even from where he was, he could smell the fumes. Setting the trap off would probably kill everyone on the platform.

Of course, with the hostages having already been murdered, that just left them and the terrorists. But Flanagan wasn't particularly interested in making that kind of a statement. He'd much rather kill the terrorists and walk away alive.

"We've got to bypass this somehow," he whispered.

"I'm open to suggestions," Wade replied, continuing to scan over his shoulder. "They've been pretty thorough about covering most avenues, so far."

"Well, they got smart with this one, so if we try to disarm it, it's probably going to blow up in our faces," Flanagan said, bringing his rifle back up. He looked around, knowing that their options weren't great. "Fortunately, it's set pretty low, so we might be able to step over the beam."

Wade didn't stare at him incredulously, but his tone when he spoke communicated the sentiment pretty well. "Just like that? Step over the beam we can't see and hope the field-expedient claymore doesn't turn us into pink mist?"

"Haven't you ever stepped over the beam to get out of a garage while the door was closing?" Flanagan asked.

"That's a little different, don't you think?" Wade retorted.

"Only because we'll die if we screw it up instead of having to re-close the garage door when it starts to open again," Flanagan said, standing. "But if we don't deal with these bastards, we'll all die, anyway." Lifting a sodden boot, he took a deep breath.

At least if I'm wrong, I'll probably never know it. He kept one hand on his rifle, muzzle high, and grabbed hold of the hatch coaming with the other, to make sure he didn't fall and accidentally break the beam that way.

"You crazy jarhead son of a bitch," Wade started to say, but Flanagan was already committed. He half-stepped, half-

196

hopped over the line of the beam, just about lost his balance as he put his weight on his lead foot, then had to throw himself flat as a bullet smacked off the wall just a few inches from his hand, having missed his head by a scant hair. The *snap* of its passage was drowned out by the loud *bang* of the impact.

He hit hard, just about driving the wind out of himself. He'd had the presence of mind to keep his rifle up, so that he didn't land on it, but he was out of position, and acutely aware of just how little cover he had, even as Wade opened fire in response, the muzzle blasts from the M6 slapping at him where he lay on the metal deck.

Flanagan rolled to his right, getting away from the door, and hopefully away from the charge before something set it off. Wade was still inside the hatch, shooting through it, even as more bullets hammered against the pipes and girders around Flanagan.

"I can't see him; I'm just laying fire!" Wade bellowed, as Flanagan got himself behind a brace of thick steel I-beams that would at least provide *some* cover from the incoming bullets. Getting his equilibrium back, he lifted his rifle again and eased one eye out from behind the beam, looking desperately for the shooter.

He spotted the blue-gray shape, kneeling on one of the upper decks on the far side of the derricks, at just about the same time that the Blackhearts up on the top deck did. More fire roared and hammered from up there, and the incoming shots ceased, as the camouflaged terrorist was forced back from his firing position.

With the fire died down, Flanagan braced himself around the side of the I-beam, pointing his rifle up, scanning for more threats. "Set!" he yelled to Wade. "Come on!"

He barely heard Wade's reply. "If I get blown up, Joe, I'm gonna find some way to come back and haunt you for the rest of your damned life. And I don't even believe in ghosts."

There was a crash behind him as Wade overbalanced the same way he had. The beam was just high enough that it wasn't possible to have both feet on the deck while straddling it. But nothing exploded, so Wade had managed to clear the beam without interrupting it.

He slammed into the angled, bracing I-beam near Flanagan's knees. "Now what?" he asked. He sounded a little out of breath, probably because of the hairiness of what they'd just done. "We're just about at the derricks. Are we defusing, or hunting?"

"Hunting," Flanagan replied, without looking down. Was that more movement up there, or was he imagining it in the play of sunlight and shadow? "We won't do anybody any good if we get shot trying to defuse the damn bombs."

"Lead on, then," Wade said.

That was going to be the tricky part. From what he'd seen so far, most of the terrorist shooters seemed to be on the higher decks behind the derricks. There had to be one or two closer in, if the bombs really were supposed to be bait for an ambush, but the ones on the upper decks were the more immediate threats. And there was a relatively open stretch of catwalk around the seaward side of the derrick, that was going to be pretty easily covered by a shooter up above.

"Cover me," Flanagan said. "I'm moving to that next ladderwell." There were steel mesh steps leading up into the open tower of decking, pipes, and support equipment on the far side of the derrick.

"I've got you," Wade said. He stepped back, behind Flanagan, pointing his rifle up toward the higher decks. He spared another glance at the crane above them, but it was still bullet-riddled and abandoned. The dead terrorist's bullpup rifle was lying on the deck not far in front of them.

Flanagan took a deep breath, then came around the main girder and the base of the derrick, pounding down the catwalk toward the next bit of dubious cover.

It wasn't a long run; the catwalk was only about twenty yards long. It just felt a lot longer. And even as he neared the steel pillars that framed the structure, movement to his left caught his eye.

There was a terrorist crouched amid the pipes leading out of the derrick, his rifle already leveled.

Flanagan threw himself flat on the deck, hitting his shoulder for the second time in the last few minutes with bruising impact, even as a three-round burst *snap*ped overhead. If he hadn't been moving as fast as he had been, he'd have been dead.

Unfortunately, even as he pointed his rifle, he saw that he didn't have a shot. The terrorist didn't, either, but he was effectively pinned behind the maze of pipes and supporting girders, which were now providing the bad guy as much cover as they were providing him. And the bad guy knew just where he was, too.

Gunshots thundered, and he faintly heard the *crack*s as several bullets went high over his head. He glanced back to see Wade shooting around the side of the derrick, aiming above him. There must be another one up there, trying to shoot down at him.

Scrambling, wincing a little as his elbows and knees beat against the hard deck, he side-crawled toward the ladderwell. The pipes were fairly level; none of them were going to provide more cover than he already had. But he wanted to get the hell away from the last spot his would-be killer had seen him.

He got close up by the pipes, still in the "side prone," and briefly tried to look underneath. At first, all he could make out was more pipes, along with some of the structural members keeping them level over the deck. Then he spotted a boot.

The owner of the boot shifted a little, and he saw a bit of the blue-gray camouflage pantleg above it. It wasn't much of a target, but it was a target. And if he did this right, it would be enough.

He snugged his rifle into his shoulder, putting the red dot on the black boot, his finger tightening on the trigger. He knew that it wasn't going to quite be point of aim, point of impact; the offset of the sight from the barrel wasn't intended for sideways shooting like this. But at that range, it wasn't going to matter.

He fired, the LWRC bucking into his shoulder, the muzzle blast concentrated in the narrow space between pipe and decking, slapping him in the face. He kept pulling the trigger, pumping five shots at the terrorist's foot and lower leg as fast as the trigger could reset.

The man screamed as bullets tore through his boot, pulping muscle and tendon and smashing bones to splinters. He collapsed, and Flanagan pumped three more rounds into him as he hit the deck. The last one tore through his heart and lungs, and he slowly shuddered to utter stillness, blood pumping out onto the steel.

Footsteps pounded on the decking, and Flanagan rolled onto his back, bringing his rifle around, but stopped himself as he saw it was Wade, dashing along the catwalk he'd already crossed.

Wade slowed as he got closer, his rifle and eyes still trained up toward the decks and girders above. "You good?" he asked.

"I'm great," Flanagan growled, as he rolled back over and heaved himself to his feet. His entire body felt like one enormous bruise, and he was pretty sure the saltwater that hadn't dried in his cammies was slowly eroding his skin away with every move he made. He still got to his feet, carefully, scanning for any more terrorists hiding in the pipes.

Wade was set up on the ladderwell, his rifle pointed up toward the first landing, waiting for him. Fighting to keep from limping—his knee was suddenly throbbing, and he hadn't even realized he'd hit it that hard—Flanagan moved to join him.

Together, trying to cover every angle at once, the two men started up.

CHAPTER 17

"I think I can see one of the bombs," Jenkins said.

Santelli and the rest were lying prone behind their rifles on the helideck, and Santelli was cussing at great length and with a viciousness that would have made Melissa blanch to hear him. He was kicking himself for getting his element into that position in the first place; they hadn't been able to cross the helideck fast enough, and now they were pinned down by one or two sons of bitches hiding in the superstructure across the platform.

Another shot cracked by, and a second nicked the edge of the deck with a *bang*. Fortunately, that guy was situated in a position that was lower than the top deck, or else they'd really be fucked. As it was, though, they didn't dare get up or get too close to the edge.

"How the hell can you see one of the bombs?" Curtis demanded. "If they're on the wells, then they're below us, under the derricks. And unless you're Superman, and got X-ray vision and shit, I don't think you can see through the damned helideck."

Santelli was about to tell them both to shut up when Hancock's voice crackled over his radio, the sound of which was muffled from being stuffed in a pouch in his chest rig, presently pressed between his barrel chest and the deck.

"Goodfella, Surfer," Hancock was calling.

With a renewed torrent of bit-off cursing, Santelli rolled halfway over to get the radio. Another shot went by overhead, close enough that he didn't just hear the *snap*, he *felt* it. "Go for Goodfella," he answered.

"Woodsrunner and Angry Ragnar just went down below," Hancock told him. "They're going after the bad guys who have firing positions on us, so watch your shots."

What shots? We can't see shit, much less shoot at it. "Roger that," Santelli replied.

"Contact, high!" Childress snapped, his voice practically drowned out by the report as he opened fire. Santelli looked up from the radio, squinting as he tried to spot whatever Sam was shooting at. But he was in a bad spot; he couldn't see anything, unless the bad guy Childress was lighting up was on the far side of the derrick. Or maybe the crane.

"Hey, Carlo," Hart said. He'd wriggled over on his belly until he was next to and behind Santelli. Santelli craned his neck around to look back at him. "What if I went down below?" he said. "I might be able to sneak in there and start defusing bombs."

"Were you not paying attention, Don?" Santelli asked. "They *want* us to try that!"

"I can get in there," Hart insisted, sounding a bit petulant. Or maybe that was Santelli's imagination. "They're gonna be focused on you guys up here, and John and Joe over on the other side. If I can get close enough, they might not even notice me."

Santelli actually considered it. They were in a tight spot, there was no doubt of that. But it was a long shot, and one that he really wasn't willing to take, not with Hart. The guy had shown flashes of competence, but he found he really didn't trust him to stay steady, particularly not on his own, and with that hole in his shoulder.

Then he heard the thump of rotor blades above and behind them.

***

Wade stayed in the lead as he and Flanagan climbed the stairs. He knew there was at least one shooter up there; he'd gotten

202

a few shots off at the guy, but his target had ducked back behind the thick steel support beam, and he wasn't sure if he'd hit him at all.

It made him mad. It hadn't been that long a shot. He should have cored the bastard's brains out and been done with it. That it had been a really small target, and he'd been snap-shooting with a red dot, didn't enter into his calculations. He should have hit the guy and killed him, he hadn't, and it pissed him off.

He was climbing as fast as he could while still being reasonably sure he could shoot accurately. They really should be clearing systematically, but he knew where he'd last seen his quarry, and he wanted that one dead. So he bypassed the first two decks, continuing upward, his rifle up, on the hunt. Flanagan didn't say anything, didn't even hesitate. Whether or not the other man knew what he was doing, he stuck with him.

Wade didn't even slow down as he hit the landing he was aiming for. He pounded up the steps and out onto the deck full of girders, pipes, cables, and equipment, his weapon up, his finger just outside the trigger guard, looking for his quarry. Flanagan was right behind him, turning the opposite direction and spreading out.

There was no sign of the terrorist. A quick check showed him that the guy wasn't still behind the support beam where he'd last seen him. He glanced over just long enough to make eye contact with Flanagan and signaled that he was going to start moving along the deck. He wanted his kill. Flanagan inclined his head fractionally, and they started to glide forward, leaning into their weapons.

Wade found he liked working with Flanagan. The guy was a pro, and could have been the poster child for "quiet professional." He was sparing with his words, and always watching, always calculating. Wade could see it; just like him, he knew that Flanagan looked at everyone with the same question in his mind: "If things go south, how am I going to kill this person?"

He stopped just behind a towering jumble of pipes and power conduits. Something wasn't quite right; something was warning him not to just go right around the next corner. He sank to a knee, even as he saw Flanagan out of the corner of his eye, angling around another corner and vanishing.

Shots rang out. A fast pair, then a rolling thunder of four or five shots, hammering at something just out of sight. He surged to his feet and went around the corner, following his rifle muzzle.

The terrorist was on his side, twitching, blood pouring out of ragged holes in his neck and head. Flanagan was advancing on the body, rifle leveled.

Wade didn't have time to yell, as he saw another blue-gray-clad shape pop up over the railing at the far edge of the platform. He just snapped his rifle up and fired. He only had one shot, but he saw the terrorist's head snap backward, spraying red obscenity into the air, and then he was gone.

The two of them continued to advance on the one Flanagan had shot, who was going still. That one was gone. Unfortunately, they had no idea just how many were on the platform.

Wade wanted to pull the guy's balaclava down, see who he was. But they weren't out of the woods yet; there could still be several more lurking around.

Then the man's radio crackled. "Recall, recall, recall," said the voice that had taunted them over the rig's PA system. "Time's up, lowlifes. Move your asses."

Wade looked up and around. Where the hell were they going to go? The Blackhearts were between them and the boat decks, and held the helideck.

Then he just about kicked himself. Of course there were other boat decks; if something went wrong, the builders weren't going to condemn everyone on half the platform to die. There would be lifeboats on all sides, just in case. They had to be heading for the north boat deck.

A glance at Flanagan told him that the other man had reached the same conclusion. Rifles coming up, they started toward the edge of the platform.

They still had to move carefully, checking corners and dead spaces, trying to cover every gap and loophole as they passed it. They saw no more charges, and no more terrorists, until they got to the edge, nearing the railing that stood between the deck and the drop toward the Gulf of Mexico below.

No sooner had they reached the rail than a long burst of automatic fire hammered at the deck, the railing, and the pipes, forcing them back. It was coming from down below, and Wade knew he'd been right. The bad guys were down on the boat deck.

Which meant that as soon as they were clear, they were probably going to blow the platform.

He tried to force his way forward to get a shot, at least to try to disable the lifeboats, but the terrorists knew they were there, and another long, ravening burst forced him back, bullets slamming into sheet metal and piping around him. Crude oil and drilling mud was seeping out of some of the holes, and the fumes were getting bad.

Flanagan was flattened against one of the bigger steel beams holding the decks up, and had his radio out of its pouch. "Surfer, Woodsrunner," he was yelling into the mic, trying to make himself heard over the noise of the machinegun fire. "The bad guys are making a break for it from the north boat deck. If they get clear, they're going to blow the charges. Get in there, now!"

Wade realized what Flanagan was aiming at. The terrorists bugging out meant that they wouldn't have anyone covering the bombs themselves anymore. It might be their only window.

Provided that Hancock and the others could get past the booby traps between them and the wells. He was suddenly thinking about the fact that they hadn't disarmed the one they'd bypassed on the way out of the superstructure.

Before he could say anything about it, though, a massive gray shape roared overhead. Wade had to duck back as the Mexican Mi-17 thumped past the platform, the door gunner hanging out of the open side door.

***

Hancock hadn't waited for Flanagan's radio call. The fire from across the platform had died down, and Santelli and the rest of his element had quickly scrambled across the helipad to join Hancock, Gomez, and Bianco in the shelter of the machinery and containers. By then, the helicopters were clearly visible and getting closer. "Everybody get down below," Hancock ordered. "I really, *really* don't want to have gone through all this just to get lit up by the Mexican Marines."

So, by the time Flanagan was calling his warning, the rest of the Blackhearts were inside the superstructure, in the room where Brannigan and Tanaka were strongpointed, and Flanagan's signal was a weak, broken mass of static and disconnected syllables.

Meanwhile, the fuses on the bombs were burning.

***

Huerta was standing in the door, braced with one hand against the overhead and the other clenched around a strap next to the doorframe itself. He was hovering just behind the door gunner, who was leaning into the MG21 mounted on a scissor mount.

He watched the platform get closer and closer, looking for human figures. He didn't know if they'd be the terrorists or the gringo mercenaries; it was pretty clear that the gringo mercenary, Brannigan, had boarded the platform and engaged the terrorists.

And he didn't know what he'd do if his men spotted the gringos first.

You know the right thing to do, Diego. Was it strange that his conscience seemed to have his mother's voice?

But he waited and watched. *Let the situation develop. Maybe the gringos will secure the platform by the time we reach it,*

206

and will have the good sense to put their weapons down when we get close.

The door gunner was leaning into the gun, his eyes already at the sights, and Huerta realized that he was getting ready to burn down anything that moved. Knowing what had happened to the first helicopters that had attempted to storm the platform, he couldn't say he blamed the younger man. But it could turn out to be disastrous if he killed the wrong people.

Or it could be a blessing in disguise. He shunned the thought, but it stayed there, lingering in the back of his mind. It could all be over quickly, once they got onto the platform. It might be strange, two different sets of dead terrorists, but he was sure they could think of a suitable explanation, if they even needed to explain anything to anyone. They could just throw the bodies in the water and be done with it. No questions asked, nothing pointing back to him, no evidence that he had gone over the line, against orders, and hired *Norteamericanos* to do his dirty work.

No evidence except what that Van Zandt might have documented. But Van Zandt was a gringo, and Mexicans would believe a Mexican officer before they believed a gringo.

But as they swooped in toward the helideck, with no signs of RPGs or MANPADS reaching up to swat them out of the sky, he saw no one in the open, and started to breathe a little easier. At least he wouldn't have to tell the door gunner to hold his fire, and deal with the questions from that.

But he didn't entirely relax, especially as the formation began to do a circuit around the platform, the next helo behind starting to pull ahead. He didn't know where the mercenaries might be, and he still didn't dare tell anyone to hold their fire.

As they circled around the north side of the platform, he was very glad that he hadn't issued that order after all.

The lead helicopter rounded the corner and promptly banked hard over, diving for the water and away from the platform. The faint sound of automatic weapons fire reached Huerta's ears, even through his earmuffs and the roar of the Mi-17's engines. A moment later, he got a look at what had made the lead pilot take such a wild evasive maneuver.

There was a long, low, black shape in the water at the north side of the platform, just to one side of the long boom leading to the burnoff stack. Its cylindrical hull was slightly flattened along the top, with a streamlined, vertical sail jutting from it, about two thirds of the way toward the bow.

And there was a machinegunner crouched on top of that sail, firing long bursts at the Mexican helicopters as they got close.

The machinegunner turned his sights on Huerta's helicopter as it started to swing around the corner. Seeing the threat, the pilot banked hard away, throwing the door gunner's aim off, even as he triggered a burst from the MG21 that went wild, the tracers arcing out over the water. Huerta held on for dear life, his hand clamped in a death grip around the strap by the door.

The pilot kept the hard bank, turning around to bring the bird behind the cover of the platform. The engines were howling, and Huerta couldn't hear if the enemy machinegunner was still at it, but all he needed to do was hold them off for a few seconds until the submarine could dive.

The rest of the flight of helicopters had pulled up hard, circling away from the platform and the submarine. Huerta was cursing, but the pilots were understandably a little nervous after the losses their *compadres* had already taken in the last few days.

Pulling his headset's microphone up to his mouth, he keyed the intercom. "Get us around so that we can fire on that submarine!" he bellowed.

"*Sí, Contralmirante*," the pilot replied. There might have been a distinct note of reluctance in his voice. But he banked back toward the platform and the burnoff stack.

They didn't take any more machinegun fire. They were too late. The wake of the strange submarine was fading, and the craft itself was gone. As soon as the helicopters had broken off, the machinegunner must have gone below, and the sub had started its dive.

"Land us on the platform," Huerta said grimly. The pilot obediently began to climb, circling around to make an approach onto the helideck.

Huerta looked down at the platform as they flew around it. He might have spied a couple of figures moving through the pipes and girders down there. He took a deep breath and made his decision. *I hope it does not mean ruin for me and my family.*

"*Teniente* Medina," he called over the radio. Hopefully, the Lieutenant had his radio on, and was listening.

"*Sì, Contralmirante?*" Medina replied promptly. His voice was scratchy and muffled by the helicopters' noise.

"I have information that there might be a private security force, hired by the oil company, on the platform," he said. "They are not to be considered hostile. Tell your men to be careful who they engage."

There was a long pause, as Medina digested the information. Huerta realized that his lie was a bit transparent; most of the platforms on the Gulf, in Mexican waters, were owned and operated by Pemex, the state-owned Mexican oil conglomerate. That Pemex would hire contractors to clear a platform instead of relying on the Mexican Naval Infantry seemed to be a bit of a stretch.

But then, he'd hired mercenaries, and there really was no such thing as standard procedure in such matters in Mexico. *Everyone* had contacts, *everyone* did deals outside the law. That was the way things were done in Mexico.

The only people who didn't play that game were the very poor. And that was why they were very poor.

"Understood, *Contralmirante*," Medina answered, his voice flat. "How are we to recognize this private security force?"

"They will be wearing green, and carrying M4 carbines," Huerta said. "As far as we know, the terrorists are using bullpup rifles."

There was another pause. It wasn't the most useful information, especially in a close-quarters fight. But Medina would use it as he felt he needed to. And if he just mowed the mercenaries down anyway, well, Huerta had tried.

Not good enough, Diego. He unplugged the intercom cable to his headset as his helicopter began its flare to land on the helideck. The lead helo had already touched down, disgorged its cargo of Naval Infantrymen, and was pulling away. Checking his P90, he prepared to step off and get in front of the Marines going down into the platform as quickly as possible.

Hopefully, for his conscience's sake, he could head off the bloodbath that was about to happen.

***

Flint stepped off the ladder and handed off the hot Mk 48 to Scrap without a word. Turning forward, he took about ten steps through the crowded Kilo-class submarine's control room, to where the captain was standing next to the periscope.

The Kilo had clearly seen better days. Paint was peeling on the bulkheads and the piping on the overhead, several of the lights were out, and there was a lingering stench in the air of sweat, piss, and ass. He knew that their employers had gotten their hands on it in some shady part of Eastern Europe, but he didn't know where.

"It's about fucking time," he snarled, as the captain turned to look at him. The guy looked a frog; bulging eyes, fat lips, and as pale as a fish's belly. And he was fat, which just made Flint instinctively despise him even more. "What the hell happened? You were supposed to be here three *fucking* days ago!"

"We had mechanical difficulties," the man replied, in a thick German accent. It sounded weird, surrounded by instruments marked in Cyrillic. "And then, when we got closer, the frigate out there was all over us. We were maneuvering for a day and a half to get in here."

Flint snorted. "Bullshit," he said. "You think the fucking *Mexican Navy* knows shit about antisub warfare? You were just scared." He let his hand drop close to the Field Pistol on his hip. He saw the captain's froggy eyes drop to follow the movement, and then widen a little as he saw where Flint's hand was resting.

"They have been dealing with many of these 'narco-subs' over the last few years…" the man said, visibly trying not to stammer. Sweat was standing out on his thick upper lip. And it wasn't even that hot in the control room.

"And how many of them have you heard that they've caught at sea, huh?" Flint asked, his voice low and dangerous. "A whole lot of my team got wasted up there, waiting for you." In truth, Flint really didn't give a damn for the dead. They'd known what they'd been getting into. He was just pissed that he'd been waiting around long enough for somebody to actually get a rescue force aboard the platform, ruining his picture-perfect op.

At least they'll all burn up soon, the ones who don't get blown to pink mist when the charges go off. He kept the satisfaction the thought gave him off his face.

"I am sorry," the captain stammered. "But we are here now, we are away, and we are submerged. By the time the frigate comes looking for us, we will be in deep water and well away."

Flint just stared at him for a long moment, letting him sweat. The guy was right, as much as he was a sniveling, slimy little frog. Finally, he nodded, and folded his arms. He saw the captain go a little wobbly in the knees as his hand moved away from the FK BRNO pistol.

"Fine," he said. "Head for the designated rendezvous site." He shouldered past the captain and started forward, toward the torpedo room. The torpedoes had long-since been stripped out, and that was where his team was going to stage.

He was a little disappointed that he hadn't found an excuse to cap the goggle-eyed captain, but reflected that it was probably all for the best. They still needed a captain; the sub wasn't going to sail itself. And the little 7.5mm bullets were probably a little too zippy to make firing them inside of a submerged submarine a good idea.

CHAPTER 18

Hancock had just reached the room where Tanaka and Brannigan were strongpointed, yelling, "Friendly!" at the top of his lungs as he approached, when the roar of the Mi-17s coming down on the helideck reverberated through the platform.

He glanced up at the sound and stifled a curse. He wasn't under any illusions that the Mexican Marines were going to be any less of a threat to the Blackhearts than the terrorists were. They might have a rep for being hard for the cartels to bribe or corrupt, but he hadn't heard anything about them that suggested that target discrimination was one of their strong suits. And they were going to be coming in shooting, either unaware that there was anyone except the armed terrorists on the platform, or specifically ordered to bury the evidence that Huerta had gone around the chain of command.

Meanwhile, there might still be terrorists on board, and there were definitely bombs with the fuses burning down near the wells. Which would kill them all if they went off.

"Looks like Huerta decided to double-cross us after all," Gomez muttered.

Hancock declined to comment. Brannigan was sitting up against the wall, his eyes open and still breathing, his rifle in his hands, but his eyes were a little glassy; he'd lost a lot of blood, and the shock had to be hitting his system pretty hard.

It's your show now, Roger. Bet you didn't think it was going to come to this so early, didja?

"All right," he said, thinking fast. "Carlo, you stay here with John and the rest. Don, you and Kev are with me. We're going to link up with Joe and Wade and see if we can't get those bombs defused."

"Roger," Brannigan croaked.

Hancock looked down at him. Brannigan was in rough shape, but he was looking up at him, and shook his head, fractionally.

Hancock's lips thinned. He knew what the Colonel was saying. *Guess you've still got some progress to make on this whole leadership thing, huh?* There were two serious threats facing them, and as the acting "Blackheart Six," he was going to have to put himself in a position to deal with the hairier one. The bombs were bad business, but deconflicting with the Mexican Marines—if it was even possible—had to come first.

"Fine," he grunted. "Carlo, you take Don and Kev, go link up with Wade and Joe, and get those bombs defused. Watch for stragglers. The bad guys might have slacked down on the shooting some, but that doesn't mean they're gone." He took a deep breath. It tasted of salt, blood, and gunsmoke. "I'll go try and make contact with our new friends up top."

Santelli didn't say anything, but waved at Hart and Curtis, and headed out the hatch. There wasn't time to waste; none of them wanted to be sitting around in the middle of the conflagration that the platform would become if those charges went off.

As they were leaving, Hancock flipped his rifle sling over his head and leaned the weapon against the wall next to Brannigan, then pulled off his still-wet chest rig, followed by his pistol belt.

"What are you doing, Rog?" Childress asked.

"We don't have any way of establishing comms with the Mexicans," he explained, trying to keep his voice bland and steady, "and they're probably going to ID weapons and shoot. So I'm going to go out and surrender, in the hopes that we can get this sorted out before we have a green-on-blue." "Green-on-blue" was

214

the usual wording for fratricide between allied forces. It had come to have a bit of a different meaning in recent years, given the number of Islamist infiltrators in Afghanistan who had murdered American and British troops under the guise of the Afghan National Army. And Hancock had to reflect that this situation potentially wasn't that much different. For all he knew, the Mexicans were there to kill *everybody*, regardless.

"You think they're going to be reasonable?" Jenkins asked. "These ain't SEALs we're talking about."

Wasn't "Sucks To Be A Hostage" a SEAL catchphrase? Hancock kept the thought to himself. It wasn't the time, and he was supposed to be a leader right then.

"I think there's a fifty-fifty chance they're going to blow my head off on sight," he admitted. "But we've got to take the chance. Otherwise there's a hundred percent chance we're not getting off this platform alive."

He didn't want to go out there. Not just because there was a risk that he'd get gunned down without a chance to take some of the bastards with him. Death wasn't something that scared Roger Hancock. He wouldn't have done some of the crazy stuff he'd done over the years if it was.

No, it was the part that came after that he didn't want to do, the part that would only happen if he survived the next few minutes. Talking and deconflicting while the boys were down below trying desperately to defuse the bombs that would kill them all.

Some might say that his thought processes had rubbed off from Brannigan and his "lead from the front" mentality. But that wasn't the case. Hancock had always been that way; it was the way he'd been taught from his first days as a Private. It was why he'd always gotten along with Brannigan, even as a platoon sergeant dealing with a Battalion Commander.

He stepped through the hatch, even as the engine noise of the Mi-17 above faded, to be replaced by the rising thunder of a second. Did he hear boots thudding on the ladderwell at the end of the passageway, or was that his imagination?

Then there was movement in the hatchway, and he held his hands out, open and empty, and waited.

He shut his eyes as the small object *clunked* onto the decking just inside the hatch off the landing, and the flashbang's concussion slapped him in the face, even several yards away. The flash was a bright light against his eyelids, but had been muted enough that there was no bright purple blotch in his vision when he opened his eyes again, to see the Mexican Marines flowing through the opening, pushing through the still-rising smoke from the banger, their P90s up, their faces covered by black balaclavas.

He sank to his knees as the submachineguns were leveled at him, keeping his hands up and visible. *"No fuego!"* he called out, hoping that it got the message across. His command of Spanish wasn't great.

The lead Marines closed on him but didn't shoot. The ones behind them flowed into the rooms as they passed, but at least one had his 5.7mm barrel pointed rock-solid at Hancock's head the entire time.

The fourth man back hadn't joined the stacks flowing into rooms. He put a hand on the lead Marine's shoulder and said something in Spanish. The P90 barrel lowered fractionally, but didn't move *too* far away from him.

The man then let his own P90 hang on its single-point sling and reached up to pull down his balaclava. He was an older man, his face jowly and lined, with a thin, graying mustache. "Who are you?" he asked, in accented but clear English.

"I'm Hancock," he replied. "I'm Brannigan's second in command."

"Where is Brannigan?" the older man demanded.

"He's wounded," Hancock replied. "My men are keeping him secured." That it was only a few paces behind him wasn't something he was going to explain, not just yet. Not until he knew that they weren't all going to be executed.

"So you are in charge?" the older man asked.

"I am," he replied.

"I am *Contralmirante* Huerta, Mexican Naval Infantry," the older man said. "What is the status of the platform?"

"The hostages are dead," Hancock said, as the Marines appeared to relax a little. None of the gun muzzles had moved far, but none of them were quite pointed at him anymore. He still wasn't going to relax. The Mexicans might just make sure everything was copacetic before wasting all of them. "It appears they were executed shortly after the terrorists arrived on the platform; they've been dead for days. There are explosive booby traps all over the place, though we've disarmed the ones we've found in the superstructure here. We believe that there are larger charges set on the oil wells themselves; I've sent several of my men down to defuse them."

Huerta nodded. He barked instructions to the Marines, and soon they were moving down the hall. "Come with us, *Señor* Hancock," he said. "We will need you and your men to keep close to me." He pointedly didn't say anything about assisting in the clearance of the platform, and Hancock noticed. The Blackhearts' role in the incident might well be over.

Just as long as it didn't end with a bullet and a drop into the Gulf.

"Friendlies coming in!" he called out as they neared the blood-smeared hatch where Aziz had died.

"Come ahead," Bianco replied.

Hancock stepped through, followed by Huerta. The Marines, somewhat to his surprise, stayed outside.

As Hancock retrieved his gear and weapons, Huerta looked down at Aziz' body and the wounded Brannigan. Hancock noticed that Huerta didn't object to his rearming; though that might just be confidence born of superior numbers.

The man's next words belied that, or at least they were calculated to do so. "Notice that I came in here alone," he said quietly. "My life is now in your hands. None of my men know that I contracted you to board the Tourmaline-Delta. I do this so that you know that you can trust me." The message was pretty clear. Huerta had imagined the thought that was going through every Blackheart's mind as the helos had descended; that they were expendable assets that were now to be swept under the rug. And he was going out of his way, putting himself in their hands, to assure them that he had no such intentions.

Hancock had to admit, he was impressed. He hadn't expected that kind of honor from a Mexican officer. There were too many stories of corruption floating around from the drug war.

"Do you have a medic, Admiral?" he asked. "Colonel Brannigan is in a bit of a bad way."

"*Sí*," Huerta replied. "I also have a few explosives experts, though they are not true EOD. I can send them down to help your men. It would not be good if we were all incinerated after securing the platform, would it?"

"No, it wouldn't be," Hancock replied. He glanced around at the rest. Bianco and Jenkins were still posted up on the hatch, while the rest were pointedly spread out around the room, eyes on Huerta, hands on guns. "Tell them that they need to be careful, though. We don't know how many of the terrorists are left."

"I do not believe that any of them are," Huerta said. "We took fire from a submarine that was loading them aboard on our final approach. The submarine dove as we came around; I believe that they have made their escape."

"Dammit," Hancock said, as a similar chorus of profanity floated around the room.

"The ARM *Hermengildo Galeana* is just off to the seaward side of the platform, and is closing in," Huerta explained. "Their escape might not be as permanent as they hope. In the meantime, however, we need to get those explosives defused."

"Agreed," Hancock said. "Let's get topside and see if I can raise the rest of my boys on the radio." It felt a little strange, saying it like that. They were Brannigan's "boys." But he was in charge at the moment, so they were his.

Huerta simply nodded, and the two of them stepped out into the passageway, turning toward the ladderwell leading up to the roof.

***

Flanagan and Wade didn't waste time heading back toward the wells, but they weren't rushing, either. They'd seen the sub slip beneath the water, but that didn't mean that the terrorists hadn't left anyone behind. They might not have been intentionally abandoned, but they'd be no less dangerous in that case.

Neither man spoke as they leapfrogged back toward the derricks. Both men were thinking, but it wasn't the time nor the place for chitchat.

I'm pretty sure that was a Kilo. Were these assholes Russians? Nah, that dude sounded American. So what kind of terrorists are using top-of-the-line gear and using a fucking Kilo-class submarine *as their getaway vehicle?* Flanagan didn't have answers to any of those questions, and it bugged him. Sure, targets were targets, bad guys were bad guys, but he'd generally prided himself on having some working knowledge of who was who in the bad guy scene. There were Islamists, drug dealers, Communists, and gangsters. Sure, he knew that the Russians and Chinese weren't exactly America's friends, but most of that sparring had been over shithole countries overseas, proxy-war type stuff. This was something different. And none of it was adding up.

All of this was a compartmentalized background note in his mind as he moved from cover to cover, pivoting to check corners and adjacent spaces as he passed them.

"Woodsrunner, Angry Ragnar, this is Goodfella," Santelli's voice crackled over the radio. It was scratchy and barely readable, but it was definitely Santelli.

"Go for Angry Ragnar," Wade replied. He was at the landing, waiting for Flanagan to catch up before descending.

"We're coming out at the base of the west derrick," Santelli called. "What's your location?"

"We're on the stairs just across from you," Wade replied, as Flanagan came up next to him, covering the opposite angles. "Be advised, there's a booby trap on that door that we weren't able to disarm before coming through. You're either going to have to go over it or find another way. It doesn't look like it was intended to *be* disarmed."

Which, given that the bad guys had put barrel bombs on the derricks, made sense. They must have planned to send the whole platform sky-high in the first place.

"Roger," Santelli replied. He sounded pissed. "We'll see if we can find a way around. Any idea how much time's left on the bombs?"

"No clue," Wade replied. "Though it looks like our little friends just made a run for it in a submarine, of all things. What's the status with the Mexican Marines we just saw fly in?"

"Surfer was going to make contact and deconflict," Santelli answered. "Get to those wells, we can chat later."

If there is a later.

Wade had already started down the steps as soon as Flanagan had reached him. Both men were feeling the press of time; with the terrorists having abandoned the platform, they might only have seconds left.

They clattered down the stairs as quickly as they could without completely abandoning security. Any adjacent space got a quick glance and a sweep with a rifle barrel, and then they were past and pushing into the derrick itself.

The first bomb was pretty easy to spot. It was set up the same way the ones that they'd encountered set up on the main avenues around the superstructure had been; a fifty-five-gallon drum with an initiation system having been lowered into an open flange in the lid.

Wade slung his rifle as he quickly advanced on the bomb. If he was feeling the strain of being that close to that much explosive, he didn't show it. He just sized up the construction, then reached for the initiation system.

There was no digital readout to say how much time was left. There was smoke coming from the igniter; and that was definitely time fuse going down into the drum. Wade carefully pulled on the time fuse until it came loose, still smoking. He pulled out his knife, cut it, then dropped it on the deck and stamped it out.

For a second, both men waited, not quite daring to breathe. The terrorists hadn't double-primed any of their charges so far, but they'd had more time to set the bombs in the wells, so that wasn't necessarily going to last.

But nothing went boom. At least, not yet. If there was a backup initiation system, it wasn't obvious, and they were still running out of time. There hadn't been all that much length left on that time fuse.

There wasn't a lot of room down in the guts of the well; there was a lot of piping, cables, and machinery to weave through. But Wade lifted his rifle and started moving toward the next bomb, while Flanagan covered him.

***

It had taken entirely too long to get to the second well; Hart had finally had to risk snipping the wires on another booby trap in a doorway. None of them had breathed much until the leads were in his hand, and the charge hadn't gone off. All three had been all too familiar with too many IEDs with failsafes in the sandbox. Snip one wire, and the interruption of the current sets off another switch. Boom. Game over. That it didn't happen in this case told

Santelli that these guys had been in something of a hurry, and hadn't really counted on sticking around. The traps were there to slow them down, more than anything else.

Hart had just straightened from the improvised claymore when boots clattered on the deck behind them, and Santelli spun to join Curtis, his rifle pointed down the passageway.

There were six Mexican Marines closing in on them, P90s leveled. "Lower your weapon, Kevin," Santelli said quietly, as he did the same. It went against the grain, but they had to treat these guys as friendlies.

That they wouldn't be able to respond fast enough if they turned out to be hostiles wasn't something he fretted over. Melissa would mourn him, but he'd be dead, and Carlo Santelli had had enough practice at resigning himself to his eventual, probably violent, demise that he didn't get too tensed up.

The lead Mexican Marine barked at them in Spanish. Santelli wasn't very good with the language, and the guy was talking too fast for even his limited vocabulary to keep up, so he just held out his hands. "Calm down, son," he said. "We're the good guys."

A Marine with hard black eyes, the only part of him visible under his balaclava, let his P90 hang and stepped forward. "You are the contractors?" he asked haltingly.

"Yeah, that's us," Santelli answered. "Now, we gotta get moving." He jerked a thumb over his shoulder to indicate the derrick beyond the hatch. "There are bombs on the oil wells, and the fuses are burning."

"Bombs?" the black-eyed man asked. Santelli nodded emphatically, widening his eyes as if to stress the urgency of the matter.

"Yeah, bombs," he said. "As in, they go boom, we all get incinerated. Come on, we gotta move!"

"You stay here," the Mexican said. "We have explosive experts."

Out of the corner of his eye, Santelli saw Curtis twitch. He didn't dare spare the moment to glare at him, but fortunately, their resident class clown held his peace. "They need to hurry up," Santelli said. "Tell them to look for barrel bombs, fifty-five-gallon drums."

The Mexican Marine nodded again, spat out orders at his men, and pointed down at the deck at their feet. "You stay here," he repeated. "Do not move."

When the Marines started pushing through the hatch, they left two behind, their P90s held at the low ready. Which told Santelli all he needed to know about where they stood with these guys. The Mexicans weren't happy about gringo mercenaries being on the platform, much less having accomplished what they hadn't been able to in two tries.

He leaned against the bulkhead, watching their minders, his hand on the buttstock of his LWRC. "May as well get comfortable, gents," he said. "If they screw it up and kill us all, we won't be able to do a damned thing about it."

Curtis was shaking a little. "*Explosive experts*," he whispered, chuckling. He looked up at Santelli.

"Yeah, I know, Kevin, you could have gotten so much mileage out of that," Santelli sighed. "Just give it a rest for now, okay?"

***

Wade dropped the second bomb's fuse on the deck and stamped it out, careful to get all the sparks that threatened to set the thin layer of crude oil on the metal ablaze. "That's two," he said. "You see a third one?"

Flanagan had already been looking. He shook his head. "Maybe they finally ran out of explosives," he said. "I hope they did."

"You and me both," Wade replied. "I hate this IED bullshit."

Flanagan already had his radio held to his mouth. "Goodfella, Woodsrunner," he called. "The eastern derrick appears to be clear. What's your status?"

"We're holding just inside the superstructure," Santelli answered. "The Mexican Marines are disarming the charges on the western well. They didn't want to bring us along."

"Roger," Flanagan replied. "I guess we'll hold here until..."

He was cut off by a thunderous *boom*, as an explosion rocked the entire platform. Both Wade and Flanagan were nearly thrown flat, as a roiling fireball consumed the western derrick. In seconds, the well was wreathed in orange flame and thick, choking, black smoke.

CHAPTER 19

If the Mexican Marines had seemed like they were wound a little tight, the explosion only made matters worse. Hancock tensed as P90 muzzles started to rise. He turned to Huerta, but the *Contralmirante* was already ahead of him. He was on his own radio, speaking rapidly in Spanish.

He looked at Hancock. "It seems that some of my men were too late getting to one of the charges," he said flatly. His eyes were empty and dead; Hancock couldn't read him at all, and it made him nervous. He wanted to sweep the rest of the Mexican Marines with his eyes, double-checking positions and dispositions, just in case this turned pear-shaped in the next few seconds. He knew that the rest of the Blackhearts in the room were doing just that, including Brannigan, where he was still sitting propped up against the bulkhead.

Another explosion rumbled through the platform. "Admiral," Hancock said carefully, "I think we'd better see about getting off this platform. There's a *lot* of explosives around here, as well as all the crude oil. That fire's gonna spread *fast*."

Huerta just looked at him for a second, before finally nodding. "You are certain that the hostages are all dead?" he asked.

"I saw 'em myself," Childress replied shortly. "They're bug food. Why the hell would we lie about that?"

Not now, Sam. Faced with twitchy Mexican Marines, not known for their restraint in the first place, and a completely unknown quantity of an employer who had those same Mexican Marines' leash in his fist, was not the time nor the place for Childress' infamous lack of mind-to-mouth filter. Hancock just held Huerta's gaze.

"We need to go now, Admiral," he repeated.

Huerta nodded again. "Call your people," he said. "Tell them that if they are not on the helideck in the next five minutes, they are going to go down with the platform."

***

A wave of heat slapped Flanagan in the face. The west derrick was completely involved, and the fire was spreading fast. It was going to reach the east derrick and the two bombs that Wade had successfully defused soon. They had to move.

He heard Hancock's broken recall transmission over the radio, just barely managing to decipher enough of the static-laced transmission over the growing roar of the flames to get the gist of it. He grabbed Wade by the vest.

"Back the way we came!" he said. "And watch for that booby trap in the hatch!" He was sure Wade hadn't forgotten about it, but it wasn't going to be a good idea to ignore random explosives with that fire spreading. Better safe than sorry.

Wade didn't respond except to turn to follow. Coughing as the caustic black smoke got thicker, they drove toward the exit from the derrick and the catwalk that would lead them back toward the superstructure.

"Goodfella, Angry Ragnar!" Wade was yelling into the radio.

"This is Goodfella," Santelli's voice came back. "We're alive and moving up. The Mexicans were on the derrick, not us. We've got two shell-shocked Mexican Marines with us."

Flanagan was almost to the hatch. Something else blew up behind them with a loud *bang*, and flaming crude started to spew out of the well to splash against the superstructure just to their right.

Flanagan felt the hair on his face and arm starting to crisp and curl as the flames crackled.

It was Wade's turn to grab him, dragging him down toward the deck. "Hold up!" the big man snapped. "That fire's too close!"

A moment later, Wade was proved right, as either the charge got too hot, or the circuits in the IR sensor melted. The charge in the hatchway detonated, the shockwave tearing at them as ball bearings whizzed overhead. Flanagan felt a fiery *thump* in his leg. The shock traveled up the limb, and for a second he thought that he'd taken a catastrophic hit.

Wade saw him flinch, and immediately started checking his leg. He slapped him on the calf and got to his feet, holding out a hand. "You're good, brother," he said. "It just trimmed you."

Flanagan took the proffered hand, and let Wade help him haul himself to his feet. Then they were moving toward the hatch, Flanagan limping a little as he went. It might have been a relatively minor wound, but it still hurt like hell.

The hatch coaming was blackened and twisted from the blast. The shockwave had actually driven the pool of burning oil back a little bit, though both men still got cooked a little as they plunged through the opening and into the darkened interior of the superstructure.

The fire was getting worse, and another massive explosion behind them made the entire platform shudder again. Another one of the wellhead bombs had gone off, which probably meant the last one was next. They could feel the heat through the walls.

The two of them hit the ladderwell running, pounding up the steps right behind the Mexican Marines who were one flight ahead of them. Nobody who wanted to live was going to stick around.

Both men were coughing and choking, tears streaming from their eyes and their lungs burning, by the time they reached the top of the steps. The smoke was suffocating, and only getting thicker. If they didn't get off the platform quickly, they were all going to choke to death in the next few minutes.

The roar of the fire made it almost impossible to hear, and the smoke was so thick that they almost didn't see the knot of men crouched at the edge of the helipad until they were right on top of them. Mexican Marines and American mercenaries alike were crouched on the deck, their faces blackened, streaming sweat, trying to breathe through cammies pulled over their mouths and noses, waiting for the helicopters.

The first Mi-17 thumped down out of the sky, its rotors kicking up wild, surrealistic whorls of black smoke as it descended. It wobbled alarmingly, drifting first to one side, then another, and Flanagan suddenly realized that the pilot was having a hard time seeing through the smoke.

Flanagan started to worry as the helicopter dipped lower. The pilot was clearly at the ragged edge of flying blind, and he was wavering at the edge of the helipad. If he tried to set down, he was going to put one set of landing gear over the edge, and quite possibly send the bird over into the water.

But the pilot must have figured that out, because he added power and pulled up, away from the platform, swinging the helicopter's tail around to try to get a better view. Smoke swirled, and the rotor wash thumped at the pad, blasting the crouched mercenaries and Mexican Marines with soot and heat.

Flanagan looked around. One of the Mexican Marines was bent over Brannigan, alongside Tanaka, who seemed to be checking the bandages and tourniquet after having moved him. Brannigan was trying to say something, but it was just too loud, between the helicopter and the roar of the growing conflagration below, for Flanagan to tell what he was saying. At least the Colonel was still alive.

The rest of the Blackhearts were there; Santelli, Hart, and Curtis had made it up intact. Flanagan felt a flash of relief at seeing Curtis there. He hadn't been sure how close the others had been when that west derrick had gone up. But his friend seemed to be none the worse for wear, though his eyes were clearly bloodshot, and he was hacking up a lung from the smoke.

There was no sign of Aziz' body. They had simply had to move too fast to retrieve it. The man's final resting place would be on the bottom of the Gulf of Mexico.

The helo pilot crept toward the pad again, keeping his nose high, peering through the cockpit windows and trying to get a feel for where he was. The rotor wash beat at the swirling whorls of smoke, but couldn't quite disperse any of it.

Finally, the wheels touched down. The pilot didn't alter the pitch of the rotors; he was clearly ready to lift as soon as possible. It meant that the rotor wash never died down, but kept hammering at the men crouched next to the pad, threatening to beat them back and possibly knock one of them over the side. But Huerta struggled to his feet, waving at the Blackhearts to come with him. Childress and Tanaka got Brannigan up, each man getting under one of the Colonel's armpits, and started hauling him toward the bird. The rest followed, keeping their weapons up and watching the Mexican Marines carefully. It was enough of a nightmare sitting on a burning oil platform; Flanagan could only imagine what was going through those men's heads, watching their commander and a bunch of gringos getting off ahead of them.

Clearly, this Huerta cat didn't follow the Brannigan school of combat leadership. Brannigan would have been the last one to step on the bird.

Of course, since they weren't in the Mexican Marines' chain of command, Flanagan didn't have any problem letting the Marines catch the next bird.

He hauled himself up into the big helicopter's troop compartment, turning to grab Wade's extended hand and drag him up inside as well. The rotor blast was brutal, and he felt like he'd been sandblasted, just by the sheer force of the wind alone. On top of the salt, the bruising, and the first degree burns he'd already endured, he just *hurt*.

The pilot was already pulling pitch as he got Wade all the way aboard. Flanagan looked around in a moment of near-panic; he hadn't seen if everyone else was on the bird yet. It wasn't his responsibility, technically, and he saw Hancock already counting heads, but as the helicopter rose away from the helideck, he couldn't see any more on the pad.

Hancock saw him looking, made eye contact, and nodded. Flanagan just nodded back; they wouldn't be able to say anything intelligible over the scream of the Mi-17's engines. But they were all on.

As the helicopter pulled away from the stricken oil platform, clearing the billowing cloud of black smoke, Flanagan looked back through streaming eyes. Another explosion rocked the platform, somewhere back by the derricks. The derricks were probably tearing themselves apart, and it was entirely possible that the wells themselves were on fire by then.

The enemy had not only slaughtered their hostages, they'd triggered another disaster along the same lines as the *Deepwater Horizon*. That fire was going to burn for a long, long time, and the oil spill was going to be huge.

Flanagan didn't care all that much about the destruction itself. Disasters happened, they were eventually cleaned up, and life went on. He had no illusions that it was the end of the world. The dead hostages, however, were something he cared about. They hadn't killed enough of the bad guys to make up for that.

He held his peace, though, holding onto a strap next to the troop door, as the helicopter banked away from the roaring conflagration and toward the low, gray shape of a frigate presently cruising toward the Tourmaline-Delta platform's funeral pyre. Another Mi-17 was dropping down into the pall of smoke, heading for the helideck to get more of the Mexican Marines off.

He looked down at the water. Somewhere down there, their enemies were still lurking, making their getaway.

I sure hope this hunt ain't over.

***

The ARM *Hermenegildo Galeana* wasn't an assault ship, or even a destroyer. There wasn't even enough room on the aft deck for the Mi-17 to touch down. Instead, the pilot, in a rather impressive display of finesse at the controls, brought the bird to a hover a couple of feet above the deck, the nose and tail both hanging off on either side of the ship.

Huerta led the way off the bird, dropping down to the deck with the help of a couple of the Mexican Navy ratings who were waiting for them, along with several of the *Hermengildo Galeana*'s small complement of Naval Infantry. He waved at Hancock to follow him, and he did, first giving instructions to Tanaka and Childress to help the wounded Brannigan get down. Brannigan was doing some moving under his own power; the pressure dressing was keeping the bleeding under control, while giving him some use of the leg.

It took a minute to get down, while the helicopter hovered and swayed, the deck rising and falling beneath it with the waves. Getting Brannigan down was a production; he stepped off just as a trough dropped the ship beneath the helicopter, and a gust of cross-wind made the helicopter side-slip a couple of feet. As a result, he dropped like a rock, and Childress was barely able to catch him, collapsing under the bigger man's weight with a crash.

Huerta was shouting orders over the noise, and a pair of Mexican sailors with medical insignia on their uniforms and aid bags over their shoulders were hurrying to Brannigan's side, even as Brannigan rolled himself off of Childress.

Hancock was about to object, but Huerta grabbed him by the upper arm and yelled into his ear, "He will have better care in the *Hermengildo Galeana*'s sickbay than out here on the deck.

One of your men can stay with him. Now, we need to talk." He jerked his head toward the frigate's superstructure and led the way.

Hancock watched him with narrowed eyes for a moment, then looked back at Brannigan. The Colonel met his gaze, and nodded fractionally. Brannigan was out of the fight for the moment, but Hancock still wanted his okay.

Turning, he followed Huerta into the frigate's superstructure.

***

Huerta clearly knew the ship well enough; he moved quickly through the narrow passageways and hatches, dodging sailors and ducking under pipes, making his way quickly toward the wardroom.

The frigate's wardroom was not large. Hancock had seen smaller, but there was just enough room around the table for one man to walk behind the chairs. The bulkheads were half-paneled with light wood, the rest painted white.

Huerta moved to the end of the table and leaned on the back of a chair. "The *Capitàn* is on his way here," he said. "But you and I need to speak, first."

"You have us at something of a disadvantage, Admiral," Hancock pointed out. He was standing across the table from Huerta, his rifle slung in front of him, one hand on the buttstock.

"As do you," Huerta pointed out. "You are still armed, and I am quite sure that, should I order your arrest, at least one of you will probably fight."

Not just one of us, buddy.

"You also know that I hired you," Huerta continued, lowering his voice. "I could try to have you all killed—it has been done before—but that has its own problems. And if you go before a Mexican judge, you can ruin me."

Which was also true. If he was being honest, Hancock hadn't even quite thought of that. He hadn't quite shifted gears from combat to legalities.

"Here is what I want to discuss," Huerta said, in the same tone. "I lost nearly a squad of Naval Infantrymen when that bomb exploded. Time is pressing; I am sure that the *Hermenegildo Galeana* can track the enemy's submarine, but we have limited assets that I can call upon. I will make a deal with you; help me to hunt these men down, and I guarantee that I will get you out of Mexico and back to the *Estados Unidos* quietly and without incident."

Hancock eyed him for a moment. "I hope that guarantee is worth more than your family company's logistical support, Admiral," he said.

Huerta stiffened. "That was not my fault," he said, "and I promise you that it will not happen again."

Hancock thought about it, uncomfortable that he was having to make this call himself, on the fly. At the very least, he wanted to consult with Brannigan before committing the team to *another* mission, especially after how badly the platform boarding had gone.

"I'm going to have to talk to the rest of the boys," he temporized. "We're contractors, not soldiers. They're going to have to agree."

Huerta looked impatient. "There isn't time," he insisted. "*El Capitàn* will be here any moment, and if he suspects that you are anything but a team of American Special Forces commandos, operating under a silent agreement between Washington and Mexico City, then we are dead. A commando leader would not consult with his men before taking on a mission."

"But he *would* have to consult with his higher headquarters," Hancock pointed out. "Even SOF has oversight. Tell him that that's what I'm doing."

Huerta was starting to look angry, but a rap on the hatch behind Hancock interrupted them. "*Entrar*," Huerta called. The hatch swung open, and the *Hermenegildo Galeana*'s captain stepped inside. He was a small, balding man, with a blatant comb-over. He looked like a clerk.

Huerta fired questions at the captain, as the little man closed the hatch behind him. The frigate's commander responded in a soft voice.

"He says that they have had intermittent sonar contact with what he believes is the submarine," Huerta told Hancock. "It is very quiet, but they have been using the frigate's active sonar to maintain contact. If he is not mistaken, the submarine is currently ten nautical miles ahead, moving to the southeast, into the deeper waters of the Gulf of Mexico."

Hancock nodded, watching Huerta even as he was all too aware of the Mexican captain's eyes on him. "I'll have an answer for you within the next few minutes, Admiral," he said.

It was clearly not the response that Huerta had been hoping for. But he simply inclined his head in agreement, and motioned toward the hatch.

Feeling both Mexican officers' eyes on his back, Hancock headed back toward the stern.

***

"I'm all for it," Santelli said. "But the price is gonna have to go up."

"I'm not sure it's such a good idea," Wade suggested. Jenkins nodded in agreement, apparently forgetting his earlier clash with Wade over the tattoos. "We're *way* out in the cold here, and we've already lost two. Are they gonna rearm us, or would we be going in with just what we've got? And what's to stop them from arresting us as soon as the bad guys are dealt with?"

Hancock glanced over his shoulder. None of the Mexican Marines or sailors appeared to be within earshot. "If he tries it, Huerta knows that his head is on the chopping block right next to ours," he said. "He doesn't want to stir that pot."

"And we should just trust his word on that?" Childress asked. "Look what happened with his family business."

"What's the Colonel have to say?" Flanagan asked quietly. He hadn't said a word so far, but only listened. Him and Gomez, both.

"He said it's our call," Hancock admitted. "He's out of the fight for the moment, so he won't say 'yes' or 'no.' We're independent contractors, so he told me that we've got to figure it out."

"I'm not comfortable going in there without the Colonel," Curtis said. He was unusually solemn. It could be that being on a potentially hostile ship and steaming away from the US had put a damper on his usual high spirits. Or maybe being nearly blown sky-high by a detonating oil rig, which was still putting up a towering column of black smoke on the horizon behind them, had done it.

"Those bastards murdered the people we went in to rescue," Santelli said bluntly. "I want my pound of flesh."

"Let's face it, gents," Flanagan said, "we don't actually have that much choice in the matter."

"What do you mean?" Childress asked, frowning.

"Simple," Flanagan said. "We're technically illegal combatants, aboard a Mexican warship. Huerta might not try to arrest us, or even have us murdered, but if we don't help him out, he's under no particular obligation to help us get home, either. He could just drop us in some port in the middle of Mexico, gear and all, and say, 'Good luck!' Then we'd be just as screwed as if he'd decided to throw us into a deep, dark hole somewhere."

None of the rest of them spoke, thinking over what he'd said. A few nodded. Hancock blew out a sigh.

"Fine," he said. "I'll go tell him we're in."

CHAPTER 20

The sun went down over the Gulf of Mexico, disappearing into the waters to the west, as the ARM *Hermenegildo Galeana* left the Mexican coast behind. The Blackhearts had found a place to settle in just forward of the aft quarterdeck, most of them sitting against the bulkheads, trying to stay out of the Mexican sailors' way.

Two of the Mexican Marines were stationed at the hatch leading toward the bridge and the rest of the ship. They held their P90s across their bodies, watching the Blackhearts.

Most of the mercenaries were zonked out. It had been a long, brutal day, and Bianco, Jenkins, Curtis, and Childress were all asleep, sprawled in various uncomfortable and contorted positions on the deck. Curtis' head was back against the bulkhead, his mouth open, snoring. Childress was bent forward, his chin on his chest, and looked like he was going to fall over any second.

Wade was sitting up, watching the Mexican Marines, his pale eyes almost unblinking.

"I don't think a staring contest is going to accomplish much, John," Flanagan said quietly. He was leaning back against the bulkhead in a corner, his rifle across his knees. He was placed so that he could casually watch the Marines without looking like he was ready to get in a fight, like Wade was.

"They want our fucking help, but they're gonna watch us like detainees?" Wade countered without turning his basilisk stare away from the two masked Naval Infantrymen. "I'm telling you, I think we're being set up."

"Could be," Santelli said. He was flat on his back, his own M6 leaning against the bulkhead next to him, his eyes on the overhead. "It sure would be simple to wrap things up in a neat little bow, lay the whole thing on us."

"Except that we'd be too likely to talk, point out who hired us in the first place," Hancock said. "We've been over this. Huerta doesn't want that."

"Who says he'd let it go to trial?" Wade countered. "We're on a damned ship in the middle of the Gulf, a ship where he's the ranking officer. We could just disappear, and he'd tell his men what to say happened afterward. They'd probably believe it, too. They don't know us."

"And I'm sure he's considered it," Hancock said. "In fact, I'm ninety-nine percent certain that he's been real, *real* tempted. But I talked to him. I don't think he's going to."

Wade finally turned his eyes away from the Mexican Marines. "What makes you so sure?" he asked.

Hancock just shrugged. "Gut call," was all he said.

Wade didn't look impressed, but then he thought for a moment and shrugged back. "I guess I can't really talk shit," he said. "I've done some objectively stupid shit that worked out, based on gut calls."

"We don't really have an option besides rolling with the punches anyway," Santelli said. "We're stuck on a ship, outnumbered and outgunned. Maybe Huerta will try having us killed. Maybe he'll be true to his word. Ain't shit we can do about it right now."

Conversation subsided. Wade went back to mean-mugging the Mexican Marines. Flanagan put his head back against the steel of the bulkhead, his eyes hooded, watching while he rested.

Outside, night descended on the Gulf of Mexico as they cruised southeast, the *Hermenegildo Galeana*'s wake almost luminous in the dark.

***

Huerta's eyes stung with fatigue, but he couldn't sleep. He wouldn't sleep. Not until he had exacted vengeance on the terrorists who had almost slipped through his fingers. Instead, he lurked around the *Hermengildo Galeana*'s bridge, a constant, brooding presence that had the sailors and watchstanders looking over their shoulders constantly.

He was rotating between the plotting table and the ASW station, where a rating was monitoring the AN/SQS-26 bow-mounted sonar. The display was a waterfall of multi-colored noise, indecipherable to Huerta, who had come up through the Naval Infantry. But it meant something to the rating, who was staring intently at it, his head buried in his headphones.

It was entirely likely that some of the sailor's intense concentration was an effort to ignore the looming presence of his superior officer looking over his shoulder. He was doing a good job of feigning absolute focus, if that was the case.

The presence of the gringo mercenaries on the aft deck was nagging at Huerta almost as much as the hunt for the terrorist submarine. *They will be the death of you, Diego.* But as much as he knew that he should simply dispose of them, hoping that none of the sailors or Marines said anything about it, he could not bring himself to do so. He knew at least one of them had been killed, and their commander severely wounded. They'd incurred those losses and wounds doing what he'd been otherwise unable to do.

You cannot afford to be soft. They are mercenaries, they knew what they were getting into in the first place.

Your honor is all you have, Diego. He could have sworn he still heard his mother saying that.

The rating pointed at a bright red point in the waterfall of the sonar display. "There, *Contralmirante*," he said. "That has to be the target."

"Are you sure?" he asked.

The rating hesitated. Admitting that he was guessing to a *Contralmirante*, especially under such circumstances, was rarely a good idea.

"It isn't sea floor noise," he said hesitantly, "and it is moving, along the same line that the submarine was the last time we had contact with it."

"But we've lost contact four times in as many hours," Huerta pointed out.

"Which is why we switched to the active sonar, *Señor*," the captain said, appearing at Huerta's elbow. "The submarine is simply too quiet to track using only the passive sonar." He nodded at the display. "It is not quite on the same track, though. It's turned due east, which has opened up the distance between us. It will take several hours to close that distance."

"Close in as fast as you can," Huerta said. "As much as I wish to kill these men in person, sinking the submarine will accomplish the same thing."

***

But it didn't turn out to be that simple. The submarine captain had heard the *Hermenegildo Galeana*'s sonar pings, and had taken steps to evade. Since they were well out into the Gulf, where the sea bottom was more than twelve thousand feet deep—well below crush depth for any operational sub—simply heading for the bottom wasn't an option. But after a couple more hours, the sonar couldn't pick the submarine out anymore.

"They may have gone below the thermocline," the sonar operator said. "The different density of the colder water is like a wall to sonar."

"Start a search pattern," Huerta demanded. "Find that submarine."

***

Brannigan opened his eyes blearily. He'd been drifting in and out for a while. He didn't think that was a good sign, with his head wound, but the Mexican orderly hadn't seemed too concerned. Of course, the man also hadn't seemed too solicitous of Brannigan's life at all, so he didn't think that was a good measuring stick to go by concerning the severity of his wounds.

He turned his aching head, and made out Hart, leaning against the wall, still armed to the teeth, his shoulder looking slightly misshapen from the pressure bandage around it. Looking around, he saw that he had been stripped of his gear, but it was piled next to the bed, with his FN-45 pistol sitting on the bed next to his hand. That had to be his boys' doing; he was sure the orderly never would have gone for it without some pressure.

"Where are we?" he croaked.

Hart looked over at him. "Somewhere in the Gulf, Colonel," he answered. "Couldn't tell you more than that. This Admiral Huerta guy is dead-set on catching the bad guys who got off the platform, and Hancock's decided we're going to help him."

Brannigan nodded slowly, the pain almost bringing tears to his eyes. He didn't know the whole situation, of course, but he suspected that he knew Hancock's reasons for going along with Huerta's vendetta. He couldn't say that he disagreed, though the circumstances were rather less than ideal.

"We lose anyone else on the way off?" he asked. He didn't think they had, but he'd been a little foggy since getting smacked in the side of the head with a bullet.

"No," Hart replied. "We couldn't get Aziz' body off, though. It went up with the platform."

Brannigan closed his eyes as he nodded fractionally. The fire and explosions were little more than snapshot impressions in his memory.

Damn, I must have gotten hit harder than I thought. I've definitely got a concussion.

241

"Can you go get Roger or Carlo?" he asked.

"Sorry, Colonel," Hart answered. "Hancock doesn't want you left alone. I don't think he entirely trusts our hosts."

I wouldn't, either.

"Well, if he comes up while I'm out of it again," Brannigan said, "wake me up." *We've got to figure out our exit plan.* He wasn't going to trust Huerta any more than Hancock apparently did, and while he might be out of action, the Blackhearts were still his boys, and he'd be damned if he left their fate to the whims of a Mexican military officer.

Hart just nodded, watching Brannigan for a moment before turning back to the door.

Brannigan felt himself start to drift again.

***

The night passed slowly, as the *Hermenegildo Galeana* cut back and forth, lashing the water with her bow sonar, searching for the mysterious submarine. Three times she picked up the sub's trail, only to lose it again. The sub's skipper was being canny, but he could only go so fast underwater without making enough noise to give his position away.

Huerta was up on the weather deck, smoking a cigarette. He'd lost track of exactly what time it was, but the eastern horizon was starting to lighten.

"*Contralmirante!*" the watch officer shouted from below.

Huerta didn't bother to respond; he just flung the lit cigarette out to sea and pounded down the ladderwell.

"We think they have surfaced, *Contralmirante*," the captain said. "We got a sonar hit near a radar contact, about twenty kilometers away."

"Show me," Huerta demanded.

The captain pointed to the plot, which was crisscrossed with paths of freighters, tankers, cruise liners, fishing boats, and yachts. There was still a lot of sea traffic in the Gulf of Mexico, despite the wars raging on the mainland.

The mark for the possible surfaced submarine was next to another track, that of a large yacht named the *Carla Espinoza*.

"They are making rendezvous," Huerta said. He didn't know that for certain, but it seemed like the most likely course of action. Why else would the submarine surface out there? If it was a diesel sub, it still wouldn't need to surface to run its engines; all modern diesels had snorkels. It had to be meeting the *Carla Espinoza* for some reason.

"Full speed ahead," he ordered. "Close in on that submarine." He turned to leave the bridge. "Let me know when we are within visual range."

He had to get the assaulters ready. All of them.

He left the bridge and headed below, to where *Teniente* Medina's Marines had set up, not far from the aft compartment where the gringo mercenaries were waiting. He stuck his head in the hatch, managing not to recoil from the stench of sweat, saltwater, and smoke. He'd smelled far worse.

"*Teniente* Medina!" he called. The hard-eyed young officer stood and came to the hatch. "We are nearing the enemy submarine," he explained. "They appear to be boarding a yacht. We are going to board that yacht, secure it, and seize the rest of the terrorists."

Medina nodded, his eyes already calculating what they would need to do to prepare.

"And *Teniente*?" Huerta continued quietly. "I have some special instructions for you, concerning the gringo contractors we brought aboard…"

***

Flint climbed up on top of the Kilo's sail and squinted against the morning light. He'd been below all night, and the sunlight stung a bit.

The *Carla Espinoza* was registered as a luxury yacht, but that didn't quite explain just what she was. She looked like a yacht from the outside, but that was where the similarities ended. She wasn't quite as fast as a hydrofoil, but she was faster than just about any other vessel of her size. Most of her interior had also been torn out to carry more cocaine, heroin, and methamphetamine. She'd smuggled a *lot* of drugs into Florida and Louisiana over the years.

Narcotics smuggling was still a large part of the *Carla Espinoza*'s business. But Flint's employers had enough money to hire her to do some other stuff on the side. Like picking up Flint and the rest of his team. The more stops and drops they made, the less likely their pursuers could find them.

And they were being pursued. The sub's captain had assured him of that. That damned Mexican frigate had been hounding their steps, rattling the sub's hull with ear-piercing sonar pings for hours.

He paused at the top of the sail, looking behind them. The smoke of the Tourmaline-Delta platform's funeral pyre was long gone, below the horizon. But the horizon itself wasn't as empty as he'd hoped it would be.

He squinted, trying to force his eyes to see better. He couldn't be absolutely sure, but that looked like a warship behind them. It wasn't much more than a ship-shaped speck on the horizon, barely visible in the morning light, but it was tall, and it was coming straight at them.

"Hurry the fuck up," he snarled at Scrap. "That piece of shit sub captain didn't manage to lose the hounds, after all." *I ought to go put a bullet in that shitstain's brain and leave the sub for the Mexicans to capture.*

Less than half the crew was left. Whoever those shooters had been who'd managed to get aboard the platform, they'd been good. Really good.

Not good enough, though. I still won, fucksticks. Now they just had to break contact and get away.

He'd been hoping that they'd surface far enough away that the Mexicans couldn't spot them. That hadn't worked out. And only the fact that they were pressed for time kept him climbing down the ladder on the side of the sail, to the gangplank that had been placed between the sub and the *Carla Espinoza*, instead of indulging his violent streak on the sub's crew.

He had to slow down on the gangplank. The sub was rolling a bit on the surface chop, and the *Carla Espinoza* wasn't exactly standing still, either. The gangplank twisted, flexed, and rose and fell. But he got up onto the yacht without going in the water, and then waited impatiently as the rest of the crew followed.

Once they were all aboard, he stepped back as one of the *Carla Espinoza*'s crew pulled in the gangplank. He looked across the gap at the sub's captain, who was standing atop the sail, and muttered, "Thanks for nothing, shithead."

The gangplank stowed, the *Carla Espinoza* turned toward the coast to the south and opened the throttle, racing away from the sub that was still wallowing on the surface.

***

"Roger?" Tanaka ventured. It felt weird to him, broaching this subject. He'd always thought of the special operations guys as some kind of demigods, even though a lot of his fellow infantrymen had resented the "operators." On top of that, he'd always been good about following orders, without bitching or complaining. This felt an awful lot like he was pushing that boundary.

"What is it, Alex?" Hancock asked, a little distractedly. They'd managed to get a little 5.56 NATO ammo from the Mexicans, and were topping off what magazines they had. It seemed like a good sign; if the Mexicans were going to double cross them the way Wade was sure they were going to, why would they give them more ammo?

"I need to go ashore," Tanaka said, blurting the words out as fast as he could. "I know that somebody's got to stay with the Colonel, but I did it last time. I need to go in with the rest of the team."

Hancock stopped jamming his magazine and looked up at Tanaka with a faint squint. For a second, he just studied him carefully, and Tanaka had to fight to maintain eye contact with the older man.

"You know that I wasn't bullshitting when I said it wasn't on you, right?" Hancock said.

"I know that," Tanaka replied, not sure if he wasn't bullshitting both of them at that moment. "But if I stay back this time, it might start to look like a trend, you know? Like I'm not really a part of the team." He took a deep breath. "Look, I know I wasn't a SEAL cool guy like Jenkins, or a Ranger like Wade…"

"Hold up right there," Hancock said. "This has nothing to do with your background."

"Yeah, it kinda does," Tanaka replied. "I was a regular 11-Bang-Bang. You guys got all the training, all the ammo allotments, and all the missions. At least, it seemed that way. I've got to get out there, or I'm always going to be the security bitch, because it's gonna start riding around in everybody's head that I'm not good enough in the field."

Hancock sighed, straightening to face Tanaka a little more fully. "You know that's bullshit, right?" he said. "This is a small team. You proved yourself in Burma, and nobody around here is going to knock you for it."

"Then let me go ashore," Tanaka said. "Don't stick me on bodyguard duty."

"Bodyguard duty could end up being even more dangerous, if the Mexicans decide to make us disappear," Hancock pointed out.

"And you're proving that I'm not worrying about bullshit by arguing in favor of me staying back," Tanaka said. "If I'm really just as good as the rest of you, why are you trying to convince me to stay back?"

Hancock shook his head with another sigh. "All right, fine," he said. "You're on the shore team. Don's up there right now; he can stay with the Colonel." He looked at Tanaka. "Since you're so insistent, you can go up and tell Don he's staying back." When Tanaka started to look a little uncertain, he snapped, "For fuck's sake, Alex! Just go tell him! We're not going to leave you behind in the next five minutes! We're nowhere near the coast yet!"

Tanaka ducked his head in a fast, rueful nod, and turned to head down to sickbay.

***

The *Carla Espinoza* kept her distance from the *Hermenegildo Galeana* for most of the rest of the day. A stern chase is a long chase, and while the frigate might have greater endurance, unless she could close the distance, the pursuit was just going to go on and on.

Just before sundown, the speedy yacht turned in toward shore. She had passed by the border of Yucatan State, and was nearing the tip of the peninsula. If she was heading to Cancùn, she could lose herself in the tourist traffic.

But instead of rounding the peninsula, the yacht turned into the bay just short of the small coastal town of Holbox. There was no way out of that bay, but there was a lot of jungle inland.

The ARM *Hermenildo Galeana* pursued. And on her aft deck, the Blackhearts and Mexican Marines prepared to go ashore.

CHAPTER 21

The frigate couldn't get too far into the bay; the water got too shallow, too quickly. Not being set up as an assault ship, she didn't have the boats to get the entire ground complement ashore in one trip, so the Mexican Marines launched with the first pair, and motored in to secure the Chiquilà pier. The *Carla Espinoza* was conspicuously tied up at that same pier. Then the boats returned to the *Hermenegildo Galeana* to pick up another team.

The Marines approached the docked yacht cautiously. There hadn't been a lot of activity in Chiquilà, but the Yucatan Peninsula was *Los Zetas* territory, for the most part. There was no love lost between the *Zetas* and the Marines.

Hancock hugged the gunwale of the rubber boat as it motored toward the pier, watching the tiny figures of the Mexican Marines surrounding the yacht and preparing to make entry. Part of him was tensed up, waiting for something to explode as soon as the first camouflage-clad figure went over the gangplank and disappeared into the boat. It seemed to be the terrorists' style.

But nothing happened. The yacht didn't explode. And even as the boats came alongside the pier, one of the Marines came out of the yacht and waved the all-clear. The yacht was empty.

Hancock figured they should have expected that. The terrorists had to know that they were still in pursuit. The *Hermenegildo Galeana* wasn't exactly a low-profile ship.

The Mexican coxswain drew the boat against the side of the pier, angling the outboard to hold it in place, and Hancock hauled himself up onto the concrete. His rifle scraped against the pier as he climbed, but he was too tired to care at that point. The optics were still good, and they'd all cleaned and lubed the hell out of the guns while they were aboard the frigate.

Huerta was with them, though he waited until the rest of the Blackhearts and Marines were on the pier before climbing up after them. He was in his kit, though he wasn't carrying a P90 like the other Marines; he had stuck with his holstered HK USP. To Hancock that spoke volumes about the man, though he had to admit that the number of American flag officers who would have done differently was vanishingly small. Hell, just the fact that Huerta was on the ground for this hunt was to his credit.

They moved down the pier to join the Marines at the *Carla Espinoza*. The one who had waved was waiting for them; the rest were facing Chiquilà itself.

The marina was lined with palm trees, most of the cement of the structures painted white. Cars lined the parking lot, and there were people lounging on the beach, watching the Marines curiously. Some were hastily moving away, having apparently put two and two together. When a bunch of armed men get off a yacht, followed by a unit of Mexican Marines, backed up by a frigate out in the bay, it's probably a good time to get inside and stay low.

The Mexican Marine spoke rapidly in Spanish to the Marine lieutenant, named Medina. Gomez was next to Hancock, listening.

"He says the boat is completely empty," Gomez translated quietly. "No sign of where they might have gone. The lieutenant is talking about questioning the locals."

Hancock looked around. Most of the locals in sight looked more like tourists, there to lie on the beach and tour the Mayan ruins inland. The gringos especially probably couldn't tell them much. But he knew that the Mexican Marines weren't going to want to hear it.

The Marines led the way down the pier, and the Blackhearts followed, their weapons at the ready.

Hancock glanced over at Gomez. The other man was silent and watchful, as was Flanagan, on the other side. He could hear Curtis muttering behind him; the short, stocky man wasn't loud enough to be overheard, but he didn't sound happy.

Hancock found he couldn't really blame him. The Marines didn't seem to want them there. There hadn't even been an attempt to fill them in about what they were doing. As of that moment, the Blackhearts were tagging along for the ride.

They came off the pier and into a plaza. The road around the manicured traffic circle, which bore shiny brass letters that spelled out, "Bienvenido Chiquilà," was cobblestone. Chiquilà wasn't a new town.

There were a few faces in the nearby windows, watching them, but they vanished as soon as a Marine or a mercenary looked at them. The street was suddenly and conspicuously empty.

"You think these people are siding with the bad guys?" Tanaka asked.

"Nah," Curtis replied. "It's Mexico, dude. They just know better than to hang out in the street when guys with guns show up."

Huerta stepped forward, calling out to Medina. The two men consulted briefly, as the Marines spread out around the traffic circle, their weapons at the ready, watching doors, windows, and alleyways.

Hancock and the Blackhearts hadn't waited; they were already inside the traffic circle itself, up against the stone planter circle in the center. It wasn't ideal as far as cover went, but Hancock figured that if all hell broke loose, they could pile inside. It was better than nothing.

Besides, the Mexican Marines out on the outer perimeter were probably going to buy them a few seconds, anyway.

"*Señor* Hancock," Huerta called. When Hancock looked over at him, the Mexican Admiral waved him over.

251

Four of the Marines were pushing inside a palm-roofed café, the walls covered in red and white stucco with a big "Coca-Cola" sign painted on the wall inside the shaded veranda. A few moments later, they came out, dragging an older man with them. The guy looked like he was about ninety; his dark face was deeply lined, and he had the characteristic Mayan nose.

Medina snapped a series of questions at him. The man shook his head, speaking rapidly in Spanish. Hancock was only picking out one or two words in a dozen, but he was gathering that the old man was insisting that he hadn't seen anything.

One of the Marines hit the old man in the back of the head. He staggered and almost fell; he would have face-planted on the cobblestones if two Marines hadn't been holding him roughly by the arms. Huerta held out a hand and said something sharply in Spanish that made the Marine draw back, looking a little ashamed.

Huerta stepped forward and faced the man, looking into his eyes, and spoke flatly and levelly. At first, the old man wouldn't meet the *Contralmirante*'s eyes, but at a snapped command, he looked up at him. Huerta repeated his question. The old man shook his head mutely.

He doesn't want to risk getting involved. Hancock had seen it a thousand times, across the Middle East and Central Asia. When the "good guys" could be as ruthless and destructive as the "bad guys," getting stuck in the middle was often a death sentence for the little guy. Tribal affiliation, ethnic groups, sectarian rivalries; it all boiled down to the same thing. If the old man had seen something and told the Marines, he might be murdered by the *Zetas* for talking to them, if he wasn't killed by the terrorists or their allies for ratting them out. If he didn't talk, he could end up vanishing into a dark, concrete room somewhere to have electrodes put on his testicles. It was a lose-lose situation for an old man.

Huerta repeated his question, with an addition that Hancock was pretty sure was a threat. The old man shook his head again, but less firmly this time. Hancock could see the hands on his upper arms tightening.

Huerta straightened up and took a step back. That had to be a bad sign for the old man. Hancock was starting to wonder if he should interfere. He wasn't in a good position to do so; he was outnumbered, outgunned, and hardly on the best footing to make moral pronouncements to a Mexican flag officer about the treatment of prisoners.

But he couldn't stand by and watch them torture an old man. He'd stood by for worse when he'd been part of a chain of command, rather than *being* the chain of command. *And how did that work out?*

Never particularly well.

But the old man hung his head, almost dangling from the hands of the Mexican Marines, and spoke softly, pointing to the south, inland.

Huerta asked another sharp question. The old man shrugged, or tried to. Huerta repeated the question by way of reply. Finally, the old man spoke again, though he sounded hesitant, like he wasn't sure of what he was saying, but knew that he had to give the *Contralmirante* something.

The *Contralmirante* patted the old man on the shoulder and jerked his head at the Marines holding him. They let the old man go, and he slumped, almost falling over in the street. Huerta barked orders at his men, then turned to Hancock. "He says that they went south," he said, unnecessarily. Hancock had gotten that part. "He also says that there is a farm about six kilometers from here, where there has been a lot of traffic and construction lately. He thinks they might be going there."

"Makes sense," Hancock replied. Huerta didn't look happy; he probably didn't think he needed a mercenary's input. Hancock didn't care. "I doubt they would have come here if they didn't have a contingency plan set up for this place to begin with. They've been pretty thoroughly prepared so far."

"We will acquire local transport and pursue," Huerta continued, as if Hancock hadn't spoken. He looked past Hancock's shoulder, and when Roger turned to follow his gaze, he saw pairs of Marines jogging toward the marina parking lot. There were going to be some tourists and locals without their rides pretty soon. "You and your men will ride in the back vehicles. I want to keep you in reserve, in case we need support when we attack the farm."

Meaning you want us to have as little to do with this operation as possible. You want to have us around, in case you need our firepower, but you don't have to like it. He was becoming increasingly convinced that Huerta was deeply conflicted about the handling of this entire operation, and it was making the hackles go up on Hancock's neck. It didn't bode well for the Blackhearts' immediate future.

But as Santelli had pointed out, they only had so many options. So long as they stayed on Huerta's good side, they still had time. They just had to keep their eyes open.

And if they got to help kill the terrorists who'd murdered all those hostages and blown up the Tourmaline-Delta platform, so much the better. As long as they got paid, they'd all be fine with letting the Mexicans take the credit.

Hancock just nodded his agreement. He wasn't interested in getting into a debate with Huerta about it; that would only hurt their chances of getting away once the smoke cleared. Huerta waved a dismissal. Hancock bit back his reflexive anger at the gesture; he wasn't one of Huerta's underlings. But then, he reminded himself, they *were* working for the man, for the moment.

He jogged back to the circle, where Santelli had the rest of the team. "We're carjacking and going inland," he said quickly. "Word is, the bad guys went south; we've got a possible target at a farm, that the old man says has seen a lot of activity in the last few weeks."

"How sure are we that that's the target?" Wade asked.

"No idea," Hancock replied. "Could be our guys, could be *Los Zetas*. We won't know until we get there."

Wade nodded, still without taking his eyes off his sector of the perimeter. Something about his attitude made Hancock follow his gaze. His eyes narrowed.

Wade wasn't watching the town. He was watching the Mexican Marines. Several specific Mexican Marines, for that matter. They weren't watching the town, either.

They were watching the Blackhearts.

Wade seemed to have sensed that Hancock had seen the same thing he had. He glanced over at him. Hancock shrugged. "If we had foreign contractors with us when we were in the mil, we'd probably have minders on 'em, too," he pointed out quietly.

Which doesn't mean I'm comfortable with them. The Mexican Marines might have a good track record for resisting corruption by the cartels, but that doesn't make 'em our friends. And I know a bit about their track record otherwise, too.

He saw the same thought mirrored in Wade's eyes, as the man simply raised his eyebrows briefly before turning his icy stare back on their escort.

Behind them, in the parking lot, they started to hear breaking glass, the occasional car alarm, and shouts as several of Huerta's Marines started "acquiring" local transportation. The Blackhearts, not having been invited to help, kept their hands on their rifles and their eyes outboard.

***

The Blackhearts ended up in two trucks, blue and white, both older, mid-'90s Ford F150s. The Mexican Marines were driving, with Hancock in one cab, Santelli in the other. The Marines had wanted to just put all the mercs in the beds, but Hancock and Santelli had been adamant that that wasn't going to happen. When the lieutenant, Medina, had tried insisting, through Gomez, Huerta had seen them getting heated and come over to intervene. He'd shut Medina down, and Hancock and Santelli were up front.

"I always hated these trucks," Childress said, sitting in the bed of the blue truck as they waited for the rest of the vehicle column to start down the main road through Chiquilà. "This body style always looked like a half-melted plastic toy to me."

"How old were you when these were all over the roads, Sam?" Wade asked. "Five?"

"I was ten when the new body style came out in '97," Childress said. He felt like he should be annoyed, but he'd gotten mistaken for a much younger man for years. He was kind of used to it.

Wade did a bit of a double-take, and looked over at him. "Damn, I thought you were younger than that."

"Clean living, John, clean living," Childress said. Bianco snorted. Wade lifted his eyebrows doubtfully. Tanaka glanced around at the rest of them, but didn't say anything, and quickly turned his eyes back outward.

"Keep your eyes open back there," Santelli said from up front. He'd pulled the rear sliding window open. "Our little buddies might have left a nasty surprise for us on the way out, if they saw us coming after them."

The men subsided, the tension returning. They were surrounded by, if not enemies, definitely not friends. And there was probably a firefight coming up.

Finally, the Blackhearts' vehicles started moving. Huerta had been serious; they were the last two trucks in the stack. The column itself was a motley assortment of pickup trucks and SUVs. Most of them looked nearly brand new; the Marines had been picky when it came to carjacking for the op.

Somehow, Childress doubted that most of the vehicles' owners were ever going to see their trucks again.

He turned his attention to the left side of the truck as they followed the white F150 in front of them. Flanagan, Curtis,

Jenkins and Gomez were set up in the back of that one. He couldn't hear him, but he could see Curtis engaged in an animated, nearly one-way conversation with Jenkins, who didn't look like he could get a word in edgewise. Flanagan and Gomez appeared to be pointedly ignoring him in favor of watching their surroundings, which only seemed to make the smaller man more agitated.

But Childress had gotten to know Curtis well enough that he knew that it was just par for the course. If he couldn't get a rise out of Flanagan, he turned to pestering someone else.

Watch your sector. He was tired; the little bit of sleep he'd gotten aboard the frigate didn't seem like it had been nearly enough, and the sun was awfully bright without sunglasses. None of them had brought shades; they'd been diving in. It hadn't been practical. But Childress really, really wished he had some as he squinted at the side of the street. A lot of the buildings were whitewashed or painted bright colors, though the paint was peeling. Doors and windows were dark blocks in the bright walls, even under corrugated metal awnings. They were also all barred. Clearly, tourist location or not, the residents of Chiquilà were more than a little concerned about crime.

Gunfire suddenly rattled up ahead, near the head of the column. It sounded like a single burst, but it was definitely an AK on automatic. The Marines returned fire in an instant, their P90s chattering rapidly, the 5.7mms making a lighter crackling noise compared to the AK's heavier, slower action.

Childress perked up a bit, lifting his rifle to his shoulder, watching the shadows to either side of the road over the sights.

Frankly, the place reminded him a lot of the Middle East, just with more trees. The buildings were rough, plastered concrete blocks, often with outbuildings and awnings made of corrugated tin over rough-cut poles. Yards were mostly bare dirt and rocks. The road itself was pocked with potholes, and he wasn't sure how accurate he was going to be if he did have to start shooting while they were moving.

Movement caught his eye as the truck hit a particularly deep pothole with a tooth-rattling jar. For a second, as he bounced against the cab, Childress' heart almost stopped. He thought he'd seen a door swing partway open in a house a few yards back from the road. It had just been wide enough for a shooter to see without exposing himself.

But as he got his focus back after the impact with the pothole, he saw a little kid peering out of the crack for a moment, before a pair of brown hands grabbed him and pulled him back, shutting the door.

He let out a ragged breath. He wasn't sure if one of the Mexican Marines wouldn't have opened fire, from what he'd seen already. The driver sure seemed keyed up, with his own P90 sticking out of the open window beside him.

Childress might have a justified reputation for being a wise-ass and a mouthy son of a bitch. The number of men he absolutely *wouldn't* snap off to if he thought they were in the wrong was a small group, pretty well limited to Santelli and Brannigan, in that order. But there were reasons why those who could see past his bluntness and abrasiveness called him a "good dude." And the fact that accidentally shooting a kid was one of his recurring nightmares was one of those reasons.

The gunfire up ahead had died down, but they stayed alert, trying to watch every door, window, or crack in the often-crumbling concrete walls as they passed. Near the edge of town, he saw where the engagement had happened. There was a low, flat-roofed, white building with a roughly-painted patch of blue on the front, half-hidden by bushes and palm trees, on the right. Childress glanced over as he saw the sun glinting off the brass in the road, and saw the dozens of bullet pockmarks in the plaster around the single window. There was no sign of a shooter, living or dead.

Then they were past, and heading into the hinterlands, the sides of the road getting overgrown with jungle foliage. Whoever the bad guys had left behind to delay pursuit hadn't done a very good job.

CHAPTER 22

"Listen up, shitheads," Flint barked, as he swung out of the pickup's cab, dropping to the dusty concrete floor of the barn. The place was a mess, littered with parts and barrels, all of it covered in a thin layer of oil and dirt. "Time's wasting, and those Mexican Marines are on their way. You know as well as I do that they'll interrogate the shit out of the locals until one of 'em tells 'em which way we went." Not that there were a lot of possibilities; the only major road went south. Everything else was jungle or mangrove swamp.

"Everybody's got their go bags," he continued. "Ditch your cammies, get in civilian clothes, and grab the bikes we've got stashed in the other garage." He glared around at the lot of them. "Nobody pairs up, nobody gets in a pack. You scatter to the winds and come into Cancun or Playa del Carmen individually. It's gonna mean being unarmed, but if you're just a tourist in Mexico, you can't be a hitter. They won't be looking for you."

"What about the *Zetas*?" Gibbet asked.

"What about 'em?" Flint replied. "They don't fuck with tourists, unless it looks like they've got a lot of money for a ransom. Trust me, none of you monkeys looks like the type." He folded his arms impatiently. "Does anyone else have any stupid questions, or can we hit the road before the Mexicans' Goon Squad gets here?"

Flint was generally self-assured to the point of overweening arrogance, but even he knew that, outnumbered as they were, they didn't stand the greatest of chances against the

Mexican Marines. They'd take a lot of the bastards with them, but the Mexican Naval Infantry wasn't known for pussyfooting around.

Fortunately, nobody ventured any more questions or opinions, so he pointed toward the opposite outbuilding, where a dozen beat-up motorcycles of various years and makes were waiting for just this eventuality. "Let's go, then! What the hell are you waiting for?"

Funnyman was almost to the barn doors when there was a flash and a deep, bone-jarring *thud* outside. The entire team stopped in their tracks.

That was the pressure plate out front. Shit! *We're out of time.* "Defensive positions!" he snapped. "Now!"

***

Tanaka saw the sudden black cloud appear ahead, a split second before the shockwave hit the rear vehicles with a tooth-rattling *wham.* The explosion was like a slap in the face; the shock made everyone just sort of freeze for a second.

But then he realized that the two trucks full of Brannigan's Blackhearts weren't moving, while the rest were continuing to advance. "Hey, what the hell?" he asked.

He could hear Gomez rattling off a harsh question at the driver of the front truck. The answer didn't seem to be satisfactory, since Gomez' reply was considerably less than friendly. But the trucks still weren't moving, even as the rest of the motorcade moved forward, becoming little more than dim, hazy silhouettes in the still-settling smoke of the explosion and the burning truck that had hit the IED. Gunfire was starting to rattle and bark up ahead.

"He says that his orders are to hang back in reserve," Gomez reported, loudly enough that he could be heard in the rear truck as well.

"I don't give a damn what his orders are," Santelli said, his head sticking out the window. "We're not sitting here on the road waiting for something to happen."

"Agreed," Hancock called back, his voice faintly muffled from having to turn around and yell back through his open window. "Everybody out. Push right."

Hancock's driver must have said something. Standing in the bed, Gomez snapped a reply in Spanish, and tapped the action of his M6. The driver subsided.

By then, Tanaka was jumping over the side of the F150's bed, bending his knees to absorb the shock as he hit. His cammies were stiff with salt, and getting damp again from his own sweat. Maybe it was the nearly three days they'd gone without a decent night's sleep by then, but his gear and weapons all felt heavier.

He rounded the front of the truck, only realizing as he did so that none of the others were going that way; they were moving behind the vehicle. Only when he saw just how easy it would have been for the rear driver to pin him against the lead truck's tailgate did he really see what he'd done wrong, and he flushed a little. *Rookie mistake. Can't be doing that shit.*

The gunfire from the farm was getting more intense, and bullets were starting to *snap* overhead and rip through the foliage above them. They were pretty close to the target already, and from the sounds of it, the Marines were trying to make a frontal assault. And the bad guys were putting up a hell of a fight.

"What did you say?" he asked Gomez, as they plunged into the jungle.

"Just that he had three options," Gomez replied shortly. "Let us go, come with us, or get shot."

Tanaka glanced at his comrade, realizing that he had no idea if Gomez would really have killed the man. The dark-eyed former Recon Marine could be a little scary sometimes, and his determination to play the cold, silent, hardass Apache made it hard to read him. Tanaka certainly didn't know the man well enough to know if he was just quiet, or if he was really as scary as he seemed.

None of us really know him, do we? I'm pretty sure even the Colonel only knows that he's good in a fight.

It was a passing thought, as disquieting as it might have been. They were in a fight, and Tanaka knew that he needed to be on his game if he was going to keep up. He'd already embarrassed himself getting out of the truck. Nobody had said anything, but he could feel their eyes on him.

Their movement got slower as they got deeper into the greenery. The foliage was thick, a mass of tangled branches, leaves, and vines, and they were soon in a couple of single-file columns, forcing their way through the brush, even as the firefight off to their left seemed to be intensifying.

Tanaka found himself the second man in one of the columns, fighting through right behind Gomez. He felt clumsy as hell compared to the quiet man, who seemed to swim through the foliage without too much effort. Tanaka felt like he was getting slapped in the face with every branch that Gomez slid past, his gear catching every half a step.

Gomez slowed, holding up a fist. Tanaka came up next to him, with Santelli close behind. He peered through the foliage, looking for whatever Gomez had seen, but just saw leaves and branches.

Gomez pointed. Slowly, peering through the tiny gaps in the vegetation, Tanaka started to make out the shape of a building. It looked like little more than a shack, but there was a bright muzzle flash coming from inside. The shooter was hidden, but the muzzle flash in the shadows was what finally showed Tanaka what he was looking at.

Without a word, Gomez lifted his rifle, bringing the red dot to his eye. Tanaka looked around, catching his breath, even as Santelli did the same, putting a meaty hand on Gomez' shoulder.

The Blackhearts were slowly working their way through the undergrowth, spreading out in a line, facing the building. Tanaka started to feel the growing sense of urgency; the fire coming from the Mexican Marines seemed to be getting slower and more ragged. The enemy was keeping the pressure on, and movement dimly seen through the foliage suggested that they were starting to maneuver.

How many of these bastards are there? How are they beating up a company of Mexican Marines?

Gomez lowered his rifle and whispered to Santelli, who nodded, and spoke softly over his radio. There was way too much noise out in the clearing for them to be overheard, but caution was ingrained in most of them.

Most of the SOF guys, anyway.

"Surfer, Goodfella," Santelli was saying. "Chato says that he sees some fire coming from the shed in front of us, and a bunch more from the big barn about fifty yards past it. He also says that it looks like it's all open once we clear the treeline."

"Chato's got good eyes," Hancock's crackling voice replied. "We move to the shed, clear it, and deconflict with the Marines before we move on the barn."

"Roger," Santelli said, before turning and making sure that everyone in earshot knew the plan. It wasn't detailed, and Tanaka was a little nervous about it. He wasn't sure where he should go, precisely.

Knock it off. You did fine in Burma. Find a job and fill it. That's what Hancock said during the train-up. It wasn't what he'd been used to in the regular Infantry, but he was getting a taste for it.

Santelli thumped Gomez in the shoulder. It was go time.

Almost as one, the Blackhearts rose from their kneeling positions and started to move forward. It wasn't a fast advance; there was too much vegetation in the way. But they kept a ragged line abreast as they approached the cleared farm.

Tanaka found himself fighting for every step. It seemed as if the greenery was actively trying to trip and strangle him, now that he had to force his own way through. His rifle muzzle kept getting caught up and was nearly pulled out of his hands more than once. But he fought through, determined not to let either Gomez or Jenkins, the men to either side of him, get too far ahead.

In fact, he was so intent on not falling behind that he didn't quite notice that he'd pushed ahead, until he suddenly stepped past a wide-leafed bush and into the open.

There were three outbuildings and what looked like a farmhouse grouped around the clearing. The grass and weeds around the clearing were nearly knee-high, except where they'd been worn away down to the bare dirt.

Intense, sustained automatic fire was coming from the biggest outbuilding, a metal-roofed, metal-sided barn or machine shop with a tall rollup door. A tailgate was clearly visible in the doorway, and the enemy shooters were firing past it, at the Mexican Marines out by the gate.

The Marines were in a bad way. Backed by a burning truck, they had moved forward onto open ground and found no cover. Whether that was by design was impossible to say; the farm looked like just another backwoods Mexican farm, rather than a prepared position. But there had clearly been *some* preparation involved, judging by the fact that there had been an IED waiting for them.

Bodies were strewn on the ground, where men weren't huddled down in the prone, some behind the corpses of their comrades, firing back at the barn and the shed with their P90s. Bullets were whipping back and forth across the cleared farmyard, hissing and cracking, striking the metal of the barn and the vehicles inside with loud *bang*s that were dimly audible even where Tanaka stood.

He suddenly realized that, while he was still backed up to the greenery of the jungle behind him, he was in fact standing upright in the open, and he could see inside the shed in front of him, where a whole lot of motorbikes were lined up and waiting.

He could also see the man in blue-gray camouflage, his face still covered, turning his bullpup rifle toward him.

Tanaka snapped his rifle to his shoulder, his heart thumping, as he saw the muzzle stare at him like a bottomless black pit. It was a good fifty yards away, but somehow he could see the muzzle clearly, even as he searched for the red dot with his eye.

The dot tracked up over the man's torso, and Tanaka spasmodically mashed the trigger, at the same instant that a flash and a faint puff of muzzle blast came from the other man's rifle.

His M6 barked, the recoil pushing slightly back into his shoulder, even as the enemy's bullet went past his ear with a harsh, painful *snap*.

He flinched away from the near miss, and then stared for a fraction of a second as he saw that the terrorist was still on his feet. He'd missed completely. In that instant, he knew he was dead.

Then Jenkins and Gomez opened fire on either side of him, smashing the terrorist off his feet with nearly a dozen rounds. The man jerked as bullets plucked at his chest and his assault vest, then toppled backward, knocking one of the bikes over as he hit it. The bike tipped, struck another one next to it, and then it was a domino cascade of falling motorcycles inside the shed.

"On me," Gomez snapped, taking the lead. He put his head down and sprinted toward the shed. Tanaka followed, less than a pace behind him, just as determined as ever to keep up.

The Mexican Marines had picked up their fire, seeing the Blackhearts advancing out of the trees. They still didn't have as many guns in the fight as they'd started with, but they managed to put enough lead on the big barn that the fire coming from there was starting to slacken.

In between gulped breaths as he pounded across the open ground toward the shed, Tanaka was briefly thankful that the Mexicans hadn't simply opened fire on them, too.

Gomez slowed slightly as he neared the doorway leading into the shed, his rifle up and his black eyes scanning every shadow inside. He paused just long enough to drop his muzzle and put an insurance round through the dead terrorist's skull, barely visible over the wreck of the motorcycle he'd knocked over when he'd fallen, then stepped across the threshold, pivoting to cover the corner he couldn't see.

Tanaka was half a step behind him.

They rounded the corner together and came face-to-face with another terrorist. The man was in his camouflage trousers and a black t-shirt, having apparently stripped off his gear and his jacket before all hell had broken loose. His face was uncovered; he looked vaguely Hispanic.

Gomez charged into him before Tanaka could shoot, batting the muzzle of the terrorist's bullpup rifle aside with his own weapon. The terrorist fired even as his weapon was knocked aside, the muzzle blast tearing a ragged, smoking hole in Gomez' sleeve, the bullet hitting the doorframe with a *bang*.

In a second, Gomez and the terrorist were clenched together, fighting to keep each other's weapon offline, even as they tried to shoot each other. For a moment, Tanaka just stared, unsure what to do. Gomez was too close; he didn't want to risk shooting him.

Then he gritted his teeth, stepped in, punched the terrorist in the face with his own rifle muzzle, and pulled the trigger.

Gore splashed both him and Gomez with a fine, reddish mist. The muzzle blast blew a ragged, bloody crater in the terrorist's cheek, and the overpressure actually popped the man's eyeball halfway out with another surge of blood. Hair, blood, bits of skull, and pulverized brain matter splashed against the wall behind him.

But the man wasn't dead. He collapsed with a strangled noise, clearly in shock, but he was blinking up at the two of them out of his surviving eye. Blood was pouring out of the wound, and he was starting to spasm. But he wasn't dead yet.

Gomez extricated himself from the terrorist's weakening grip, lifted his blood-misted rifle, and reached down to wrest the terrorist's weapon away from him. He tossed the bullpup clear, as the dying man's spasms got worse, then faded away.

He reached up, wiped some of the blood off his face, and turned toward the doorway without comment.

Tanaka kind of wished he'd said something.

Deciding that he probably needed to do the same, even as he dragged a sleeve across his own face, feeling the salt stinging his skin and his eyes, Tanaka swept his eyes across the rest of the shed. It was crowded with motorcycles, and only he, Gomez, and Jenkins had made entry; the rest were nowhere to be seen.

***

Flint knew that things were going from bad to worse when the fire from the Mexican Marines out front intensified. He ducked down behind the trucks as more 5.7mm rounds smashed through the thin metal walls, and through the man called Gore, smashing him back into the tailgate of the nearest truck before dumping him on the grimy floor.

The only reason they could be hosing the barn down the way they were was if they were covering for a maneuver element. Which meant he and his crew were about to be flanked.

He wormed across the floor, grinding oily mud into his camouflage combat shirt, and peered out through a gap in the wall, toward the shed with the motorcycles. There didn't seem to be any shooting coming from there anymore, and he swore under his breath. Those two clowns of Dingo's...

But then he saw movement around the back. Too much movement to be the two who had gotten out of the barn just before the IED had gone off. Which meant only one thing.

Scuttling backward, he looked for the trap door in the floor. It had been carefully camouflaged when they'd first gotten this place from the *Zetas*, for a considerable sum of money, but he'd been smart enough to sniff it out. The *Zetas* should have known better.

Dragging the trap door open, he reached down and pulled out the MG21 machinegun nestled in the crate beneath. There was a lot more in the weapons cache, but the machinegun was what he needed right at the moment. Scooping up a can of linked 7.62x51mm ammunition, he scrambled back toward the gap.

It wasn't a wide gap, but he didn't need a big loophole. He didn't even bother to deploy the MG21's bipod, but rested the barrel on the edge of the foundation. Hastily loading the machinegun and getting as low behind it as he could, he put the sights on the shed and held down the trigger.

***

Tanaka never knew what hit him. He was moving past Jenkins to barricade on the door and see if he could get a shot at the barn, when a long, ravening burst of machinegun fire tore through the thin, sheet-metal wall of the shed, tracking across as Flint expertly traversed the MG21.

Jenkins was just barely low enough to avoid getting hit, crouching on a knee by the pile of motorcycles. Tanaka was standing, and took three rounds across the upper chest. One shattered ribs, driving fragments of bone into his lung. The next two obliterated his heart and half of his other lung.

He was dead by the time he hit the floor.

CHAPTER 23

Flanagan hadn't seen Tanaka go down. It wouldn't have changed anything if he had.

He did, however, see the muzzle blast and hear the report of what had to be a belt-fed machinegun firing from inside the metal-walled barn. Already on his belly in the weeds behind the shed, he simply reacted. Shifting his body to bring his rifle to bear, he put his red dot right on the muzzle blast and opened fire, dumping half a magazine at the machinegunner as fast as he could pull the trigger. In the prone, the recoil did little to move his muzzle away from his target.

***

Flint jerked back, letting his finger off the trigger, as he flinched away from the bullets punching through the sheet metal wall overhead. *Somebody* had him dialed in, a lot closer than he was comfortable with. As he flattened himself against the filthy floor, the volume of fire on his position only increased, bullets smacking small, bright holes through the metal with loud *bangs* that reverberated through the entire barn. Several went past to punch into the side panels of the truck behind him. They weren't going to do much more damage than the Mexicans were already doing, but then, Flint and his guys had no intention of using the trucks again, anyway.

He looked around at what was left of his team. Scrap, Funnyman, Lunatic, and Gibbet were about the only ones left. He could only see Funnyman and Lunatic from where he was lying, still trying to keep away from the gunfire that was turning the metal wall above him into a sieve. And they were all looking away, toward the Mexican Marines, trying to return the increasingly overwhelming fire coming at them.

A plan started to form in his mind.

***

With the machinegun silenced, and the fire coming from the barn slackening sharply, the Blackhearts had an opening.

"Moving!" Hancock bellowed. He got to his feet, keeping his rifle pointed at the barn. It was a lot more of a laborious movement than he'd anticipated; the last forty-eight hours were taking their toll. *Getting old, Rog.* With his feet under him, he dashed forward, his lungs burning, managing only a few yards in about three seconds, before throwing himself prone again, immediately opening fire on the barn. He didn't want that machinegunner to get enough breathing room to open up on them again, especially not as they were crossing the open ground.

He hadn't seen Tanaka get dumped, either. He'd been on the other side of Flanagan, around the back of the shed. But like Flanagan, it wouldn't have changed anything if he had. Both of them had developed the ability to compartmentalize their emotions in combat. It was a survival skill for any soldier.

Flanagan and Wade pounded past him, both men circling around behind him, in order to avoid crossing into his line of fire. They both hit the ground with heavy grunts, then started shooting.

***

Flint stayed on his belly, worming his way under the truck and toward the back of the barn. It was a tight fit; the truck wasn't really lifted, and Flint wasn't a small man. But it gave him a little bit of cover, and he hoped that it would keep him low enough to avoid getting shot.

A sudden fiery impact in his right leg put the lie to that hope. "*Fuck!*" He couldn't look down to see how bad he'd been hit; his cheek was pressed into the thin layer of greasy mud on the concrete floor of the barn. But it felt like his calf. Hopefully it hadn't taken too much meat with it. He didn't go into shock. It just made him mad.

It wasn't the first time he'd been shot.

He kept going, scraping his back on the truck's undercarriage, and came out under the headlights, to see Scrap doing the same thing, only a few feet away.

For a second, the two men just stared at each other.

Flint didn't know Scrap any better than he knew any of the rest. He didn't even know his real name. They'd never met before the team had been set up and started training. It was the way the employer liked to operate. He knew that it had its cons; he'd spent enough time on small teams over the last couple of decades to know that a group of brothers performed better than a pack of complete strangers. But since it was the way this gig went, he hadn't questioned it. He'd just altered his mindset accordingly. There was only one non-expendable member of Flint's team: Flint.

He'd gotten to know Scrap enough over the last couple of months to know that they were kindred spirits, of a sort. Which mean that Scrap was thinking the exact same thing.

"What the hell are you doing?" Scrap asked.

Flint didn't answer. There was no need. He wasn't in a good position, halfway out from under a truck, still flat on the ground, but Scrap was still on his belly, while Flint had managed to turn halfway over onto his side. And his holster was on his high side.

He drew the Field Pistol as quickly as he could under the circumstances, knowing that Scrap wasn't going to be able to roll to one side and draw on him before it was all over. Even so, he didn't want Scrap to yell. Better to do him and get out.

The FK BRNO pistol barked as Scrap tried to shove himself back under the other truck. He was simply too slow; even a man as fast as Flint would be hard pressed to crawl backward that quickly. The first 7.5mm bullet punched through his mouth, blowing a bloody hole through his lower jaw and leaving it hanging.

The second round went through his right eye and blasted half his brain out the exit hole. The remains of his head slumped over his shoulder to rest on the floor.

Then Flint was scrambling out from under the truck and scuttling over to the rolling toolbox that covered the escape tunnel. Staying as low as he could—the gunfire from outside was only intensifying, with bullets crisscrossing through the barn, shattering already broken windows and riddling trucks and walls alike—he heaved the toolbox to one side, then dove headfirst into the narrow, muddy hole. He paused just long enough to pull the igniters on the failsafe, and then he was doing his best impression of a gopher, wriggling down the tunnel, away from his team's last stand.

***

Hancock had barely gotten up to a knee when the barn exploded.

The blast blew the roof off and sent twisted pieces of corrugated sheet metal flying. Hancock threw himself flat, dropping backward and rolling over to shield his face, even as a metal fragment that sounded like it was the size of a lawnmower blade ripped past overhead, whickering through the air with an ugly sound to hit the dirt behind him with a savage impact before tumbling another ten yards.

He looked up. The barn was engulfed in flame and ugly black smoke. All that was visible outside the fire was a few twisted remains of sheet-metal walls and bent, twisted, and blackened structural beams. What might have been a burning truck could be dimly seen through the wall of flame and blackened framework. The weeds outside were starting to catch, too; if it hadn't been so damp, he would have worried that they were about to get caught in a wildfire.

A secondary explosion from inside the fire shook the ground with a heavy *whump*. Loud *pops* could only be ammunition cooking off. But there were no more gunshots coming from the barn.

"Well, fuck," Wade said, as he pried himself off the ground. "I didn't think they were going to go all hard-core, *Scarface* on us."

"Means we still don't know who the hell they were," Childress said from behind Hancock.

"We've got bigger problems for now," Hancock said grimly. He turned his eye toward the line of Mexican Marines that was spreading out across the clearing from the gate, their P90s at the ready. "Let's get back to the shed." It wasn't a lot of cover, but it was better than nothing.

Hancock still didn't entirely trust Huerta, and he didn't want to imagine Brannigan's disappointment if he got the team killed or stuck in a Mexican jail for life times two. Even if he died in the process, he still didn't want to imagine it.

It was a little strange, he reflected, as they moved quickly but carefully back toward the shed. He'd never met an officer who inspired that kind of loyalty before Brannigan. Most of them had been ladder-climbers who could be trusted only to do and say what would look good for their careers. Some had been arrogant bastards who treated their men like dirt. The really good ones had had a tendency to act not unlike his best Sergeants, and, in similar manner, gotten out after five to ten years, usually as Captains. A man making it to full bird Colonel and still being the kind of leader that Brannigan was, was vanishingly rare.

He briefly wondered if he wasn't putting his loyalty to Brannigan over his responsibilities to Tammy and the kids. If he was dead, who was going to take care of them?

Kinda too late for that, ain't it? This is the third time you've stuck your neck out for Brannigan, knowing you might not make it back.

Inside the shed, he found Gomez on a knee, his rifle at the ready, facing out the entrance. Tanaka's body was lying behind him; it looked like Gomez was guarding their fallen comrade.

"Oh, hell," Hancock said. "What happened?"

"That first burst took him out," Jenkins said matter-of-factly. "He stuck his head up and got schwacked."

"He was moving up and got shot through the wall," Gomez said, without turning around. "Wasn't anything he could have done; wasn't anything he did wrong. It was just his time." It was probably the longest speech any of them had heard from Gomez yet, and the tone of rebuke aimed at Jenkins was unmistakable.

"What's the plan now, Boss?" Curtis asked. Like Gomez, he was facing the door and the advancing Mexican Marines. "We gonna get to go home?"

"That depends on Huerta," Hancock said, as he stepped up to stand next to Gomez, letting his rifle hang. "Keep your eyes open."

Is there really anything you're going to be able to do, if he decides to bury us? We're outnumbered ten to one.

He doubted it. But he wasn't going to disappear into a Mexican prison without a fight, either. Especially not when it had been Huerta who had hired them in the first place.

He could see the Admiral, most easily distinguishable by the fact that he wasn't carrying a submachine gun or rifle. But the man wasn't approaching them; he wasn't even looking in their direction. He was walking toward the burning barn, flanked by four Marines on his Personal Security Detachment, and accompanied by two of his lieutenants.

There was a group of five Mexican Marines approaching the shed, however. They held their P90s at the low ready, but they weren't pointing them at the Blackhearts. They still had their balaclavas up; that seemed to be standard procedure for the Marines. Hancock supposed that it was only common sense in a country where the enemy had a well-deserved reputation for going after the families of people who stood up to them.

There was something familiar about the guy in the middle. After a moment, he thought he recognized him as that lieutenant, Medina. As much as he could recognize him by height and demeanor, anyway.

"You are Hancock?" the man asked. His English was heavily accented but intelligible. Hancock just nodded.

"This is the best time," the man continued. "If you go back the way you came, and wait near the road, there will be two vans coming for you. They will have Ciela International stickers on the sides. Get in them. They will take you to Cancùn, and then you can get transportation back to *Los Estados Unidos* from there."

Hancock raised an eyebrow. "Ciela?" he asked.

The man just nodded. "You can thank *Contralmirante* Huerta later," he said. Without another word, he turned and walked away. A couple of the Marines stood there and watched the Blackhearts for a moment, then followed.

"Who the hell is this Dalca chick?" Santelli muttered from the back of the shed. "And how the hell did Huerta get this shit moving so fast?"

"I don't know," Hancock said. "But for the moment, I'm not looking a gift horse in the mouth. If the Mexican Marines are going to look the other way while we get out, then let's not overstay our welcome." He looked down at Tanaka's bloody corpse. "We'll take turns carrying Alex," he said. "We're not leaving him behind."

***

Hart had been dozing in his chair next to the single bed in the *Hermenegildo Galeana*'s tiny sickbay. Brannigan himself had been in and out, but looked up, his hand resting on his FN-45 under the covers at his side, as a pair of Mexican Marines appeared in the hatchway.

"*Don,*" he hissed. Hart's head snapped up, and he almost pointed his M6 at the two men entering sickbay. Neither one of them had a P90, though; they were only carrying their sidearms, and those were holstered. They were otherwise kitted up, except for their helmets and balaclavas.

"*Coronel* Brannigan, you need to come with us," the taller Mexican Marine said. "Orders from *Contralmirante* Huerta."

Hart looked at him, then looked back at the Mexican Marines, his hands flexing on his M6. Brannigan, even through the haze of pain, could see that Hart wasn't sure how to handle this.

Hell, I'm *not sure how to handle this. I trust these guys about as far as I can throw them.*

"Where are we going?" he asked.

"We need to get you off the ship before she enters port, *Coronel,*" the Marine said respectfully. "*Contralmirante* Huerta is not certain that he can protect you otherwise. Arrangements have been made to have you picked up." The man spread his hands. "I do not know what your arrangement with the *Contralmirante* was, and it is not my business to ask. I only follow orders."

Hart was still looking a little shaky. From some of the outbursts he'd seen, Brannigan wasn't entirely sure how the man was going to react if he decided that their oft-discussed paranoia was legit. On the one hand, if they really were being marched off to be shot in the head and dumped to the sharks, then a bit of a flip-out might be warranted. *Just keep it together, Don.*

He sat up and swung his legs out of bed. He nearly passed out with the effort; he was in a dizzying amount of pain. Hancock and Santelli had flatly refused to allow the Mexican corpsman near him, and he'd refused painkillers, both out of distrust of the Mexican drugs and a desire to try to stay as clear as possible while they were still in harm's way. And even on board an ostensibly friendly vessel, Brannigan considered them to be in harm's way. The *Hermenegildo Galeana* could turn into enemy territory in an eyeblink if Huerta decided to make it that way.

"Give me a hand, Don," he rasped, as he tucked the FN-45 in his belt. He just barely saw the Mexican Marine's eyes flicker as he saw it. The Marines hadn't known that he was still armed.

Hart helped him off the gurney, getting a shoulder under his armpit and supporting him as he slowly, painfully, stood up, his head swimming. "Okay, *Señor*," he said to the Mexican Marine. "Lead on."

The man just nodded, stuck his head out the hatchway, looked both ways, then beckoned and stepped out into the passageway.

Both Marines acted like a protection detail as they threaded their way through the *Hermenegildo Galeana*, heading for the aft decks. The one who had done all the talking led the way, checking each open hatch and intersection before waving them through. Brannigan thought he was starting to get the idea.

The Marines didn't trust that the sailors would keep their mouths shut. Or at least, Huerta didn't. Possibly he didn't trust all of his Marines, either. This little bit of skullduggery was as much to cover Huerta's ass as it was to get them off the ship safely. Let someone leak the fact that American mercenaries had been involved in the Tourmaline-Delta incident, *and* aboard a Mexican Navy frigate, and all hell would break loose, if Huerta had been telling the truth about the political aspects. He'd be disgraced, and his family would probably suffer for it.

Not that they'd suffer the same way they would if they had, say, crossed a cartel. But they would lose influence, and to an aristocratic Mexican family, that could be almost as bad.

Brannigan wasn't particularly sympathetic to the loss of political clout; he'd known too many officers with the same sort of mindset. Granted, few of them would have stuck their necks out nearly as far as Huerta already had, but there were a lot of men already dead who had suffered far worse than Huerta would face, even if this little affair saw the light of day.

The Marines checked the aft deck, then moved out, beckoning Hart and Brannigan to follow. They made a beeline for the stern, where a life-raft had already been inflated, and immediately began prepping it for launch.

Looking around as they hobbled across the deck, Brannigan saw that the *Hermenildo Galeana* was still in the bay. Chiquilà lay off to the starboard side, Holbox to port. It was early afternoon, but there weren't many boats in view; the frigate's presence seemed to be deterring most of the locals from going out on the water.

As they approached, the Marines lowered the boat off the side and into the water. One of them lowered a chain ladder down to where the life-raft was bobbing slightly on the faint swell inside the bay, and clambered down to hold it close by the side of the ship. The lead Marine reached over and helped Hart and Brannigan onto the ladder. Brannigan went first, followed by Hart, who was almost as stiff and clumsy getting down the ladder as his commander, with his prosthetic. As soon as both of them were aboard, the first Marine clambered quickly up the ladder and onto the deck.

There was no outboard, but there were paddles lying on the deck inside the raft. It might have been all that they could spare without too many questions being asked. It could also simply be all they were willing to offer.

"*Vaya con Dios*," the first Marine said. He sounded sincere. He pointed toward Holbox. "Your pickup will be over there. It will not approach until you are well away from the ship. I'm sorry that you have to row, but that is the way it is."

Hart was muttering about how messed up it was, but Brannigan just waved his thanks, and took up a paddle.

"Sir, should you be doing that?" Hart asked.

"You see any oarlocks on this thing, Don?" Brannigan asked. "If I pass out, just splash some seawater on me."

The two men started paddling, slowly and painfully, gradually pulling away from the frigate. Brannigan felt like a bug on a plate; there was no way a lookout wasn't going to see them. He also had no idea whether paddling was even going to work; he didn't know what time it was, or whether the tide was coming in or going out.

But they started to open the gap, and more rapidly than he'd expected. The tide must have been in their favor; it was possible, however unlikely, that the Marines had timed their drop-off to make sure of it. Either way, he was thankful.

Paddling was agony. His chest wound was a pit of fire, pulling open with every stroke, and it hurt to breathe. Several times he simply had to stop, letting them drift on the faint current of the outgoing tide.

It felt like an eternity, but was probably less than an hour, judging by the position of the sun, when a yacht pulled alongside. It didn't look much different from the various yachts and sailboats that had been tied up alongside the pier at Chiquilà. But there was a familiar, and very female, figure standing in the bow as it came closer.

"Fancy meeting you here, John," Erika Dalca called down. "Would you care for a ride?"

EPILOGUE

It was raining as they lowered Alex Tanaka's coffin into the ground. Just like at Aziz' funeral, and Doc Villareal's before it, the Blackhearts were gathered near the back rows of mourners, their faces blank, most of them with their hands clasped in front of them.

Brannigan was still in a wheelchair, though he chafed at it. He could walk; he was just under strict instructions not to go far on his own while the hole in his chest healed. He'd been lucky; that kind of wound had been the death knell for many men before him.

All eyes watched the casket as it was ratcheted down into the grave. Most of them had attended Aziz' funeral out of a sense of duty; he'd been one of theirs, no matter what kind of a pain in the ass he had been. Some made themselves remember the things he had done, like going alone into Khadarkh City. That had taken guts, no matter how many other times he'd disappointed them.

But losing Tanaka had *hurt*, almost as bad as losing Doc. He probably had never realized it, but he'd become something of a little brother to all of them. Not only because of his age, but because he hadn't had the experience that the rest of them did. He'd had heart, though, he'd learned quickly, and he'd been plenty competent as a soldier without having the Special Operations background that many of them shared. They'd had as much confidence in him as they had with any of the rest of the Blackhearts, whether he'd been able to see it or not.

Hart was weeping openly. Brannigan glanced over at him, then traded a look with Hancock. Hancock nodded ever so slightly. They'd have to keep an eye on Hart for a while. They all mourned Tanaka, but it was clear that Hart had already started hitting the bottle pretty hard as part of his grieving process.

Chavez was standing behind Brannigan's wheelchair. As the preacher finished the service, and the mourners started dispersing, Brannigan turned to look up at him.

"Anything new?" he asked quietly. The rest of the Blackhearts turned away from the grave to gather around. The graveyard was a private enough place to have this discussion.

"Nothing," Chavez replied. "Every claim of responsibility has been a false flag. The Mexicans aren't talking to anybody, not even Van Zandt. Huerta's been 'unavailable' for days."

"Hope he doesn't get in too much trouble for helping us out," Santelli commented. "He wasn't a bad guy."

"I think he's keeping his head down for a while," Chavez said. "He needs to let the dust settle and the rumors of gringos running around with guns die down. But even so, the Mexican government is refusing to share any intel."

"Probably because they don't have any, either," Hancock growled.

"Probably," Chavez agreed. "Especially considering that most of the bodies got blown to charred chunks."

"There were those two in the shed," Childress pointed out. "Unless they blew those up, too."

Chavez shrugged. "No idea."

"What it all boils down to is that *somebody* managed a wide-reaching, highly-coordinated terrorist attack, all without leaving any definite fingerprints on it," Brannigan said grimly.

"Exactly," Chavez said. "It doesn't smell like jihadis; they can't keep their mouths shut even when they *do* stage an attack." He shook his head. "Some people are thinking the Russians.

Chaos and disruption is definitely their style. And they'll deny, deny, deny if called on it."

"Maybe," Brannigan said. "There's a worse possibility, though."

"What's that?" Chavez asked.

"Somebody new," Flanagan said, before Brannigan could answer. "Somebody nobody's ever heard of, who's been watching and learning for a while."

"If that's the case," Chavez said into the sudden silence, "we're going to have to do some serious digging." He looked down at Brannigan. "Are you guys going to be up for it, after you finish recovering?"

"That could take a few months," Brannigan said with a wince. "But I'm sure that if something pops up sooner, Roger can handle it."

Hancock blinked. All eyes turned to him for a moment, but nobody gainsaid the Colonel. There were just a few nods.

"But yeah," Brannigan continued, as if he hadn't said anything out of the ordinary. "Consider us on call if something comes up that might lead us to these bastards. We've got some scores to settle."

***

The room looked like just about every other corporate conference room in the developed world. Half-paneled walls, sound-absorbent ceiling tiles, faux-leather chairs around a gray, lozenge-shaped table on a blue-gray carpet that felt too thin. A single TV hung on the wall, though it was currently dark.

Four people were gathered around the table, looking at the printouts in front of them.

The portly, gray-haired man leaned back in his chair, pushing the papers away. "Well, that was a disaster," he said.

"Was it?" asked the middle-aged blond woman.

"It was a good dry run," said the third man. He looked positively ancient compared to the other three, with longer, snow-white hair. Heavy bags hung beneath rheumy eyes. "It proved that we could conduct a dispersed operation, using multiple proxies, coordinated down to the hour, and leave no traces that the authorities could pick up on. I'd call that a win, not a disaster."

"We lost the entire direct-action team we sent to Matamoros," the gray-haired man protested.

"They were expendable from the outset," the ancient replied. "It isn't the first team that Flint has broken, and it won't be the last. At least he survived. He'll be building a new team within the week. And we succeeded in the other main objective of the operation; there are a lot of people running scared. The governments involved are all loudly proclaiming that they know exactly what happened and who was responsible, but the fact of the matter is, except for those within those governments whom we own, none of them have the faintest idea. And when it happens again, the authority of those governments will be further eroded."

There was a pause. The fourth person at the table, an older woman with hatchet features and a short haircut, had still said nothing.

"This isn't just about creating instability," the blond woman said.

"Of course not, but that instability is a vital part of the plan's opening stages," the ancient said calmly. "Trust me; this has all been in the works for a very, very long time. This is the long game, my friends. I fully expect that I will not live to see the plan come to fruition. Have patience.

"All will go our way, in the end. History is on our side."

Made in the USA
Las Vegas, NV
24 April 2021